DEATH IN
DOUGLAS GLADE

By G B Ralph

The Rise and Shine Series
Duck and Dive
Slip and Slide
Over and Out

The Milverton Mysteries
Murder on Milverton Square
Poison at Penshaw Hall
Death in Douglas Glade

DEATH IN DOUGLAS GLADE
A Milverton Mystery

G B RALPH

ISBN 978-1-99-118296-8 (Paperback POD)
ISBN 978-1-99-118297-5 (Ebook EPUB)

A catalogue record for this book is available
from the National Library of New Zealand.

G B Ralph
www.gbralph.com

For Karl and Hannah, my best friends right from the start.

Chapter 1

Addison was determined not to slip, trip, or otherwise make a fool of himself in front of Sergeant Jake Murphy. Or behind him, for that matter. As was the case here, with Jake leading the way and Addison following closely behind.

He concentrated on placing one foot in front of the other. It wasn't the walking that was the issue, as he tended to get most places on foot. Neither was it his general fitness. He kept up the modest pace, breathing remaining steady, no troubles there. Even his allergies seemed to be taking the day off, no doubt helped along by the extra hay fever tablet he'd been sure to take that morning.

The issue was the trail itself – a far cry from the smooth city pavement. Narrow, criss-crossed by tree roots and small trenches eroded by rainwater, with depressions where water pooled, occasionally turning the dirt track into a mud pit. Faced with such hazards, it was his shocking lack of coordination and tendency to attract misfortune that had Addison's anxieties up around the level of the forest canopy.

He was grateful to be bringing up the rear for a few reasons. The first was being able to follow his hiking companion's lead with footing placement through any tricky sections. The second was that his many minor slips or stumbles could occur without an audience. But the key appeal of being *behind* Jake, in Addison's opinion, was the man's, well, his behind.

When his gaze inevitably drifted upwards, Addison's view went from the muscles of Jake's powerful legs bunching and stretching to power him up the slopes all the way up to his backside. It was right there, frequently at eye level on the steeper sections. Looking up further, the shape of Jake's back was lost behind the pack strapped to it. Addison might have felt deprived by such a barrier, but the pack held their picnic lunch, so he let it slide. And besides, Jake's broad shoulders were still in clear view out either side.

Now, a scenic nature walk may not have been Addison's idea of a good time, certainly not his first choice for a date, but he had to admit that, with Jake constantly within view, this walk was more scenic than most.

On the practical side of things, Jake had promised he had everything sorted and that Addison only needed to bring himself. Confident he could manage that much, Addison had been determined to do a good job – that is, not make himself an embarrassment or a liability.

The first step had been to ensure he came prepared with the appropriate attire. In the absence of hiking boots – which he did not own – Addison wore his running shoes, hoping they'd be up to the task. The closest they'd previously been to off-road was the gravelled riverside walkway, which was a far cry from the uneven, unsurfaced trail winding its way along the forest floor. At least he didn't have to fear for the survival of his calf muscles – his years living in Wellington, with its many hills, had prepared him for such steep terrain.

But again, this was a dirt path he was working with, not city pavements.

Then there was the hat. Addison wasn't normally one for hats – they just never seemed to fit, perching ridiculously atop his head. The one time in recent memory when he'd attempted a hat, it had caught in the notorious Wellington winds, skittered along the boardwalk, and leapt into the harbour. But he wasn't in the capital anymore, and he had the added shelter of the forest.

The hat had been a practical decision made out of necessity. The wavy, loose curls of Addison's hair were getting out of control, and what had been an occasional minor irritant had grown into a near-constant annoyance. If his hair wasn't flopping about and obscuring his vision, then it was pricking him in the eyes. He'd been meaning to get it cut for weeks, but between one thing and another, he hadn't found a spare minute. To avoid spending the entire walk batting hair out of the way, he came prepared with something to tuck it under. Once again, his late great-uncle's wardrobe had produced the goods, this time in the form of a wide-brimmed straw hat. It may have been a little folksy for Addison's liking but it seemed to fit and even had a drawcord. Having the option to pull that tight in high winds might have been where he'd gone wrong in the past in keeping control of rogue hats, not that it was necessary with only the light breeze amongst the thick vegetation of the forest.

When Jake had proposed this outing, Addison had checked online to get an idea of what he was in for. According to the Department of Conservation website, the track was approximately four kilometres long, forming a loop on the southern slopes of the Manawatū Gorge, with an estimated walking time of up to two hours. DOC had classified it as an 'easy walk', though there was an alert saying current conditions were slippery – which Addison could confirm – and that care should be taken in the wet. There had been plenty enough rain lately for track conditions to be wet and slippery, even if the weather had since cleared.

The forecast that morning indicated they were in for a fine day, with light easterlies to start, easing late morning, and temperatures that suggested a single layer of clothing would suffice. The density of the bush may have served to shelter them from the breeze, but it also meant there were stretches of the track where little to no direct sunlight reached the forest floor. Addison hadn't factored that into his assessment. Not for the first time a chill ran through him, goosebumps prickling his forearms and the back of his neck, and he faintly regretted not wearing more than just shorts and a T-shirt. Though Jake was dressed similarly, so he hadn't been too far off the mark.

Addison made do with surreptitiously rubbing warmth into his arms and soaking up the handful of rays that broke through the canopy to dapple the ground as he passed. If he found himself getting chilled, they'd just have to pick up the pace a little – that'd get the blood pumping. Addison couldn't help thinking what else might help get the blood pumping – with Jake's assistance, obviously – but he promptly quashed the salacious thought. This was not the time nor the place, even if the outing was a date, which Addison hoped he wasn't being presumptuous in thinking.

He'd already gone over his preparations for the day, taken stock of his attire, justifying his decisions to himself, and expended considerable mental energy coordinating his limbs so as not to embarrass himself. With anxieties successfully assuaged, or at least managed to his satisfaction, the mental capacity that remained was apparently rather *thirsty...*

Thirsty for Jake.

He would have to make do with water. Again, Addison had come prepared. He took another sip from the bottle he'd insisted on carrying himself. A token gesture, his sense of self-respect refusing to allow Jake to carry *everything*.

How did people occupy themselves while out for a walk? His need to stay upright and moving forwards had kept him occupied so far, but by this point they'd reached a smoother section of the track, relatively flat and firm, with few obstacles, so he didn't even need to concentrate too hard on the walk. People chose to go on nature walks, didn't they? Not just for exercise or to spend time with others, but to enjoy being in nature itself. Addison didn't understand it, but thought perhaps he ought to give it a go...

He lifted his focus from the path directly ahead of him, beyond Jake, and widened it to the world around them dominated by lush greens and deep, earthy browns. The leaves and mulch blanketing the ground amongst the undergrowth. Ferns and palms and all sorts of other plants Addison couldn't put names to – some mere saplings, some coming up to his knee, his chest, or well over his head. Tree trunks, some thick and imposing, others spindly and sinuous, but all playing host to mosses and other plant life.

He took in the faint rustle of leaves in the gentle breeze above, the creak of tree limbs and scrambling vines. Addison half expected Tarzan to come swinging by on those thick natural ropes, strung apparently at random between the trees and from the canopy.

This was a drastic change from the walls of glass and concrete he was accustomed to. The air in the city was almost stale by comparison. Recycled, it picked up whiffs of whatever it blew past. Here, a deep breath brought scents of life, fresh and clear, with an underlying earthy dampness.

If anything, being out in the bush was possibly louder even than the city, with the air dominated by the overlapping cacophony of bird calls. Addison recognised the distinctive warble of the tūī, but wouldn't have known where to start with any of the many others battling for supremacy. All he knew was that there was a full, rich chorus of calls. In the occasional brief gaps in the song, an eerie quiet would settle on the forest. Not even the distant rumble of the highway reached this far into the bush, and it was but a moment before the calls started up again.

It was in one of these quiet moments that a crashing, rhythmic thump broke into Addison's consciousness. The sound quickly grew louder, closing in from the way they'd come. He was still turning to see what it was when someone called out, short and sharp. 'On your right.'

Unfortunately, all Addison heard was 'right'. And so, Addison stepped to his right, directly into the path of the rapidly approaching runner.

Chapter 2

The runner's chest slammed into Addison's shoulder, and their legs tangled together beneath them. The sudden impact threw Addison off balance, sending him sprawling into the damp and scratchy undergrowth, squashing a poor, unsuspecting fern in the process. He lost control of his drink bottle and hat in the turmoil, and was also pretty sure he'd let out a hideous, choked squawk.

The runner's momentum carried him further off course, ending up in a jumble of limbs and curses a few steps beyond Addison, his bright red top stark against the background of greens and browns, even if it now had a smear of mud on it.

'What happened?' Jake said, eyes darting between Addison and his unintentional assailant as they both recovered. Jake stood with hands out, hovering uncertainly to either side of Addison's shoulders, but ready to leap into action as required. 'Are you OK?'

'Yeah, yes,' Addison said, looking himself up and down, taking stock. Just a couple of minor scratches on his forearms and knees. But otherwise, physically he was fine.

It was the shock of the collision and the immediate

disorientation that had Addison out of sorts, a little rattled. And now that he was upright again, with Jake before him – eyes bright with concern, searching Addison's face – he realised there was nothing to worry about.

He'd made a fool of himself and unintentionally drawn this man's attention enough times now that he ought to be used to it. In this instance, though, he had to admit he didn't mind the attention, even if it was a bit much. Really, he was fine.

The difference here was that his own ineptitude wasn't wholly responsible for the situation. Sure, he'd misinterpreted the warning, but he didn't think he was being unreasonable in laying the lion's share of the blame at the feet of the aggressive runner.

So, instead of his customary embarrassment, Addison felt an unexpected and uncharacteristic flare of animosity. Who did this guy think he was? This guy who apparently thought he owned the trail? Addison, having made it through the immediate shock, was about to say as much, but the runner was already filling the air with his own string of curses, interspersed with words like 'split' and 'form' and 'PB' – whatever that was. He wasn't directing any of it towards Addison, as he was facing the other way, tapping and swiping furiously at the watch on his wrist. He picked his way out of the undergrowth, returned to the track, and took off again.

Addison pulled his gaze back from the runner to focus on Jake, his short-lived flash of anger giving way to confusion. He lowered his voice and said, 'What does peanut butter have to do with anything?'

Jake's look of mild concern leapt up to one of proper alarm. 'Come here,' he said, stepping closer and reaching

14

up.

'What—'

'Just hold still.' Jake held one hand on each side of Addison's head, his grip firm yet gentle.

What was this sudden and strange intimacy? Addison was too shocked – for the second time in a minute – to do anything about it. It was when Jake started lifting and parting Addison's hair that he snapped out of it, pushing him away. 'What are you doing?'

'I'm checking your head—'

'I can see that. I don't have lice, if that's what you're worried about. And it hardly seems like—'

'I thought you might have hit your head. I was checking for cuts.'

'What?' Addison said, patting his own head now, not turning up anything wet or sticky, just some literal sticks that had caught in his hair. 'I had a pretty soft landing, all things considered.'

Jake's expression – usually so under control – was unguarded, and clearly communicated that he remained unconvinced. 'Then why are you asking about peanut butter? I thought you didn't even like peanut butter?'

Addison's eyes narrowed. 'How do you know that?'

'You mentioned it once.'

'Did I?' Addison said, realising not for the first time that any offhand comments made around this man were liable to come up again. Was Sergeant Jake Murphy ever off duty?

'Addison.'

'Yes?'

'Why were you asking about peanut butter?'

'Oh, right,' Addison said. 'That guy was muttering something about "PB" as he got himself up again.'

All the tension dropped out of Jake's shoulders at that. He shook his head, scooped up Addison's wide-brimmed straw hat from where it had caught on a branch, and pulled out his drink bottle from where it had lodged itself in the dirt. Jake handed them both back to Addison. 'You're all right. Come on, let's go.'

'Hang on—'

'Personal Best,' Jake said. 'PB stands for Personal Best.'

'Oh,' Addison said as he set the hat on his head, thinking back to how the runner had been tapping and swiping at his watch. 'He was timing his run.'

'I'd say so.'

'And ploughing into me probably didn't help.'

'I doubt it.' Jake's lip twitched up at the corner. 'What are we going to do with you, Addison Harper?'

'What do you mean?'

'Wrong place, wrong time, once again.'

'Hey, those had nothing to do—'

'I know, I know,' Jake said, raising his hands in a gesture of surrender. 'I shouldn't have mentioned it.'

'It's fine.' Addison didn't blame the man for such a thought, considering his recent track record. Still, he'd rather not be reminded, if he had the choice. He waved a hand along the way they had to go. 'Let's get a move on then. That picnic is calling my name.'

Jake's small smile reappeared before he turned and led the way, with Addison following close behind.

They'd been so caught up in checking for head lice and peanut butter that neither of them noticed the forest and its inhabitants had already returned to business as usual, nor that the runner was already well out of sight and earshot.

Something about the man did seem familiar though, but

Addison couldn't place it. Perhaps someone he'd seen around Milverton? He knew it would come to him later, probably when he least expected it.

Chapter 3

Addison and Jake crossed paths with a steady trickle of walkers doing the loop track in the opposite direction. Some were by themselves and others in pairs or small groups, but unlike the altercation with the keen runner, these other interactions all followed the same template. Everyone veered to the edge of the track – sometimes stepping off briefly, depending on how narrow it was through that section – to allow the oncoming party past.

Also, without fail, the passing was accompanied by a quick nod of acknowledgement and a greeting – more often than not a monosyllabic and rather ominous grunt that sounded closer to 'Mourn' than the intended 'Morning'. The thought was there, even if the enunciation wasn't.

Addison didn't know the names of anyone he was exchanging pleasantries with – *Mourn, Mourn, Mourn* – but a few faces were familiar from around town. More than a few recognised his date though, addressing Jake directly with a 'Sergeant' instead of the customary greeting.

The interactions were fleeting, with long stretches in between. And other than the occasional bird darting from one tree to the next, Addison and Jake were alone.

Jake was not known for his effusiveness, but whether it was due to being out of uniform, out in nature, or just off the clock, he seemed more relaxed and more forthcoming.

He talked about the immediate fallout following the investigation and arrest prompted by the poisoning at Penshaw Hall. He spoke of Constables Edwards and McGiffert, his latest meeting with the mayor, and even made one fleeting allusion to his life before moving to Milverton. Addison, intrigued by this rare insight into Jake's past, attempted to pursue that conversational thread. Though his efforts must have been clumsier than he even realised as Jake deftly deflected the comment, somehow turned it around, and then pressed his advantage by enquiring about any new developments in Addison's situation.

Addison might have been impressed by the swiftness of the manoeuvre if he wasn't still recovering from having the spotlight spun around onto him. Eyes wide and mouth agape, Addison was glad Jake couldn't see him at that moment. But then, if they had been facing each other – over coffee, or a meal, or maybe even a pillow? – Jake might not have been so bold as to ask in the first place.

It was not merely the asking, but everything else the question could mean. It was perfectly reasonable to ask after the very reason Addison had come to Milverton in the first instance – that is, to settle an unexpected inheritance. But coming from Jake, Addison couldn't help hearing the other, entirely unspoken questions, the most prominent being: *Will you be sticking around, or not?*

If Addison was committing to Harper House then that meant he was committing to Milverton. And if he was doing *that* then some kind of future with Jake suddenly became a very real possibility. As things stood, nobody had committed to anything – or *anyone* – and any progress thus far could be walked back by either party without too much consequence.

Milverton was far from the quiet, scenic town filled with simple folk Addison had thought it was when he'd first arrived. The casual observer only skimmed the surface. Those city dwellers enjoying weekend getaways in this idyllic setting would never know how much was going on behind the scenes – both good and ill – and that the local residents were just as complicated as those you found back in the capital.

Addison was still considering how to respond to a question for which he had no answer – not yet, anyway – when something broke through the birdsong. It grew louder with each step until they reached a bend in the track and the noise coalesced into a clamour of overlapping voices, all chattering away at full volume. The various conversations were staggered back down a line of walkers that wound out of sight.

'Ah, Sergeant! Patrolling the forest now, are we?'

Addison hadn't yet laid eyes on the speaker, but the voice was unmistakable. He ducked his head around Jake to see the woman at the head of the line – imposing despite her stature, limber despite her vintage, and mischievous despite the fact she ought to know better. It was, of course, Mabel Zhou.

'Oh! Hello, dear,' she said, stepping aside. Mabel halted her forward momentum but remained walking on the spot, her eyes flicking between the two of them. Her lips pressed into a cheeky smile as she pinned Addison with her shrewd gaze. 'I see you've found a better offer this morning.'

Addison didn't respond immediately, didn't react with

20

his first thought – that being general indignation – for which he was mildly proud of himself. He considered Mabel's group as they passed by the trio gathered at the edge of the narrow track. They came in various ages, shapes, and sizes, but all sported activewear. This lot had to be Mabel's much-touted Riverside Runners.

'You've misled me,' Addison said, his face one of mock censure.

'What are you—'

'You're hardly the "Riverside Runners", are you? We're up in the hills, can't even see the river. Not to mention the fact that nobody's running.' Addison shook his head, barely repressing the smile twitching at his lips. 'False advertising, Mabel.'

The older woman tsked and rolled her eyes. 'We can't be doing the same thing every week, can we? Have to spice things up every now and then. Besides, you're the marketing man.'

'I don't see what that has to do—'

'Oh, you know. Some of the accuracy may be lost in the pursuit of something memorable,' Mabel said, tapping Addison on the chest. 'And a little alliteration goes a long way.'

'Fair,' Addison said, shrugging as he conceded the point. 'In that case, perhaps the Wilderness Wanderers would be a better fit. How's that?'

Mabel scoffed at the suggestion. 'Sounds a little aimless to me. We walk with *purpose*.'

'Purposeful Plodders?'

She rolled her eyes again at the suggestion. 'That just comes across as angry. And dumpy.'

Addison murmured his agreement. 'Alliteration isn't

21

always for the best. Anyway, are you sure the purpose of your walks isn't just to get in a good gossip session?' He couldn't help his smile that time.

'Oh, Addison,' Mabel said, patting him on the arm as she shook her head, her grey-white bob jostling with the movement. 'It's important to keep up to date with what's going on around town, what everyone's been up to.'

'Mm-hmm.'

'Including you two,' Mabel said with a sly smile.

Addison's own smile faltered, his neck warming at the comment. He was perfectly willing and able to defend himself against playful digs when they concerned only himself, but when they involved the man beside him – especially when the man was right beside him, as he was in that very moment – Addison found himself unable to draw from his well of witty retorts.

Mabel, never one to pass up an opportunity, ploughed on. 'I'm pleased to see you getting on so well. Sergeant, perhaps you will succeed where I have so far failed?'

Jake had seemed content to keep out of the conversation, but even he couldn't ignore being addressed directly. 'How's that, Mrs Zh—'

'How *many* times have I told you?' Mabel batted him on the arm.

'Old habits.' Jake allowed a small smile. 'How do you think I might succeed where you have failed, *Mabel*? In what way?'

She acknowledged his comment with a nod. 'In what way? In convincing our Addison here to make his move to Milverton more permanent, of course.'

Addison bugged his eyes at his friend before repeating her own words back at her. 'How many times have I told *you*?'

'I wasn't pushing the topic,' Mabel said, her hands raised in an exaggerated display of contrition. 'Merely suggesting Sergeant Murphy here might take up the baton.'

'Yes, yes, OK. Thank you—'

'He has an extra weapon or two in his arsenal that might help tip the—'

'Thank you, Mabel,' Addison said quickly, cutting her off as heat flooded his cheeks. Which was made all the worse with the knowledge the unhelpful reaction would be written all over his pale skin. 'That is *quite* enough meddling for one day.'

'Oh, Addison. A little nudge in the right direction never hurt.'

Mabel meant well, and for the most part Addison thought she was fantastic – one of Milverton's very best – but on occasion she meddled a little too close to the sun. At that moment Addison didn't trust himself to respond with civility, but was saved from having to make the attempt by the last of her party drawing level.

'You still with us,' the tail-end Charlie said, 'Mabel?'

'Yes, she is,' Addison said before his interfering friend could invite herself to join him and Jake.

'I suppose I am,' Mabel said, smiling at them both before stepping back out onto the track proper.

'Don't let us keep you.'

'I look forward to a full report on Monday,' she said to Addison with a wink before turning to address Jake. 'You look after this one.'

Jake only nodded and, apparently satisfied with herself, Mabel took off after her group.

More than a little anxious, Addison shot a glance at Jake.

How would he be taking this whole interaction?

An amused smile lingered on Jake's lips before he tipped his head up the track. 'Come on,' he said. 'We're almost at the lookout.'

Addison was glad to hear it. All this walking and talking, he was dying to get into their picnic.

***

Milverton appeared in miniature, as if Addison was looking down upon a scale model. All the little buildings, the roads and the railway, and Milverton Square in pride of place, the focal point of the town. He couldn't see the people on the streets, but he could make out some of the more brightly coloured cars. He followed a truck crossing the bridge over the mighty Manawatū River, taking the road that led to the city of Palmerston North in the distance. And all around were the wide, green Manawatū Plains, dotted with trees and hedges and houses and farm buildings, paddocks full of cows, stretching all the way to the horizon.

Where everything up to the horizon was dominated by various shades of green, above that distant line it was all blue, punctuated only occasionally by wisps and puffs of white.

The clear air felt impossibly open from their vantage point at the lookout, instilling a sense of contentment and complete freedom that Addison had rarely felt before. It was made all the better by the knowledge that he was sharing this moment with someone else. He slowly turned to Jake, only to find he wasn't staring out and drinking up the scenery as Addison had been, but was already looking right at him, his face as open as the land before them.

Without conscious thought, Addison found he'd turned his entire body to position himself face to face with Jake, stepped in to close the already small distance between them, and ever-so-slightly tilted his head up.

Jake took no convincing, finishing the movement by pulling Addison against him. The softness of his lips contrasted with the roughness of his closely trimmed facial hair as it grazed Addison's skin. The hunger in the press of his mouth contrasted with the tenderness of his hands wrapped around Addison's back, holding him close. Addison felt his body heating with the proximity and the urgency, his heart thumping, his lungs snatching air whenever they could. Then he heard a growl starting from deep inside, the roar coursing through his entire body—

And suddenly his front was cold, and there was clear space between them. Jake held him at arm's length, his face a little flushed, and he glanced down Addison's front then back up to his face, a quirk of amusement twitching at the corner of his mouth.

Addison had been so caught up in their impromptu entanglement – so distracted, no matter how pleasantly – that he hadn't realised until then the noise was his own rumbling stomach. It was protesting its neglect, and had selected the most awkward and inopportune moment to do it.

Still, Addison couldn't help smiling. 'I don't appear to have died of embarrassment, which is a win.' He patted himself down, smoothing out the rumples in his top. 'But it sounds like I'm hungrier than I realised, so starvation is a very real possibility.'

Jake smiled back. 'Let's get going then,' he said, nodding his head further along the track.

'Oh, we're not eating here?' Addison said, only then glancing around them. He'd been too captivated by the view, and then by Jake, to look at their immediate surroundings. The lookout point was effectively only a widened section of track on the edge of a ridge, with some railing and a small information sign coming up to hip height. There were no seats, benches, tables, or even any clear space off the track to sit without squashing ferns in the undergrowth.

'There's a clearing with a couple of picnic tables about five minutes further along.' There was that smile again – Addison doubted he'd ever tire of it. 'Do you think you'll manage?'

'I don't think I'll starve to death before we get there, if that's what you mean.'

Jake's wry amusement was obvious as he looked at Addison once more, before shaking his head and turning to lead the way. 'Come on then. The next stop is Douglas Glade.'

Chapter 4

The track turned away from the lookout and headed back into the ranges where the forest fully enveloped them once again. Their steps returned to a steady rhythm, as did Addison's breathing and the beat of his heart.

Addison was relieved to find Jake remained interested, and in a way that was very *not* platonic. A safe assumption, he thought, based on the man's recent actions.

He hadn't been so sure after the lacklustre end to their dinner date the weekend before. Since then Addison had suspected he was in danger of being friendzoned, and he would have understood. Jake had taken him out for dinner, which by all measures had been a success. But then, after a busy and stressful week, followed by the relief of the investigation being wrapped up, and topped off with a delicious meal and a few wines, Addison had drifted off to sleep on the drive home. Bleary eyed, he'd snuffled back to wakefulness as Jake pulled up at Harper House. The ever-dutiful sergeant made sure Addison got inside all right, handing over responsibility to Keith, the resident cat, before heading home himself. It was hardly the sizzling end to the hot date Addison had hoped for. Worse, he had only himself to blame.

In the days leading up to this bushwalk, Addison hadn't known if it was just a nice outdoor activity that two new friends were doing or a wholesome daytime date. After the kiss at the lookout, he felt safe assuming it was the latter, even if it had been interrupted. Again, he only had himself to blame for that, but he was too delighted it had happened at all to be worried over the details. A minor blip, but they were back on track.

Addison was feeling more positive than he had all week – practically floating up in the tree canopy – when he spotted a hand-carved wooden sign welcoming them to Douglas Glade. A few steps later the dense forest opened up into a grassed and sun-bathed clearing – perhaps the size of two tennis courts, and roughly egg-shaped – with the forest crowding up to its edges on all sides. At its centre was a small open-sided pergola with two picnic tables nearby, and at the far side another narrow gap in the perimeter where the track continued.

Despite the number of walkers they'd encountered on the track, he and Jake had the entire glade to themselves.

'We made it!' Addison said with exaggerated fanfare, arms spread wide.

Jake's wry smile was back in place as they approached the nearest table. 'Douglas Glade marks the halfway point for the loop track.'

'It was touch and go there for a minute.' Not that Addison was unfamiliar with genuinely dicey situations, having had more than a few of late. It would be just his luck if a short stroll in nature was what finally did him in. 'Though I haven't faded away, nor has my stomach devoured me whole.'

'I am pleased,' Jake said, slinging a leg over the bench and unshouldering his pack.

'And to think you doubted me.'

'I would never.' He unzipped the pack and started pulling out small brown paper bags, setting them on the picnic table, his eyes lowered to the task. 'Though I will admit that I prefer having you present, and in one piece.' Jake had kept his tone light throughout, though to Addison's ear it sounded like he was straining to keep it so.

Addison didn't know what to say to that. Taking it seriously would be too much, but making light of the comment... Well, he didn't want to do that either. Instead, he cleared his throat more than a little self-consciously, sat down opposite Jake, and started peeking into the various brown paper bags.

They just kept on coming. And with two of each savoury item, like they were loading up an ark or something. Revealing each pair of deliciousness was practically a religious experience, and he hadn't even taken a bite yet – sausage rolls, mini quiches, club sandwiches cut into four triangles each, and mini potato-top mince pies. Then individual sweet treats, for a greater overall selection: some chocolate brownie, a custard square, a piece of Louise slice, and a slice of carrot cake with cream cheese icing.

'Lynne's outdone herself,' Addison said, having recognised the familiar hand in their creation.

Jake hadn't mentioned where he'd picked up the goodies, but should've known Addison would recognise the baker's work, considering how often he was in her cafe. 'She has. And I'm surprised they all survived the trip up here intact.'

'Barely a squish in sight,' Addison said. He appreciated a

nicely presented baked good, but really, it was the taste and the texture that were most important. 'Actually, I'm surprised you fit so many in that pack of yours. It looks like you've cleared out her cabinets.'

'She tried to foist even more on me. I had to insist this was enough.'

'Why so pushy? She's always very *supportive* of my ordering baked treats with my coffee but never overdoes it.'

Jake cleared his throat. 'She may have uncovered the reason for my order...'

'Lynne knows you were coming up here with all this?'

'She does.'

'And with me?'

'You try keeping anything from Lynne Matthews.'

Addison recognised the truth in his words. 'Don't forget we ran into Mabel too.'

Jake murmured his agreement.

'Both wonderful in their own rights, but...' Addison trailed off.

'But they aren't known for keeping their thoughts to themselves?'

Addison laughed. 'Right. Mabel has already said she expects a full report, and Lynne will no doubt require the same.'

'Of course,' Jake said. 'As long as we can report there were no rumbling stomachs *after* our picnic, otherwise Lynne will never let me hear the end of it.'

'I'd believe that,' Addison said, looking over each morsel again as Jake reached once more into his pack.

He produced a bottle of water, a large red thermos, and two enamel-coated camping mugs, one of which featured the familiar 'I Sun Milverton' that was splashed across so much of the merchandise available from Milverton's visitor centre. Addison turned the other mug around to see the design – an illustration of a steaming cup of coffee and the words 'I'd kill for caffeine'.

Addison raised the mug along with an eyebrow. 'As an officer of the law, should you really be advertising this?'

Jake looked at it and winced, apparently seeing it with fresh eyes. 'I forgot it said that,' he said, reaching out to reclaim it.

'No, no. I like it.' Addison put the threatening cup safely down on the bench next to himself, then unscrewed the thermos lid, pouring them each a cup. 'And it appears you've come prepared, so it doesn't look like I'll have to kill anyone. At least not today.'

Sergeant Jake Murphy sighed, shaking his head. 'Considering the trouble you've been in lately, you really shouldn't say things like that—'

'Oh, come on.'

'Especially not in front of an "officer of the law", as you've just said.'

'On my honour,' Addison said, hand placed ostentatiously on his heart, 'I promise to keep the gallows humour to a minimum—'

'Addison.'

Addison sighed and dropped his gaze to the picnic table. 'I know myself too well. As does Katie – you know, my housemate back in Wellington? – she likes to tell me my sense of humour is broken.'

'That's not—'

'She's not wrong, you know. If I took it all too seriously, I'd never get out of bed.' Addison looked up at Jake, a small smile on his lips. 'I'm all right, I promise. But now those two

31

deaths are behind us, I admit I may be – uhh – overcompensating? I'm sorry.'

Jake held the eye contact, his face softening at Addison's words. 'It has been… a lot.'

Addison considered his coffee as it rested on the picnic table alongside Jake's, steam coming from each mug, curling between them before dissipating in the clear air of Douglas Glade. He lifted his mug and fixed the sergeant with a look. 'To the unravelling of Milverton's mysteries.'

Jake took up his own coffee. 'May the last of them be behind us,' he said, knocking his mug against Addison's.

Chapter 5

'I met with Susan Watts this week,' Addison said, pulling out one of the club sandwiches. Shredded chicken, crispy bacon, juicy slices of tomato, ribbons of fresh lettuce, and a generous dollop of mayonnaise, all pressed between two thick slices of wholemeal bread, with another in the centre, cut on both diagonals to produce four small triangles. These club sandwiches were definitely the hearty, deluxe version, not the more humble fare you were offered in vast quantities down at the community hall—

'Oh, yeah?' Jake said, pulling Addison from his distracted sandwich inspection.

'Uh, yes. She took me through the estate inheritance paperwork. All signed,' Addison said with a smile. It was a statement of fact that relayed the purpose and outcome of his meeting with the lawyer, and the smile signified his successful completion of a task that he'd been bogged down in for so long, nothing more. He said nothing of what he planned to do next, including what he intended for Harper House – that is, move in permanently, or prepare it for sale. Not that Addison was withholding his plans from Jake either. It was just that he did not yet know what they were.

What Addison did know was that he was hungry. He lifted his club sandwich to his mouth and quickly determined the triangle, despite being only a quarter of the sandwich, would still be too big to jam into his mouth in one go. He settled on biting it in half, which was not quite enough for a mouthful, but better that than stuffing his face and choking on it.

Addison chewed his sandwich while Jake chewed over the comment. It was at the point that Addison swallowed his second bite that Jake seemed ready to respond. Addison jumped in before he could voice the first of his queries. 'I stopped in at Mayor Ferguson's office too.'

Jake took a moment before pivoting to the new topic. 'Oh, yeah?'

'She made her pitch, outlined her ambitions for Milverton – the lifestyle for locals, and the destination for visitors. She shared her thoughts about the potential role she has in mind for me, which basically boils down to helping her sell that vision. Which wouldn't be too tall of an order, I don't think. Milverton has a lot going for it, recent murders aside, of course.'

'Of course.'

'That'd be part of it too, you know? A bit of – uhh – a reputation refresh? "Hey, potential visitor with large disposable income, be sure to visit magical Milverton! It's nice, we promise. Sergeant Murphy has locked up the bad eggs, no more killers on the loose."'

Jake huffed out a laugh. 'With campaigns like that, Mayor Ferguson would be a fool not to hire you.'

'Right?' Addison laughed along. 'But let's call that campaign a work in progress.'

Jake was quiet for a time – he had opted to start with the

sausage roll – and Addison thought that might have been the end of it. But when Jake next spoke his tone was earnest, having lost any of the former lightness. 'It sounds like an interesting role...' He trailed off at the end, inviting Addison to go on.

'Yeah, I think it might be. Uses my marketing skills – communicating with people in their own language, being insightful and persuasive, all that. She said to think it over and let her know next week.'

And Addison *had* been thinking it over, a lot. Not that he was about to volunteer those thoughts, half-baked as they were, and with no clear resolution.

He was determined to come to a decision himself, without outside influence, and without feeling like he had to justify himself along the way. He hadn't even been sure he was going to mention it at all. On the one hand Addison kind of wanted Jake to know things were happening, but on the other hand he didn't want to string him along, build up an expectation that may never be realised. Though, considering he'd been with Jake when the mayor asked Addison to pop into her office, it was only a matter of time before Jake followed up by asking how it had gone.

Other aspects – namely Harper House and the various business interests he'd inherited – could continue ticking along with the help of Emily Smith, his late great-uncle's property manager. But people were different. There's only so long they could be kept in a holding pattern before Addison could justifiably be accused of stringing them along.

Her Worship the Mayor of Milverton had plans for the town. Plans that would utilise Addison's expertise and experience in marketing. And with so much recent bad press, she was motivated to implement those plans sooner rather than later, or as she'd put it, 'We need to get onto this like yesterday.' Moral of the story was she needed an answer from Addison, and soon.

Then there was Jake. Stable, solid, almost unbearably attractive, and surprisingly sweet.

Addison wasn't about to give up his life in Wellington, with its reliable yet admittedly uninspiring job, for a new role in a new town, based only on the possibility of pursuing a man, no matter how appealing he might be. He was determined to be responsible about this – no flight of fancy, upheaving his life for a bit of tail.

Though he had an inkling his subconscious might already be making moves in that direction. Earlier in the week he'd popped back to Wellington, a quick round-trip on the bus and the train to pick up his bike and a few more changes of clothes from his apartment. Not that he'd mentioned it to anyone, except for Katie of course, who'd taken the opportunity to grill him about his intentions in Milverton. He told himself and his housemate that having his bike would make getting around Milverton quicker and easier while he was in town, and the extra clothes would mean he wasn't doing laundry practically every day – again, just while he was in town. He hadn't admitted to himself, let alone Katie, that it might have been his quiet, tentative first steps in committing to the move.

Addison needed to *consciously* decide for himself first – did he want this new role and this new way of life? If they were enough to convince him to make the move to Milverton permanent, then... He'd be fooling himself if he thought he could make the decision without factoring in the possibility of Jake. That was unavoidable – he was only human. But if anything, Jake would be the icing on top, not the entire cake. Addison didn't want to get ahead of himself, but maybe one day Jake would grow to factor more heavily in his decision-making. One day Jake might achieve cake status.

Cake Jake.

Addison laughed at the thought, the outburst coming out of nowhere, or so it must have seemed to the now mildly concerned Jake, glancing up from his mini quiche to make sure his companion hadn't lost the plot. But still, the man said nothing, just quietly finished his mouthful – perhaps realising Addison had been lost in his own thoughts, and was unwilling to pry. Or realising that rushing the process would result in a knee-jerk decision. Trusting that Addison would pass on his thoughts if and when necessary.

He did raise an eyebrow though, and sipped his coffee, as if to say, *Are you going to share, or not?*

'Just thinking about cake,' Addison said, 'and the icing on top.' He chose not to elaborate on Jake's cake or his icing, and didn't trust himself to look at him. Instead, he reached to claim the carrot cake with its cream cheese icing – a top tier sweet treat if ever there was one – and took a bite.

The cake was even dreamier than Addison had imagined. He'd enjoyed many carrot cakes in his time, even made a few himself, yet it never failed to surprise him how the unassuming vegetable could produce such wonder.

His eyes drifted closed as he enjoyed the cake, only opening again after he'd swallowed the first bite. He found Jake staring back at him, looking a little stunned, and Addison just knew from that look he'd unintentionally been making noises. Noises of appreciation and satisfaction.

Noises that may not have sounded out of place in other, less family-friendly contexts. Noises that may have more aptly been described as *moans*.

Addison's ears warmed at the attention. 'So...' he said, scrambling for a change of topic to distract from his embarrassment. 'Where are we heading next?'

Being the gentleman that he was, Jake accepted the blatant attempt to move things along without question, for which Addison was endlessly grateful. 'There's another short trail which shoots off from here that I wanted to show you,' Jake said, 'but I'd forgotten the rangers have closed it off for nesting season. So we'll just carry on with the loop track. There's another lookout coming up with views over the gorge itself.'

'Oh, I think I might know the view you're talking about? We – I mean Mabel – sells the postcards at the visitor centre. Quite impressive.' Addison had admired the view in the snapshots and found himself very much looking forward to seeing it for himself. 'Wind turbines across the top of the ranges, thick native forest on both sides of the gorge, steep slopes down to the Manawatū River?'

'That's the one,' Jake said. 'You'll be able to see the old road running near the base on this side, as well as the landslides that closed it down. And the railway on the other side of the gorge—'

'Why'd they build them on different sides?'

'The road and railway?'

'Yeah.'

'You're asking the wrong guy.' Jake shrugged. 'It's a good thing they did though. There don't seem to be the same issues on the other side, and trains are still running through there fine. But you'll see all that for yourself soon enough.' Jake collected up the ransacked brown paper bags. 'If you've had enough?'

'I'm stuffed, couldn't do another bite.' Addison rested a hand on his formerly rumbling stomach. He glanced at the two remaining sweet treats – the chocolate brownie and the custard square – and wondered, maybe… 'No,' he said, shaking his head. 'We can have those later if we get peckish.'

'You're sure?' Jake said, this time with a bit of a smirk.

'Quite sure.' Addison nodded with finality. 'Crisis successfully averted. It was a close call, but you seem to have brought me back from the brink.'

'Lynne will be pleased to hear it,' Jake said, returning the thermos, mugs, slices, and picnic detritus to his pack. 'Shall we carry on then?'

'We shall,' Addison said, swinging his legs out from under the picnic table, standing and stretching.

His stomach had been getting progressively and pleasingly more full as they worked their way through the picnic, but the movement prompted his body to recognise that with all of his diligent hydrating, his bladder was also rather full.

Nothing so urgent, but it would surely need to be dealt with before they made it back to the car if he didn't want to cramp up and suffer with each jolting step. Better to take care of it now.

Addison glanced towards the dense foliage encircling the glade. 'Might just go pee quickly,' he said, already heading to the side away from the tracks that went in and out of the glade. He'd hate for some poor walker to stumble across him mid-stream.

'Ah, yeah. Sure,' Jake said. 'Just—'

'I won't go far,' Addison called back over his shoulder.

He knew better than to stray too far from the path. The New Zealand bush may have been stunning, but it was also treacherous, especially for the inexperienced. And Addison wasn't kidding anyone into thinking he was any kind of bushman. He would only take a step or two into the undergrowth.

There was a shoulder-width strip of flattened grass which Addison followed to the edge of the glade. It looked like previous picnickers had had the same idea as him.

He took one step into the undergrowth, his leg brushing against a nearby fern frond.

He went to take another step when his foot caught on something and, unbalanced by the unexpected obstruction, he stumbled, crashing into the scratchy debris lining the forest floor for the second time that day, huffing out a breath in surprise. But where before he'd been caught by the spongy, damp earth, this time his knees and forearms landed on something smoother and... warmer?

Addison pushed himself up, which only reinforced his impression that something was off. Looking down, he saw patches of unnaturally bright red beneath a blanket of greenery. Resting on his haunches, Addison brushed the fern fronds aside, expecting them to give some resistance, wanting to spring back into place. Instead, they slid right off, unattached to the plant from which they'd grown.

The red was fabric, and very much man-made. Addison swiped faster at the leaf litter and fern fronds, determined to reveal the unexpected discovery, a lump of concern already forming in his gut.

One final swipe revealed something even more unexpected than the bright red fabric.

A face.

A face belonging to the runner who'd crashed into him barely half an hour earlier.

A face that he'd previously only partially glimpsed, mostly from behind and only for the briefest of moments, yet had still stuck in Addison's memory somehow.

A face that he was now confronted with, its dead eyes wide open, staring blindly at the forest canopy overhead.

A face that he now absolutely recognised.

A face that belonged to his ex.

Chapter 6

Addison remembered only flashes from the minutes following his awful discovery, his brain in shock, refusing to engage. He did remember Jake appearing at his side, leading him back from the edge of Douglas Glade to the picnic table.

Jake had to turn walkers away a few times, sending them back the way they'd come. He was on the phone at some point too. Addison hadn't heard a word he said, but did absently wonder at how he'd picked up mobile phone reception.

With so much of his adult life spent in central Wellington, reception was not something he tended to give much thought. Like turning on the tap – of course water was going to come out. Though not all modern conveniences were available everywhere at all times, especially beyond urban areas. He'd been reminded of such things recently by the random dead spot halfway up the driveway to Harper House, and that was barely outside Milverton's town limits, not in a clearing in the middle of the forest.

That minor detail had managed to break into his shock, and he found it occupying an outsized proportion of his thoughts, at least until the rescue helicopter arrived.

The distant chop of the rotor blades had grown louder as it approached, building into a steady thrum that echoed off the surrounding trees. The grass flattened under the gusts of the blades as the helicopter lowered into the clearing, the gusts flattening the grass and sending loose leaves, dust, seeds, and pollen flying into the air.

Even from the relative safety of the picnic tables, Addison was buffeted by the blasts. And despite being turned away with his face pressed into the crook of his elbow, plenty of errant bits of nature found their way into Addison's sinuses.

The whir of the engine had shifted in pitch and the rotor blades had slowed right down by the time Addison had ceased his sneezing. There was nothing he could do about the red, bleary eyes and the splotchy face – everything would calm down, eventually. His hay fever tablets were good, but they weren't magic.

The paramedics had reappeared from amongst the trees by the time Addison had recovered from the initial shock of the discovery and the allergy-induced onslaught, then regathered his usual complement of wits. He watched the body jostling against the restraints strapping it to the stretcher as the paramedics crossed the clearing.

Addison couldn't think of him as anything other than 'the body' – it was all just too unreal.

Jake emerged from the trees next, and Addison gave him a grim, tight-lipped smile as he approached and sat at the picnic table. Jake's gaze followed the paramedics before he turned to face Addison, his eyes roving across Addison's features.

In all the commotion, they hadn't had a chance to talk

yet, not properly, not that Addison had been up for it anyway. 'So...' Addison said in an attempt to start them off and also to distract himself from Jake's scrutiny. But with no idea how to continue, his comment fizzled into nothing.

Where Addison displayed bewilderment and dismay, Jake radiated a calm reassurance. He slowly reached out a hand and rested it on Addison's thigh before saying something.

Addison didn't hear a word and had to ask Jake to repeat himself.

Thinking Addison couldn't hear him over the chopper, Jake raised his voice. In reality, there was nothing wrong with his vocal volume – it was just that Addison's ears had switched off the moment Jake's hand made contact with his thigh. 'Are you all right?' Jake said for presumably the second time.

'Oh, yeah.' Addison cleared his throat. 'Just a bit of a shock, and you know, a lot of pollen,' he said, gesturing first to the paramedics as they arrived at the chopper, then around them to nature at large.

Jake nodded but said nothing further, his reassuring hand remaining in place.

'You don't need to babysit me, you know? I'm sure you've got plenty to be doing.'

'I am right where I need to be,' Jake said, emphasising his words with an ever-so-subtle squeeze of Addison's thigh. 'And besides, I've done everything I can for the minute. I'm just waiting for the others to get here so I can hand over the scene, then we'll head back to the station where I can coordinate next steps.'

They sat without speaking after that. But with thoughts crowding in, competing with the constant barrage of signals being sent from his thigh, Addison needed a distraction. Perhaps what he needed was a way to pin down at least some of his whirling thoughts. Not really knowing what he needed to know, only that he needed to know something, Addison tried again. 'So, what... you know, what—'

'What happened?'

'Well, yeah.' He didn't see how much, if anything, could be known at this stage. Still, maybe it'd help him get a grasp on what was happening? On *why* it was happening? Help him feel like the situation wasn't completely out of control? It didn't help that he and the dead man were so similar in age, that it could so easily have been him lying lifeless on the stretcher.

Regardless, Jake appeared to recognise this need, and was already updating Addison on what he'd found out so far.

'—the paramedics have pronounced him dead. Initial assessment is the cause of death was head trauma. Very recent, within the past hour. Working theory is he tripped and hit his head, but we can't rule out that he was pushed—'

'What?' Addison said, eyes widening as he sat up straighter. 'Pushed?'

Jake held up a hand. 'Nothing to worry about. Standard procedure with incidents like this—'

'With accidental deaths?'

'Yes, *assumed* accidental deaths. It can be dangerous to go making assumptions like that, and it's just lazy police work. With everything that's been going on lately, we're being extra thorough – no cutting corners, everything by the book.'

Addison nodded at the explanation and found himself

45

appropriately reassured.

'So...' Jake said, looking off into the middle distance, tapping the picnic table, as he thought back. 'Male, early to mid-thirties, white, athletic build. Presumably not local, as I don't recognise him. He had no ID on him, though that's not unexpected. He might have left his wallet in his car before he headed out, which I'll check—'

'Dominic,' Addison said, cutting across the sergeant's summary.

Jake frowned. 'What?'

'Dominic Campbell – that's his name. And he is – was, I guess – about a year older than me.'

Addison felt the cool air on his thigh as Jake removed his hand, placing it on the picnic table, seeming to brace himself as he shifted his weight to face Addison front-on. If the loss of contact hadn't already chilled him, then the dark and troubled expression on Jake's face certainly did.

Chapter 7

'Addison,' Jake said. 'How do you know that man? And why didn't you tell me before?'

'I didn't recognise him before, when he ran into us on the track. I was too busy getting back on my feet and didn't get a good look at his face, but I did recognise him when – you know,' Addison said, swallowing as he nodded to the trees before his eyes were drawn back to the paramedics, who seemed to be almost finished loading the body into the chopper. 'And then I, well, I wasn't really thinking straight, must have forgotten to say, sorry.'

'So, Dominic Campbell,' Jake said, his voice pointedly neutral. 'How did you know him?'

Addison's stomach knotted at the question. He didn't know where to start, but what he did know was that he would very much rather not have this conversation. Not with Jake, and especially not while they were supposed to be on a date.

Unfortunately for Addison, coming face to face with a dead body from his past was rather more than your usual dating mishap.

He may have been sitting next to the handsome man

who'd taken him out for a nice walk in the bush. The man with whom he'd shared a pleasant picnic mere minutes ago. And he may have been out of uniform, but he was very much back on duty. Less Jake, more Sergeant Murphy.

'Dominic...' Addison said. Where to even start? 'Dominic and I dated, briefly. We were – it was years –'

'How many years?'

'Oh, no. No, no. Years *ago*, like maybe six or seven years ago? We only went on a handful of dates, that's it. Hardly dating. It became clear very quickly that it wasn't going anywhere.'

When Addison didn't continue, Jake prompted by asking, 'Why do you say that?'

For a brief, naive moment, Addison had hoped he could skate through with just the headlines. He didn't want to get into his failed dating history with Jake, but again, this was Milverton's sergeant he was talking to. And they were dealing with a dead man, not some noise complaint or parking infringement.

Luckily, he didn't have to reply immediately, as the noise from the helicopter ratcheted up, the rotor speeding up ready for take-off, too loud for them to hear each other.

It gave Addison a few extra seconds, enough for him to realise he was too anxious of a person to think he could get away with holding anything back, let alone lying. The worry would gnaw at him and he'd never know a moment's peace. He couldn't see how the fizzer of a courtship was relevant, but he couldn't deny it was how he knew the man, and he refused to do anything that might look dodgy, like he had something to hide. Which he did not.

'I had thought there might be something in it, at the start, anyway,' Addison said as the helicopter cleared the trees surrounding the glade. 'He was driven. I was attracted to his passion and commitment, I think. He was a professional triathlete, but off-road, you know? A cross triathlete, I think they're called – swimming in the ocean or in lakes, then mountain biking, then trail running, like cross-country, or through the bush…'

'That explains why he was timing his run earlier.'

'Yeah,' Addison said, pulling his attention back to the conversation. 'Which was a large part of why it was never going to work. He was so dedicated to the competitions and all they involved – early mornings, hours-long gym workouts, training days. He recorded everything in this gigantic spreadsheet – what he ate, what he drank, hours slept, distance run. It was his entire life, all-consuming. It soon became clear he had no room for anything else, such as a boyfriend.'

Jake nodded. 'OK. So, your relationship ran its course?'

Addison considered agreeing, just so this excruciating conversation could come to an end. It would be so easy – let Jake assume they'd done the classic 'Let's catch up again soon' and then quietly never initiated contact ever again – but that would be lying. 'It was… there was definitely an end-point,' Addison said. 'I was the one always accommodating him and his timetable, but my willingness to be flexible was wearing thin after a few last-minute cancellations and schedule changes. It was starting to look a little pathetic, and I'd just about had enough. The final straw was – it was my birthday, I think? – and he'd organised a dinner for just us two. I thought this was him making the effort. He'd booked a restaurant around the corner from his place. It had been raining, and was just getting dark outside. I was the first to arrive and was seated at a table by the window. There were candles, and they started me off with a glass of wine – it was all very cosy and had the potential to be romantic. I don't remember how long I waited there by myself, but I do remember I'd finished the entire bread basket and was on maybe my third glass of wine. I had endured polite queries from every passing waiter and pitying looks from those seated at the tables around me. When Dominic finally came crashing into the restaurant, still in his running gear, mud splashed up his legs, he said he'd lost track of time on his run in the hills, that he was just on his way back to his place for a quick shower and change, and that I should order and start eating, he'd be back in a minute.'

Jake, normally so diligent with keeping his expression in check, blew out his cheeks. 'I take it you left after that?'

'I did,' Addison said, pausing briefly before deciding that yes, he'd come this far. He didn't know how or why Jake would hear any more about that evening, but just in case he did, Addison wanted to be the one to have said it. 'I left, but not before sharing a few of my thoughts with him.'

'Oh.'

'At volume.'

'OK.'

'In the middle of the restaurant.'

'Right.'

'I am not proud of what I said, but by this point I was very embarrassed, and actually quite angry.'

Jake nodded, making it clear he thought such feelings were well within reason.

Addison took a deep breath and slowly let it out again. 'I said something along the lines of, well… I told him not to rush, because I wouldn't want him to trip on his way home, hit his head, and drown in a shallow puddle.'

'Ah,' Jake said, tense, before resuming his nodding, though more slowly this time. 'So creative—'

'Oh, please don't.'

'—and specific.'

Addison dropped his head into his hands, rubbing his face before looking back up again. 'I was angry, and obviously didn't mean it. But a lot of people were there, including – honestly, you can't make this up – the sports editor of some student magazine. And they recognised Dominic, the up-and-coming cross triathlete. It must have been a slow news week because they reported on it. I'll never forget the headline either, speaking of *creative*: "Vengeful Lover Leaves Dom for Dead".'

Jake opened his mouth to speak before changing his mind and closing it again. This happened a few times before he finally said, 'Wow, OK.'

What else could he say to that, really?

'Exactly,' Addison said. 'Anyway, I didn't want you or Sean or Manaia or anyone else in the police department just doing their due diligence and digging up that little gem. At least not without context, or my side of the story.' Addison sighed, looking down as he prodded the ground with the toe of his running shoe. 'I feel like I've had more than enough attention in the papers recently.'

'I doubt it's something we'll have to worry about here,' Jake said. 'Considering the relative remoteness of this incident, and that there wasn't a room full of observers, the papers will only have what we give them. And I don't see why that should include your discovery of the body.'

Addison wanted to believe him, to be reassured. He stopped his nervous prodding of the ground, shook his head, and looked up at Jake. 'Thanks for saying so, but really, this isn't about me, is it? It's about Dominic. He may have been a selfish, self-centred, self-whatevered jerk, but in this case he *is* the one being airlifted to the mortuary, not me.'

Jake's Adam's apple bobbed up and down and his expression shifted subtly, but Addison couldn't read it.

'Anyway,' Addison said. 'I haven't seen Dominic since that dinner, at least I hadn't until today.'

Jake took Addison's lead and returned his focus to the recently deceased. 'Does Mr Campbell still live in Wellington?'

'As far as I know. His sports club or his team or whatever, they were Wellington-based. So I don't imagine he would've moved.'

'Do you know if he was often up here training?'

'Yeah, from memory, I think he was. Up here or hereabouts. Plenty of trails across the lower North Island. Or he'd take the ferry over to Picton for the Marlborough Sounds, and the rest of the South Island, I guess. I really don't understand why he lived in the city when he spent every minute he could out of it.'

'Did he have family in Wellington?'

Addison hummed, looking skyward, trying to think back. 'I don't think so? If he did, he didn't live with them. He lived alone.' Addison's eyes went wide as more details came back to him. 'He did have some family up here though. An aunty? Or a cousin, maybe? They were somewhere around here. Or maybe that was over in Taranaki? Or the Wairarapa?' Addison bit his lip, a little embarrassed at his past self's shocking lack of interest or knowledge in anything outside the city limits.

'Don't worry, we should be able to find out—'

'Hey, boss!'

Emerging from the far side of the glade was Constable Sean McGiffert, a smile on his face and an arm waving over his head, as if they weren't the only people in the entire area and couldn't already see and hear him. At his side was Constable Manaia Edwards, who appeared to be rolling her eyes at her colleague, and behind them was a blond, bearded man in a camouflage-patterned bucket hat who Addison didn't recognise. Though, based on the uniform with its various shades of green and high-viz orange sleeves, he suspected the man was a local DOC ranger.

Jake was on his feet as they approached. 'You all right here for a bit?' he said to Addison.

'Yeah, I'm fine,' Addison said. 'You go do sergeant things.'

'I won't be long, then we can head back to town.'

Jake left Addison at the picnic table and met the newcomers part way across the glade, just out of earshot. They spoke for a while before Jake led them to the edge of the glade, Manaia giving Addison a quick nod and Sean lifting a hand once more in greeting as they crossed to where Addison had discovered the body.

They were gone for a while, out of sight behind the trees and the thick undergrowth. He itched to see what they were up to, to hear what was going on. And even though discretion was not Addison's natural inclination, he knew better than to interfere. He was already more involved in this unexpected and as-yet unexplained death than he was comfortable with.

Sean and Manaia were the first to reappear, looping police tape around and between the trees.

The scene taking shape almost reminded him of the bunting he'd strung up in Milverton Town Hall for the Spring Craft Fair... but this was decidedly more macabre. Instead of the festive triangles suspended overhead indicating some joyous occasion was in progress, they had white plastic tape with text in red block capitals, the words 'POLICE EMERGENCY' repeating indefinitely. It certainly stood out against the all-natural backdrop of greens and browns.

Presumably they were cordoning off the scene to prevent anyone bumbling their way through, much like Addison had. Speaking of, he still needed to pee. In all the drama he'd managed to dampen that impulse, at least temporarily. And now he'd had the thought, he knew there would be no dislodging it.

He considered calling out to inform the others, but he was also not a toddler who felt it necessary to announce to all nearby grownups that they were going to go potty. Addison decided that, on balance, it would be better to not interrupt or interfere, and just quietly go.

Addison headed in the opposite direction to that which he'd attempted before, making a slight adjustment to allow for a sufficient buffer between himself and the nearest trail entering Douglas Glade. He stepped under the cover of the trees and just out of sight.

After being bottled up for longer than was comfortable, it took him a moment to get going, but the second he did, the relief was immense. A shudder rippled through his body from head to toe. He was quick about it though as he didn't want Jake to return only to find Addison not there. Someone missing in the forest was cause for alarm and someone missing from near the scene of an unexpected death was cause for suspicion – neither of which Addison wanted to raise.

But he was too late.

Addison stepped back into the clearing to find Jake standing beside the picnic table, his head whipping around to face the disturbance in the undergrowth. They locked eyes, and Addison volunteered a small, apologetic smile as he watched Jake's shoulders settle ever so slightly.

'Sorry,' Addison said as he approached. 'Couldn't hold it anymore.'

'That's fine,' Jake said, but his body language communicated otherwise. He repeated his comment, attempting a reassuring smile of his own for good measure. 'You ready to go?'

'Uh, yeah? Sure.'

They spoke little on the walk back. Mostly just Jake warning other walkers they encountered that Douglas Glade was inaccessible, and that they should take an alternate route, but otherwise not providing any further details.

The second half of the loop track seemed darker than the first, with the undergrowth crowding in on either side, the trees reaching over and pressing down. The chorus of birdsong felt more distant and sparse, with any noise or scuffle in the vegetation drawing Addison's attention. He kept telling himself he was being silly, that the forest was no darker, chillier, or more dangerous than it had been before.

And besides, he wasn't alone. Still, he remained on edge.

They stopped briefly at the vantage point Jake had mentioned earlier, the one that overlooked the gorge and featured on so many of the postcards back at the visitor centre. Somehow the view managed to look even more impressive than the images he'd seen, but also more precipitous. The hulking great wind turbines thrust out of the ridgelines, monstrous and unstoppable with the powerful momentum of their sweeping blades. The forest lining the gorge, so dense and unforgiving that it could swallow you up without a trace. The steep slopes where one wrong step could send you tumbling down. Add to that, on this side of the gorge, even the land itself wasn't immune, with great scars gouged from the flanks of the ranges from successive landslides. And then far below, the churning waters of the gorge itself, with the terrible, sharp and unforgiving rocks breaking the surface, but also lurking just beneath.

A stunning, awe-inspiring scene, but Addison was all the more aware of the dangers of his position high on the hillside, a feeling he hadn't appreciated from the view as captured in the postcards. Though he did suspect the sinister aspect he now experienced was less to do with being present in person, and more to do with very recent events.

Addison had seen enough, and he could see Jake didn't want to linger, so they carried on, back to the car, then back to town.

Chapter 8

Addison sat, leaning forwards with hands clasped and forearms pressed into his thighs, left foot twitching up and down on the linoleum floor.

He leant back, the row of three plastic chairs creaking as they shifted under his weight, though they remained in place, bolted to the floor as they were.

He sat up straight, rubbing his thighs back and forth to get some warmth into them in the chilly waiting area.

But then they were too warm. He held onto his knees and his foot started tapping again.

It must have been an hour since Sergeant Jake Murphy had left his side. Addison glanced up at the plain, white clock on the wall – it had barely been ten minutes.

He could tell Jake had been reluctant to leave him there in the police station reception area, but recognised that as the sergeant, he was suddenly very much back on duty.

Jake had asked if Addison would mind hanging around for a bit while he sorted out a few things in his office. Addison had said that was fine, though he soon wished he'd enquired a little before agreeing to such a request.

Was Addison hanging around, in his capacity as a date,

while Jake did a quick bit of emergency work before they did something else? That seemed unlikely – stumbling across a dead body rather spoiled the mood, to put it lightly.

Or was Addison hanging around, in his capacity as a witness to an unexplained death, while Sergeant Murphy decided if any further input was required? Unfortunately, that seemed more likely. More so considering Addison's recent status as an apparent death magnet...

Three deaths in as many weeks? Unbelievable. Ridiculous. Absurd.

Sad too, obviously. And tragic.

But really... you couldn't write this stuff. Nonsense. It was very much an 'If I didn't laugh, I'd cry' kind of situation. Though, he doubted laughing in a police station following the discovery of a dead ex would go down well.

No matter what he thought of the man, Dominic's death was a sobering thought. Firstly, they were the same age, or close enough as to make no difference. Nothing raised the issue of one's own mortality quite like a contemporary's death.

Secondly, Dominic was a cross triathlete. With all the hours and years of training that involved, Addison thought it was safe to assume he was experienced and capable when it came to traversing mountainsides, yet that was how he met his end.

Which of the skills Addison was so confident in could be the one to do him in? Like Dominic, he also used running to keep himself fit – though the gravelled riverside path was as off-road as he got, so he had to hope he wasn't in line for a fatal tumble.

Sampling delicious baked goods? Addison liked to think himself an expert, but he wasn't, not really. He just liked to practise a lot. His enthusiasm tended to overwhelm his ability to chew properly, and he had been known to choke on occasion... If anything was going to finish him off, it would be some tasty pastry, he knew it.

Unfortunately he had nothing to choke on at that moment, just his waxy paper cup. Addison had been alternating between the awful, scalding hot machine coffee and the icy water-cooler water. Not that he was particularly thirsty, or in need of caffeine, but it was something to do. He briefly wondered how many more alternating hot and cold refills it would take before the cup disintegrated completely. There was an entire stack of them, so he'd have a replacement at the ready if it came to that.

He'd tried distracting himself with something on his phone, but couldn't focus on anything for more than a few seconds. He eventually gave up and returned it to his pocket. The small side table provided no respite either, stacked as it was with trucking, fishing, and motorbike magazines, all of which were at least three years out of date, not that it mattered as the subject matter wasn't of interest to Addison in the first place.

He needed something, anything, to distract himself from the third and most sobering thought, one which was demanding his consideration: the possibility that Dominic's death somehow involved foul play. Jake hadn't been willing to rule that out, which was a chilling thought.

Restless and determined to find something else to occupy his mind, Addison ended up glaring at the clock.

When Jake asked if he would mind hanging around for a bit... how long was 'a bit', anyway? Were they talking twenty minutes? Two hours? The rest of the day? Addison had no idea. He was mentally building himself up to approach the officer at the front desk so he could ask, rehearsing what he was going to say so he didn't get up there and fluff it, when the sliding doors whooshed open and a tall, powerful woman stormed in.

The woman's hiking boots had fresh mud clinging to the sides, partially smeared, as if a hasty attempt had been made to wipe the worst of it off on the grass before coming inside. Still, a few small muddy clumps had survived the haphazard cleaning job only to be flung across the police station linoleum as she stomped up to the front desk.

Her pair of hard-wearing dark blue work trousers also had mud splashed up the legs, though no higher than the knee. Where Jake had carried their picnic lunch in his pack, Addison reckoned this woman would've been able to accommodate the lot in her abundant trouser pockets, thermos and all.

Addison had latched on to the assessment of this new arrival not out of any particular interest, but because she represented something different to focus on. He was considering whether her polo shirt in the same dark blue as her trousers suggested this was a uniform when his ears caught the name 'Campbell', and suddenly his interest sharpened.

He couldn't hear what the officer was saying, but he could see the hair the woman had pulled back into a severe ponytail swishing back and forth with every shake of the head. And he did hear the woman's response. 'What did you call me in here for, then?' she said, waving her phone for emphasis.

Again, Addison couldn't make out the officer's response, but the newcomer was clearly not impressed.

'Fine. I guess you know where to find me,' she said, with

one final shake of the head before clomping over towards the seating area.

Chapter 9

Addison's chair jostled in place, connected as it was to the one the newcomer had dropped herself into. Her head whipped up at the movement, only then realising the chairs were fixed together. 'Sorry,' she said, raising a half-hearted hand in apology, before returning to her phone.

'No worries,' Addison said automatically. Then before he could help himself, he added, 'Did I hear you say "Campbell" just before?'

The woman continued tapping her phone, apparently having not heard him. Addison sipped his water, cleared his throat, and tried again, this time a little louder. 'Did I—'

'Yes, yes. Keep your knickers on.' Without looking up, she lifted her hand a fraction, and held it rigid for a moment before returning to her tapping. She tapped once more with finality, locked the screen, then slipped the phone into one of her many pockets, and let out a full-body sigh. 'Yes, you did.'

She turned to look at Addison and he couldn't help noticing he'd been right about the uniform, with the regional council's logo stitched on the polo, though her look of impatience tempered any satisfaction at his little deduction.

'I – uhh – I knew Dominic…' Addison trailed off, unsure quite what he wanted to say.

The woman raised an expectant eyebrow. Her eyes were red and a little glassy, but her sharp gaze pierced through the evidence of her upset, and gave Addison the alarming sensation he had a bulls-eye painted on his forehead. 'You had something to do with his death?'

'No, no,' Addison said, holding up his hands in his defence. 'Well, not no. Yes, actually…'

'What? You did or you didn't,' she said, shifting in place to face him properly. 'Which is it?'

'I discovered Dominic, his body, in the bush—'

'How did you know my cousin?' she said.

Her *cousin*? Well, he supposed that explained her presence, and confirmed that he had been right about Dominic having some family living locally.

Addison was about to explain they'd dated briefly years ago, when she held up an abrupt finger, slowly looked him up and down then pursed her lips and tsked. 'Never mind.'

'What – what do you mean by that?'

'You're his type, all right.' She rolled her eyes and leant back into her chair. 'So predictable.'

'I'm not – we weren't – we hadn't—'

'So, what was it then?' she said, glancing back at him and cocking her head. 'A lovers' tiff gone wrong?'

Addison's mouth dropped open, the shock momentarily overriding his mounting frustration before it rushed back double.

'No, I did not kill him. He was impossible, almost completely selfish, but I figured that out pretty quick. I hadn't seen him for *years*, and would have been quite content to continue *not* seeing him. But I assume *you* have seen him recently? And for family, you don't appear particularly cut up about all this?'

The woman scoffed. 'Yes, my cousin is dead. I should be upset, but I'm not, OK? Maybe that will come, but for now I'm just blinkin' riled up.' Dominic's cousin's response was not said in quite that language, her actual word choice being as filthy as her boots.

Dominic was a strong personality, and such people could evoke strong reactions from those who crossed their paths. Had Dominic's cousin crossed his path, with deadly consequences?

Addison felt a twinge of guilt as he considered what he was about to ask, but as he'd already said, this woman didn't seem particularly devastated about the news of her cousin's untimely death. And how bad could he feel when she'd already accused him of the same? 'So,' he said, 'what about you?'

'What about me? What do you mean?'

Addison paused, long enough to add weight to his words but not so long as to appear melodramatic. He focused, ready to read her reaction, and said, 'Did you kill him?'

She didn't flinch or strike back with any knee-jerk denial. Instead she gave him a long, searching look in return before slowly revealing a small smile. 'No, I didn't kill him.' She paused again, considering Addison. 'I don't think you did either. And now that I've got to know you a little better, I don't think you are Dominic's type after all.'

'Based on what?' It didn't matter, not really. And it was absolutely not relevant, but Addison couldn't help himself from asking.

'You're less of an airhead than I first assumed. You

64

weren't wowed by his charisma and athleticism, weren't taken in by his nonsense. At least, not for too long.'

Addison didn't know how he felt about the assessment of his character or his preference when it came to men. The comment was an insult wrapped in compliment's clothing. Still, he valiantly and maturely resisted the urge to respond to such backhandedness, doubting there was any merit in calling it out.

The cousin continued. 'You knew him well enough to see through the bluster. Even if the feeling wasn't mutual, he must've liked *you*. Dominic normally cycled through them fast enough that they'd never catch on, not really. At least, they didn't catch on before he dumped them, or just plain forgot about them.'

It felt uncharitable to think such things, but Addison found that easy to believe. 'And before, you had me pinned as another romantic casualty?'

'I did, just another former member of the Dominic Campbell fan club.'

Addison hadn't considered this might be the case. When he met Dominic, the sportsman was relatively unknown. But his profile had grown in the intervening years, and it appeared he'd taken advantage of that. 'It sounds like Dominic had plenty of exes he might have upset?'

'I wouldn't be surprised. Though I doubt he'd ever have upset them on purpose.'

Addison thought back to his own limited experience of the man, how Dominic had always placed himself at the centre, never considering how that might impact anyone else. If he wanted to train, he'd train, never mind the dinner date he'd organised and for which he would be very, very late. He really only cared about himself, end of story.

'You think his thoughtlessness,' Addison said, 'his unintentional cruelty, might have been enough…'

'To send someone on a vengeful rampage? To settle a score?'

'Well, yeah?'

The words were barely out of Addison's mouth and the woman was already shaking her head. 'Nah, I don't think there's anyone to blame but Dominic. He cared about himself, his career, his achievements, staying on top.'

'Surely that's an argument *against* doing himself in? That kind of passion and dedication. The success he'd worked so hard to achieve – he'd need to be alive to enjoy it.'

'Yes, a healthy dose of passion and dedication can take you far. But in the past year or two, he'd been taking it *too far*.' The woman sighed and Addison had the distinct impression she was caught somewhere between saddened and furious. She shook her head sharply and continued. 'Dominic stayed over at ours whenever he was up here training, so I could see it happening. Did he take advantage of us and our hospitality? Yes. Were my partner and I sick of him? Also yes. But at least when he was staying with us, I could keep a bit of an eye on him.'

'What was it that you could see was happening?'

'He was becoming obsessed, borderline paranoid.'

'Paranoid?'

'That he'd lose the top spot, drop in ranking. He loved that limelight, the prestige. But it was also the sponsorship deals. Brands want to see their logos splashed across the shirts of winners, not runners-up. If he lost his sponsorship, or had to take lesser offers, he'd have to get a "real" job to supplement his income. Plenty of sportspeople have day jobs, but Dominic was arrogant. For him, earning other income would impact his view of himself, what he considered a "full-time" sportsperson.'

'So, you think he was pushing himself too hard to maintain his status?' Addison said. 'Maybe taking unnecessary risks?'

The woman dropped her chin to her chest then lifted her head again in one big emphatic nod. 'There's only so many times you can go dancing naked in a storm before you're struck down by lightning.'

'Ah, sure?'

'What I mean is, low risk – so it's fine, right? But the more you do it, the more chances you have of *realising* that risk. It's Health and Safety 101. I've filled in my fair share of risk assessment forms in my time, and I can't help it if some of it stuck,' she said, tapping her head.

'So, you think he was pushing himself too hard with his training, and he's had some accident, but, well…'

'He was practically asking for it by this point?' she said, eyebrow raised, a knowing look on her face.

Addison quibbled, screwing his mouth up into a knot. 'I wouldn't put it quite like that—'

'Well, I think he was. Asking for it, that is.' She shook her head. 'An awful thing to say, I know. But I can't help but be angry at him for it.'

'That's…'

'Harsh?'

'Yeah.' Addison grimaced. 'But I can understand where you're coming from too.'

'If we're being generous, letting him *abscond* from taking any personal responsibility, looking for somewhere else to lay the blame, it's got to be those sponsors of his, hasn't it?'

Addison wanted to reject the suggestion outright –

really, what did they have to do with it? – but then he took a second to consider. 'The sponsors would be looking to recoup their costs. The pressure to get value for money from their investment.' The woman was nodding along, which Addison might have found mildly condescending if he wasn't in the midst of pursuing his train of thought. 'Sponsors want to see their brands splashed all over those on the podium, preferably the winner. They wouldn't be shy about making their expectations known. And if their expectations weren't met…'

'They might not be so willing to keep dipping into the kitty.'

'Right,' Addison said. 'So, you think the stress got to him?'

'Oh, I'm sure that didn't help matters,' she said. 'His sponsors would've been well aware of the pressure to perform. And considering their product, they might have even leaned into it.'

Addison thought back, trying to remember what Dominic had on his training shirt. He'd been a little distracted both times he'd seen it – firstly, while recovering his footing after being crashed into, and then while recovering his wits after coming face to face with the dead man on the forest floor. 'Go Something Something Wheat? What was it?'

'Go All the Whey – "whey" as in whey protein.'

That rang a bell… 'The sport supplement store?' Addison remembered seeing their shop in town not long after he'd first arrived. He'd seen it, quietly scoffed at the terrible pun while simultaneously conceding that it was rather clever, then never given it another thought.

'That's the one. Makes sense for a cross triathlete like

him to be sponsored by them, doesn't it? Dominic has great stacks of their products piled up in our spare room – don't get me started. Anyway, these sponsors, they set sky-high expectations – practically unachievable. They say "Don't worry, it's fine, we'll help you out there," then they go and pump him up with their fancy-pants supplements. Made him think he was invincible, didn't they?'

'What – did they have him on illegal, performance-enhancing—'

'No, no,' the woman said with a wave of the hand. 'Just the stuff you can get from the shop – they have to stand by their products, don't they? I'm sure they must do some good – protein shakes and electrolytes and energy plus and recovery max and all those buzzwords. But then there's a lot to be said for drinking plenty of water, eating food your great-grandmother would recognise, and getting eight hours of sleep each night.'

'Back to basics?'

'Absolutely. Nothing flash, but they're classics for a reason. Anyway, all those fancy products with their fancy promises – super this, power that – Dominic was a sucker for shameless marketing like that.'

Addison winced at the comment. Working in marketing himself, he'd become increasingly conflicted about his role in convincing people to buy things they probably didn't need. He was still figuring out how to respond to that when the woman let out a big sigh, shaking out the last of the breath as if to clear her head.

'I'm Sandra,' she said, extending a hand.

'Oh, right,' Addison said, accepting the hand and realising they really had just got stuck right in, no introductions. 'Nice to meet you, I'm Addison.'

'Ah,' Sandra said. 'Harper, right?'

'How'd you—'

'Your name has cropped up once or twice recently.' Sandra drew her lips into a tight line, and flashed her eyes wide.

Addison was on the edge of pursuing that line of questioning, but decided he probably didn't want to hear it and had enough to be dealing with already anyway. As far as Dominic went, they'd covered everything Addison could think of at the minute, so he decided to opt for general, benign chit-chat, hoping the conversation would soon die of natural causes and they could instead sit in strained silence. 'So, what do you do for the regional council, then?'

'I'm an environmental scientist,' Sandra said. 'Had a bit of fieldwork to do this morning.'

'Oh, nice, nice. Bit rough though, working on a Saturday?'

'I know, right? Had to be done though. Understaffed, overworked, you know how it is.' She rolled her eyes. 'The overtime pay is all right though, so I can't complain… much.'

She continued talking about her solo work that morning, how council policy required a minimum of two staff when out in the field for safety reasons, full risk assessments, how the boss wasn't happy about it but wasn't so unhappy that they'd be willing to fork out for two lots of overtime from the team's budget. She talked and talked and Addison found his gaze drifting, landing eventually once again on her muddy boots.

He couldn't help wondering… What were the chances? The regional council had responsibilities across the entire region – it was in the name – and Sandra could've been

70

doing her fieldwork anywhere. Anywhere in a region covering an area that it took hours to drive across. Only one way to find out, not that he *needed* to know, but he was curious, and it'd niggle at him if he didn't ask.

When he sensed a lull in Sandra's work-related venting, he said as casually as he could manage, 'So, where did your work take you this morning?'

'Oh, I was up in the ranges, just behind Milverton, taking some water samples in and around the gorge. Very handy to home, and well, when the sergeant called, it meant I could get down here to the police station nice and quick.'

So much for being anywhere in the region. Addison didn't know the hills behind Milverton well, but based on Sandra's description… could she have been in the vicinity of where they'd discovered Dominic's body? Could she have been within *striking distance*? She was working alone, after all – that is, without anyone to verify where she was or what she was doing.

'Not that it mattered, apparently,' Sandra said, looking up at the clock and grumbling as she crossed her arms and slouched back into the chair. 'Any day now would be good, Sergeant.'

It was a wild notion. He was letting his imagination get away from him. But as before, he had to know for sure. Considering he'd anticipated that not asking the previous question would've bugged him later, then not following it up would be even worse.

'So, were you working somewhere near the loop track?' Addison said, as if it were of no consequence. He was just a clueless out-of-towner trying to make conversation. 'Close to Douglas Glade?'

Sandra stilled for a moment before sharpening her focus

71

on Addison. 'Are you accusing *me*? Are you *seriously* accusing me of killing my cousin?'

'No, no,' Addison said, hands up in his defence.

'I thought we were past this.' Sandra scoffed, shaking her head. 'You've already asked me outright: "Did you kill him?"'

'I'm just, you know, trying to get the lay of the land around here.' Apparently something about his words or his tone hadn't quite hit the right note.

'Right, sure,' Sandra said, drawing out each vowel, clearly not believing a word he'd said. 'Just as I told you I didn't kill him, I thought we'd already established it was an accident? A terrible, should-not-have-happened, could-see-it-coming-from-a-mile-away accident? Otherwise what have we been talking about for the past ten minutes?'

Well, indeed. He thought Sandra's declaration was very well reasoned. Too well reasoned? And don't think he hadn't noticed that she hadn't answered the question about her proximity to Douglas Glade. Still, the last thing he wanted to do was start a fight in a police station. 'I'm sorry, I didn't mean it like that,' Addison said, letting out a sigh of his own and looking down at his hands. 'I guess I just don't want to believe that something so... so *random* could happen. He was a fit guy, doing what he was good at, and he was the same age as me—'

'Ah, there it is,' Sandra said, almost triumphant. She reached over and patted him on the knee in a way that was not at all gentle or reassuring. 'Nothing like a bit of trauma to make you confront your own mortality, is there? When someone can be snuffed out like that.' She snapped her fingers and shook her head. 'Do you know what you need?'

Addison waited, but after a moment realised the

question was not rhetorical. 'What do I need?'

'What you need is to let off some steam.'

Addison appreciated the thought, but he knew himself too well. A distraction was only good while it was distracting, because the moment it finished, the thoughts would come flooding back in. 'I'm sure you're right.'

'Blast out a big number at a karaoke bar – that's a favourite of mine.'

'Not really my style, if I'm honest—'

'Doesn't matter what it is. A few drinks at the pub? A workout at the gym? Or in the bedroom? Choose your poison. Whatever it takes to stop you jumping at shadows, seeing the bogeymen behind every bush.'

Addison appreciated the thought, shifting his lips into some semblance of a smile. But before he could come up with a response, the sliding doors swooshed open.

Chapter 10

The new arrival was a woman with hair more unruly even than Addison's, and with her torso apparently wrapped up entirely in a giant scarf of various shades of yellows, oranges, pinks, and blues. The scarf streamed from her shoulders as she crossed the reception area, its bright, springtime colours vaguely threatening, as if to say, *You'd better be cheerful, or else.*

She seemed familiar, and for the second time that day Addison was trying to pin down where he recognised someone from. At least this time around he could confidently scratch off 'former date' from his list of possibilities.

Sandra leapt up at the new arrival, the seat jolting in response, and the other woman gasped when she spotted her before rushing over. 'I'm so sorry,' she said, drawing Sandra into a tight hug. After a long moment she pulled back and held Sandra at arm's length, searching her face. 'What happened?'

Sandra sighed, shaking her head as she led her back towards the seating. 'What we thought might happen. The idiot…'

'Burning the candle from both ends?'

'As usual,' Sandra said, still shaking her head as she reclaimed her seat. 'Sounds like he put a foot wrong and hit himself in that thick skull of his for the last time.'

'Oh, honey.' The other woman took the spare seat, her back turned to Addison and her attention focused on Sandra, sympathy and concern coming off her in waves.

Addison tried to tune them out, to give the pair some privacy. At least that's what he told himself he ought to be doing. In truth he lasted all of a second before his curiosity won out. Really, he didn't have much of a choice – they were sitting directly beside him. He only had to half raise his elbow and he'd be nudging this scarf-clad woman in the lower back. The reception area was no help as it remained distinctly void of anything else to focus on.

'Yeah…' Sandra didn't have anything more to say and appeared to be caught between gratitude and discomfort. Addison wondered whether it was at the attention in general or because he was sitting *right there*. After a moment Sandra cleared her throat and said, 'Babe, this is Addison Harper there behind you.'

'Oh, I'm so sorry. Having my back to you like that,' the woman said as she shuffled around, her face brightening as she did so. 'I'm Ariana, Sandra's partner – I've seen you before, haven't I?'

'At the library,' Addison said, realising it was true the moment he said it.

'Of course! You've been in a lot the past few weeks. Coming in with your little takeaway coffee and a mildly harassed look about you.'

Addison snorted and smiled despite the situation. 'That'll be Mabel's doing, I expect.'

'Oh, yes. That's our Mabel. She has taken a shine to you.'

'She's been wonderful,' Addison said, but didn't question how Ariana knew such a thing – Mabel had been talking about him, it seemed.

'Yes, she is a special lady. Anyway, I'm one of the librarians. I'm sorry I didn't introduce myself properly before, but I never found the right moment. You always looked so focused, tapping away on your laptop, or ducking into the little meeting rooms to take calls.'

'I didn't mean to look so unapproachable—'

'Oh no, no,' Ariana said, waving a hand in reassurance. 'That's fine. I wouldn't want to disturb. Busy, busy.'

'With so many – uhh – *distractions* lately, I'm often a bit behind, plenty to catch up on.'

'I am sure, gosh. Working from "home" then, are you? Working remotely? There's more and more of that going on these days. And I'm always glad to see the library getting used by so many people for so many different things.'

'Yeah, my role is based in Wellington, but most of my work can be done remotely. And it's great that I can come in and use the space, and the internet. Though, hopefully it won't be for too much longer.'

'Oh, are you heading back to Wellington soon?'

Addison tripped over his words for a moment. That had always been the plan, but maybe not for much longer. The offer was there for the new role in Milverton. He was yet to accept, or reject for that matter, but he knew he'd have to make his decision soon. He cleared his throat and said, 'No, it's not that. I'm expecting an electrician out next week, coming to lay fibre-optic cable, connect up the house. I hadn't expected to be able to book him in so quickly. A few jobs fell through or something, so he had some gaps in his schedule. Anyway, fingers crossed I'll have proper internet access of my own very shortly.'

'Goodness, so up-to-date!'

'Right?' Addison couldn't help laughing. 'I enjoy coming in to the library though, so I expect I'll still pop in sometimes.'

'I am very happy to hear—'

'Sandra Campbell?' It was the officer on reception, calling out across their conversation. He'd said her name like a question, as if he couldn't be sure which of the three members of the public she was, and as if she hadn't checked in with him mere minutes ago.

Before Sandra could acknowledge the summons, someone else appeared through a side door. He may not have been dressed the part – still in his lightweight T-shirt and shorts from their walk – but somehow he still looked the part. Calm in a crisis, radiating competence, and wearing a look of thoughtful concentration, Sergeant Jake Murphy stepped clear and approached them. 'Hi, Sandra. Ariana, good to see you too. Thanks for coming in,' he said.

The other two stood to meet the sergeant, and feeling awkwardly like a small child looking up at all the gathered adults, Addison stood too.

'No, no,' Sandra said. 'Has to be done.'

Jake hummed, a sound that somehow communicated agreement and commiseration all in one. 'And sorry to keep you waiting. We've – uhh – had a fair bit to sort out...' His gaze drifted over to Addison for a moment, his lips drawing into a line, his eyes becoming somehow apologetic. 'And it looks like we'll be here a while longer yet—'

'I can imagine,' Sandra said, arm extending towards the door Jake had entered through. 'Shall we get to it then? No point dragging this thing out.'

Ariana nudged her partner with an elbow. 'No need to be so… so *callous*, babe.'

'Sorry,' Sandra said, clearing her throat. 'But standing around chatting isn't going to bring that idiot back, now is it?'

Ariana adjusted her scarf as she pulled on a sad smile and sighed. 'I suppose not.'

Where before Addison had awkwardly sat while everyone else stood, now he felt silly to be standing, like he'd invited himself to join a conversation he had no business being involved in.

He wasn't about to head off to Jake's office with the others. He'd just be sitting back down again in the reception area, to wait. But for how long? He had no idea.

It also didn't sound like Jake knew how much more he had to deal with, or how long it would take. Addison felt for the man – it must be a tough job. But he didn't see how he could lessen the load, and his presence possibly even added to it. He could see Jake was conscious of making him wait, and that the initial time estimate of 'a bit' had grown rather longer and more indefinite. Addison reckoned that, considering he was unable to do anything of any actual use, him heading off might take at least one thing off Jake's mind.

He'd had enough for the day, anyway – enough people, enough drama, enough talk of death – and with nothing he could do, Addison felt suddenly and overwhelmingly *tired*.

All he wanted was a calming cup of tea and a sit down, preferably somewhere quiet, perhaps with Keith at his side for added cosiness and comfort. That ginger ball of fur would know what to do. Despite being aloof by default, apart from his frequent and onerous demands, he was also very perceptive in recognising when his services were required. Keith served as Addison's unintended trauma support animal. Nothing quite like petting a cat and being rewarded with its rumble of contentment.

With a plan in place, Addison mentally returned to the room only to find the others all looking at him – Sandra with impatience, Ariana with concern, and Jake with something somewhere between sadness and hope. He had definitely missed something, but he refused to make the situation worse by asking.

'I think I'll just head back to the house,' Addison said. 'Keith might shred the curtains in protest if he doesn't get fed soon.'

Jake looked pained, but he understood. He said something about catching up again soon. Addison didn't really hear, just smiled on autopilot, nodded, and headed out the door.

Chapter 11

Sunday morning found Addison restless, a ball of nerves pinging around Harper House. He couldn't stop thinking, questioning, wondering. What was he going to do and where was he going to be next week, next month, next year?

Addison didn't have a plan. He also knew himself well enough to recognise he did not do well without a plan. He was struggling to entertain such medium- or long-term thoughts when he had so much uncertainty in the short term. He knew Dominic's death had nothing to do with him. But he couldn't ignore the fact that he'd discovered yet *another* dead body at his feet, and worse, he had personal history with this particular dead body.

He needed to get out of the house and clear his head. Going for a bike ride was something he could do immediately – that is, in the very short-term – which was well within his control.

Decision made, he was soon out the door and on his way. He pumped the pedals until he had some good pace going, then pushed that little bit more – still safe, but perhaps a bit less comfortable. Between his lungs, his legs, and the scenery, he had more than enough to focus on. As far as clearing the head and exercising the body went, a bike ride served just as well as a run, but with the added benefit of wheels carrying him faster and further.

Addison had set off in the downstream direction, leaving Milverton behind. The riverside path snaked its way along the riparian zone of the Manawatū River, with trees and shrubs lining the edges of the gravelled path. Beyond the vegetation, he took in views of the wide, powerful river to one side and lush, green farmland to the other. He'd been biking hard for maybe half an hour when he reached the Palmerston North city limits and stopbanks sprung up on one side, presumably shielding the suburbs from the river in full flood.

On the ride from Milverton, he'd practically had the path to himself, only coming across a couple of hardcore runners and one other cyclist. It had been a different story after he'd entered the city, requiring him to limit his speed and pay more attention to where he was going. With so many dogs and clusters of friends or families out for a walk, the shared path had required much more sharing on his part. The children in particular needed to be given a much wider berth than you might expect – blissfully unaware of anything beyond their current focus, their movements were so often erratic and illogical, and you never knew which direction they might leap next.

With his head sufficiently cleared and legs more than adequately exercised, Addison was considering turning back when he came across an impressive structure spanning the river just ahead. It turned out to be a walking and cycling bridge, a feature which had drawn even more of the people who were out getting some fresh air on their Sunday morning. And to cater to all these extra people, there was an ice cream and slushie caravan – and, more importantly, a coffee cart.

The first sip of his oat flat white was heaven, and he didn't even feel guilty about cheating on his regular caffeine dealer. The number of coffees and delicious pastries he'd bought from Lynne's Cafe had surely earnt him a few free passes.

Whether it was the fresh air, the exercise, or the coffee, he didn't know, but on the ride back to Milverton, Addison found himself able to make some sense of his thoughts swirling around Dominic's death. He ordered the various strands into three main categories:

The first related to the supplements Sandra had talked about. Could they really push someone to train beyond their limits? Addison thought about his own experience while running or cycling – his body would tell him when it was approaching its limit. He might be able to push beyond that point on occasion, but that would also be pushing his luck. Even if he thought he'd got away with it at the time, his body might think otherwise when he woke up the next day. And then he'd just be paying for it in recovery time. Dominic may have been arrogant, but he was also a professional athlete. If even Addison knew his own limitations, then Dominic surely could recognise and heed his own.

The second overarching issue related to how abrupt and unexpected Dominic's death was. From a self-centred point of view, the incident had forced Addison to consider his own mortality. But setting that aside, Dominic was relatively young, fit, and able, doing something well within his wheelhouse. A trip and a fall, with fatal consequences? Not impossible, but *unlikely*. The unlikeliness increased when

Addison factored in that he'd discovered the body away from any thoroughfares or gathering points. Why was Dominic there? To answer the call of nature? OK, considering Addison had been about to do the same, maybe that wasn't so unlikely after all.

Still, the idea of it being a freak accident didn't sit right with Addison, but what was the alternative? An attack? Who would have done such a thing, and why —

Actually, never mind the *why* – Addison wouldn't be surprised to find more than a few possibilities there. Regardless of who or why, one factor lending credibility to the attacker theory was something that, with everything going on, he hadn't registered at the time. Dominic's body couldn't have been lying there for long at all, yet it was already partially obscured by leaves and things. There had been a bit of wind, but not that much under the shelter of the trees and ferns and all the undergrowth. Too much coverage for it to have occurred naturally, but not nearly enough coverage for someone wanting to cover up a dead body...

The third and final item had less to do with Dominic and more to do with Addison. Addison's name was once again wrapped up in an abrupt and unexplained death, one which may or may not involve foul play. He knew he had nothing to do with it but he couldn't deny that a trend was emerging, one which locals would be sure to comment on.

It didn't help, at least in Addison's mind, that the last time they saw each other alive he'd effectively wished Dominic dead. He had to console himself that Dominic hadn't been found face down in a shallow puddle, as he'd so vividly suggested at the end of their failed final date.

Regardless, Addison didn't want any doubt of his

innocence amongst the people of Milverton, and one person in particular. He could pretend that it was because of the man's position as Milverton's sergeant, but he had to admit to himself that his driving factor was much more personal.

If there was even the whisper of a possibility of something more with Jake, Addison didn't want any lingering doubt in Jake's mind regarding Addison's sort-of ex and his untimely death.

No matter what anyone else thought, what was clear to Addison was that something was *off*. And he realised his mind would not rest until he'd figured out what.

Chapter 12

Addison woke the following morning to find his body could definitely remember being taken for a decent ride yesterday. He eased himself out of bed and was pleased to find the movement hadn't triggered any alarming pings, only reinforced the satisfying ache in his muscles. And even that ache was worked out under the still surprisingly decent pressure of the shower's hot water.

Monday was the start of a brand-new week. An arbitrary thing, but also an excuse to draw a line under the week that was, reset, start again afresh. Addison wouldn't kid himself into thinking the happenings of last week would not spill into the coming days, but he was determined to take it easy, to give himself a break, at least while he was getting ready for the day.

Fresh and clean, with a towel cinched around his waist, Addison returned to the guest bedroom where he found a change of clothes – also fresh and clean – ready to go. No hunting in the bottom of his bag, rummaging through his great-uncle Herbert's closet, or running the decrepit hairdryer back and forth over damp washing.

Ignoring for a minute the events of the weekend,

Addison was feeling good about things. He was taking his time, focusing on his morning routine, and not allowing his brain to gallop ahead, bounding from one problem to the next, bouncing off various issues and half-formed thoughts along the way, only to loop back and go through them all again.

While getting dressed, Addison did absently wonder though where Keith had got to. On his return from the shower each morning, Addison had grown accustomed to finding the surly ball of orange fur laying claim to the bed, luxuriating in the warmth of the scrunched-up duvet. His absence this morning was no matter – Addison was confident the cat would soon make his presence known.

He'd barely finished the thought when he stepped out of the bedroom and spotted Harper House's resident feline. Keith sat upright on the landing at the top of the stairs, and with eyes locked on Addison, he slowly lifted his paw and placed it firmly and unequivocally on the nearest baluster. The same warm, golden wood was used throughout the old house, but Keith was not providing a commentary on the decor – he was indicating in his usual imperious way, with no room for misinterpretation, that Addison may have been taking his time, enjoying a slower start to the day, but it was now past time to head downstairs.

'Yes, yes,' Addison said. And seeing Addison approaching the top of the stairs, Keith seemed satisfied his message had been received, dropped his paw, lifted himself up onto all fours, and with one last flick of his tail, padded his way down the carpeted stairs.

Addison and Keith may have only known each other for a matter of weeks, but they were already developing a strong relationship, one built on mutual trust and respect.

Keith *respected* that Addison was the new human representative of Harper House, and Keith *trusted* that he would be presented with suitably tasty and high-quality sustenance at regular intervals. Addison, for his part, *respected* that if he did not do so then he could *trust* Keith to demonstrate his displeasure or remind Addison of his obligations.

With those obligations in mind, Addison followed the cat downstairs, but he was only halfway down when he found himself distracted from his purpose.

The foyer was panelled wall-to-wall in timber – not to mention the cornices, doors, mantelpiece – and then across the ceiling too for good measure. The excess of wood wasn't itself the distraction – he was starting to get used to all that – it was the light streaming into the space that had caught his eye. The wood seemed to glow in the morning sun, the stained-glass windows too. Addison hadn't taken much notice of them, higher up as they were, above his eyeline, but now they shone bright.

The coloured light even played across the wood lining the ceiling, glinting off the chandelier, which was rather too *extra* for Addison's taste, but then so much about Harper House was extra. He had to focus on the carpet to avoid being dazzled by the light show, as it was the only surface that absorbed any of the light instead of glowing or reflecting it back at him. The carpet itself was a psychedelic pattern of swirls and flowers and spots in an eruption of oranges and browns straight from the 1960s – hardly restful on the eye, but less likely to blind him.

Addison made his way without further incident to the much more modest kitchen at the back of the house to find Keith waiting, paw already pressed to the fridge door and a glare of impatience once more fixed on Addison.

He wasn't sure how his great-uncle tended to do things, but Addison had set up a three-bowl system, which he thought made it easy to keep track of at a glance.

The first bowl was for water, which was easy enough to keep up. Addison had spotted the cat drinking from various other water sources around the place – most often the pond and a bird bath – so the cat wasn't about to die of thirst.

The second bowl was for jellied meat. He'd trialled a couple of alternative – that is, cheaper – products, but Keith had turned his nose up at all but Fancy Fine Feline Cuisine, which was the brand Addison had found in the fridge when he first arrived.

The third bowl was for dry food. Keith seemed quite happy with supermarket-brand biscuits, which didn't seem in keeping with his usual first-class standards, but Addison wasn't about to call him out on the inconsistency.

The first and third bowls were well stocked, but the middle bowl was polished clean and clearly the issue here. Addison promptly scooped a good portion of the tuna and chicken gloop into the bowl, which Keith pounced on before Addison even had the chance to withdraw the spoon. Any irritation that may have been building at this whole procedure evaporated the moment the purring started, almost aggressive in its volume and vibration, but very clearly communicating satisfaction.

With the little tyrant appeased for the moment, Addison moved on to his own breakfast. He flicked the electric kettle on, dropped two slices of bread in the toaster, and poured some cereal in a small bowl, topping it off with a banana and a couple of dollops of yoghurt.

He dropped a tea bag in the *I Sun Milverton* mug he'd

recently had foisted on him – at the rate he was going he'd have Milverton-branded everything. But he'd forgive it in this instance, because the mug had a good handle, and the lip was nice to drink from. The tea wouldn't cut it for long, but it would tide him over until he made it into town for a proper coffee.

He had a few mouthfuls of cereal down when the kettle clicked off, and had just poured the water in to start brewing his tea when his toast popped – it was not quite done, so he put it down for a final burst. He'd retrieved the butter dish from the pantry, and manually popped the toast before he forgot and ended up with two charcoal coasters. He caught them at that perfectly crispy, crunchy brown stage. Still hot to the touch, each slice melted the thick spreads of butter with ease, and smelt *divine*.

Next step was spreading the faintest smudge of Marmite on one piece, and a hearty coating of mānuka honey on the other. By then he'd finished off the cereal and his tea had brewed. He removed the teabag, added a dash of milk, and carried the mug and plate of toast out the kitchen door.

The ornamental garden – complete with pond, water fountain, and even a few ducks – remained in shadow, with dew still clinging to the lawn. But the sun had cleared the ranges and the orchard at the bottom of the garden enough to cast its light on the wicker chairs on the back porch. The chill air prickled Addison's arms, but he drew enough warmth from the sun for it to be a pleasant spot to sit.

The breakfast fare may have been simple, but the setting sure elevated the meal, and nobody could argue that having three courses – cereal and yoghurt entree, savoury toast main, sweet toast dessert – wasn't at least a little fancy.

Addison was halfway through his honey toast when he

absently wondered if he could keep bees... Not that he knew anything about bees, or keeping them, but there was plenty of nature around Harper House for the bees to thrive on.

The other thing taking up space in his head was the fact he hadn't heard from Jake since late on Saturday... which was fine. As Milverton's sergeant, having yet another dead body turn up meant enjoying a personal life was a luxury and any attempts at work-life balance went out the window, at least until the situation was wrapped up.

Addison knew the only way to take his mind off one thing – such as a handsome and temporarily absent sergeant – was to put it onto another. In summary, focusing on the unexplained death of a sort-of ex was for his own good. And for now, the supplements were the only thing he could look into.

He checked the time and realised that despite his leisurely start to the day, he still had a while before he needed to make an appearance online and fulfil the 'working' aspect of 'working remotely'. He might even be able to ask those few questions before he clocked in.

With a plan in hand, it only took a few minutes to finish up his breakfast, grab his work things, then check Keith was out of the house before heading out himself.

Addison pulled on his jacket, slung his laptop bag over his shoulder, and locked the recently fixed front door behind him. He stepped down onto the driveway, hearing the crunch and feeling the give of the gravel underfoot. But when the sound kept going, continuously shifting, Addison glanced up the tree-lined avenue ahead of him...

A white van had turned off the road and was heading directly towards him.

Chapter 13

Addison stepped back up onto the front porch as the van swung around the loop and crunched to a stop.

The branding on the side read 'Turn It On Electrical Services' with muscled cartoon superheroes to each side of the company name, flexing their biceps and sporting skintight bodysuits with lightning bolt motifs on their chests.

The man who emerged looked much like his mascot, and Addison could see why the business might have leapt to mind when he'd asked Mabel for recommendations.

The electrician was a tall guy who appeared to be five to ten years older than Addison. He had dark brown hair, the buzz cut making his already large ears all the more prominent. But they weren't the only large thing about the man – he was *quite* muscular, bigger even than Jake – not that it was a competition.

Addison couldn't help the brief flash of guilt at noticing such a thing, but how could he not?

The branding of the electrician's polo shirt matched the side of his van, and was more than a little tight across his chest. And to add to the fit tradie ensemble were cargo shorts that barely reached mid-thigh, his legs like tree trunks. Finally, white sports socks pulled up to mid-calf and a pair of steel-cap boots. The few steps it took the man to reach Addison were enough for him to take in the electrician, but not enough to corral his brain cells into producing a greeting before the man beat him to it. 'Addison Harper?'

Addison cleared his throat. 'That's me.'

'Kyle Thompson.' He reached out and shook Addison's hand with perhaps a little more force than strictly necessary. 'We spoke on the phone.'

'Right, of course,' Addison said, thinking back, across the great divide that was his ill-fated date, all the way to late last week. 'Sorry, Kyle. I thought you were booked in for this Thursday?'

'Yes,' he said, short and sharp, as if Addison was already trying his patience. He glanced at the house, then back up the driveway towards the road. 'I said I'd drop by earlier this week, get an idea of what I'm working with.'

'Ah, you did say something about that, sorry.'

'Mm-hmm.' The electrician was clearly annoyed he was having to repeat himself. 'Important to check with semi-rural places like this. Want to get an idea how much cable I'll need, and any issues between the road and the house that might make digging the trench tricky.'

'Right—'

'Means I can bring everything I need on the day, be in and out. Can't be working all day and night, can we? Got other things to be doing.'

'Yeah, sure.' Addison got it, really he did. But, did this guy not want the job?

'You do want the fibre-optic cable laid in a trench, I take

it?'

Addison paused. Did he? What was the alternative? He was so used to having decent internet wherever he went, whether that was good wifi or a strong mobile connection. He never had to consider how the internet got to where it needed to be. 'A trench? Yes, I guess?'

'Good. I've seen some real cowboy jobs – cables stapled along the fence line or strung up between the trees.' He shook his head. 'Installations like that, asking for trouble.'

'Right, OK. Did you – uh – did you need to get into the house for that?'

'No, not today. Details. We can sort that out on Thursday when I'm back to do the job proper,' Kyle said, waving a dismissive hand. At the movement, and despite the man's apparent attitude, Addison couldn't help noticing the size of his arms all over again – biceps, triceps, shoulders, the works. They were something, all right. Maybe even too much, if that was a thing?

Addison found himself comparing the man's physique to that of Jake's. Objectively impressive, but Addison knew it'd be tough to measure up to the sergeant, in his eyes anyway. And there he was, thinking about Jake again.

Kyle twitched under Addison's scrutiny, glancing down at himself, forcing Addison to trip over his words in order to explain himself. Though really the difficult part was coming up with something feasible that was not the truth. 'Ah, sorry. Just…' Addison couldn't help himself from looking again, but this time noticed a few small scratches up his left forearm. 'I just noticed the scratches, they look sore.' They didn't, not at all, but it was the best he could manage in the heat of the moment.

The electrician frowned, drew his lips into a line, then

lifted his arm a bit. 'Oh, they're fine. I was – uh – I was laying a cable last week, another trench. Getting power from the house out to a new spa pool – I've been picking up a few smaller jobs like that lately. The place was just up the road. Husband bought it for the wife to relax. She didn't want it – didn't seem like the type to relax – but if she had to have the spa pool, she was going to have it done properly. Had me laying the power cable through her rose bushes. Wouldn't let me trim them back either. Nightmare. And then it got too hot working in the protective gear, so this,' he said, gesturing to the scratches.

Addison let the man overexplain himself, relieved to have averted being called out on his lapse in decorum. And then his thoughts drifted to considering whether a spa pool might be what Harper House needed. If he were to set the place up as a bed and breakfast, a place for city folk looking for a nice getaway, a weekend of relaxation and rejuvenation… a spa pool might be just the ticket. And now his inheritance was being processed, he should soon have access to funds to do such a thing, make such an investment.

'Anyway,' Kyle said, lowering his arm. 'You were heading out?'

'Ah, I was, but—'

'No need to hang about. I won't be long.'

'OK, great,' Addison said, repositioning his laptop bag on his shoulder, and nodding his farewell. 'I'll see you Thursday.'

'Are you' – Kyle paused for a moment, frowning – 'are you *walking* into town?'

'Yeah? I mean, I do have my bike now.' Addison shrugged. 'The walk's not far though.'

'I suppose not,' Kyle said. 'I should only be here a few

minutes, five minutes max.' He looked at the house and driveway again, before settling his gaze back on Addison, frowning a little. 'I can give you a ride, I guess? Into town.'

Addison cleared his throat. 'No, no. I could do with the fresh air. Thanks, though.'

'All right.' Kyle shrugged, already turning away to grab something from his van. 'Bye.'

'Yeah, see you,' Addison said, pausing a moment, nodding to himself, then heading off up the driveway.

A weird start that left him feeling a little off-kilter, but it was the first real step in dragging Harper House out of the twentieth century. It was good, this was good.

Addison nodded again to himself, this time with conviction – he had a shopkeeper to see about a protein shake.

Chapter 14

Addison had been in Milverton for weeks, and despite seeing it almost every day, was yet to tire of Milverton Square. With an impressive stone clock tower at its centre the square was a focal point for the town, one which the locals were proud of, and had every right to be. He'd seen all sorts of people using the space: young and old, those in groups, pairs, or flying solo, some pushing strollers or wheelchairs, others being pulled by small children or excitable pups. Some stopped to feed the ducks or picnicked on the manicured lawns. Others ambled through the square, checking out the recently installed sculpture – an oversized, electric-blue duck – or smelling the roses, quite literally.

At that time on Monday morning, though, the only people in the square were crossing the space from one side to the other, getting to their destination as swiftly as possible.

One side of the square remained open to the powerful Manawatū River, accessed by the riverside path running from the gorge, along Milverton's boundary, downstream towards Palmerston North and beyond. The other three sides were bounded by streets, each fronted with tidy two-storey buildings of various styles from the past hundred years or more.

Addison took the footpath which ran along the side furthest from the river, passing the bus stop and public toilets – that is, the more practical and less glamorous aspect of the square. Lynne's Cafe called to him from its spot on the other side of the street, with its promises of proper coffee and mouth-watering baked treats, but Addison stayed strong and powered on. If he were being honest with himself, exhibiting strength in this matter was no trouble as he knew he'd be back very shortly anyway.

Just like practically everything in Milverton, the sport supplement store wasn't far away – just another block over. The place would be impossible to miss, with its bold and energetic branding plastered across the shop awning and front windows, propped up on footpath signage, and covering the sides of the white van parked directly out front.

Seeing the van there, Addison couldn't help thinking about the constant stream of local newspaper articles given over to parking issues. The restrictions were too tight or too lax, enforced too rigorously or not rigorously enough, and then there were too few spaces for quick visits but also too few available for extended periods, and so it went. The eye-roll-inducing articles were inevitably accompanied by photos of outraged shopkeepers standing outside their businesses, arms crossed and glaring into the camera.

Parking your own vehicle, presumably all day, in the best spot for your own shop felt like an own goal. It all seemed a bit much to Addison, but then he didn't drive, so probably wasn't the best qualified to pass judgement. Also, he had to concede parking your branded vehicle outside your own shop was a winner when it came to advertising –

nobody could say they didn't know where to find Go All the Whey.

Addison had to hope finding some answers about Dominic's supplement intake would be just as straightforward. He took a deep breath in before slowly exhaling and stepping inside.

He had only one foot across the threshold when something erupted right beside his ear. Addison lunged away to the left and raised his arms before his face, all while dropping his head into his shoulders and whipping around to catch sight of his loud assailant.

Nobody was there, no assailant, only a tall display unit stacked with products. That's all he saw before he lost his legs from underneath him and landed on his back with a lung-emptying thump, his vision filled with off-white ceiling tiles. Even that sight only lasted a moment before a wide-eyed, slack-jawed face appeared.

'Mate? You all right?'

'Yeah,' Addison said, clearing his throat and repeating himself when the word didn't come out as convincingly as it had sounded in his head. He slowly lifted himself up onto his elbows, then into a sitting position before finally getting back to his feet – checking for signs of damage at each stage of regaining verticality. His initial assessment didn't uncover any limbs where they shouldn't be, or alarming aches, though those may come later. Addison was left with a racing heart and a slowly receding tide of adrenaline that had realised its services were no longer required.

The unfamiliar man hovered uncertainly while Addison completed his mental stocktake. 'Sorry about that, my man,' the stranger said once they had both determined Addison remained in one piece.

'Yeah, it's fine,' Addison said, taking in the truncated pyramid of protein powder tubs lying in disarray behind him, with the top half of it scattered across the store. 'I'm kind of used to it by now. Sorry for knocking over your…'

It wasn't until that moment that Addison actually looked at the man before him, and his words drifted off. Head-to-toe muscle, the man bulged at every opportunity, his gym top and shorts holding on for dear life.

What was going on this morning? First the electrician, now this guy. It was like Milverton had been overrun by spinach-chugging sailors, with beefcakes springing up at every turn. It was all a bit much for a Monday morning.

'Oh no, no. You're all good,' the man said with a laugh, heading over to the tall display unit by the entrance. 'I turned it right up. Should've tested it out first. I'll turn it down a bit.' With an arm that was tattooed from wrist to shoulder he reached behind what Addison could now see was a little black box. It sat quietly and unobtrusively between two packets of some product of unknown purpose or application, and Addison could quite understand how he'd missed it. The other guy stepped back and flashed a look at Addison as if to say, *Well, let's see how we go this time*, before waving the other arm – un-tattooed but equally muscled – towards the street, in front of the little black box.

His arm was halfway through its arc when a vigorous, joyful, and very loud *Chahoo!* burst from the small unit.

'A bit more,' he said, once again reaching behind and then sticking an arm out in front of the door. The resultant *Chahoo!* was a few decibels quieter, perhaps a little less likely to induce heart attacks, but still quite enthusiastic.

Apparently satisfied with the result, the man turned to Addison, a wide smile on his face. 'My mate recorded it for me, and I set it up this morning. Hearty little speaker, far out.'

It turned out Addison's supposed assailant was in fact a personalised doorbell. 'You sure won't have anyone sneaking in or out unnoticed.'

'Too right, my man.' The other guy laughed, slapping Addison on the back before laying an arm across his shoulders and holding firm as he led Addison further into the shop. 'Wouldn't want to miss the chance to transform someone's life, would I?'

'Yeah, right…' Addison didn't have a clue what to say in the face of such earnestness. 'I guess not.'

The other guy only laughed harder. 'You're a crack-up, mate. I'm Zach by the way, and that's the missus,' he said, gesturing with his free arm at the floor-to-ceiling poster of himself and a woman, back to back, arms crossed, heads turned to look out at the open space with fierce, penetrating eyes. Across the top it read 'Go All the Whey' and just below that 'Zach Paine & Prisha Kumar-Attwood'.

'I'm Addison, nice to meet you.'

'Yeah, you too, bro,' Zach said, squeezing Addison across the shoulders and spinning them both around to face the shop floor. 'Addie, my man, we got everything you need to go *hard*. To get jacked.'

Zach suddenly relinquished his grip and stepped back, striking an exaggerating thinking pose. Addison couldn't help rolling his shoulders back and subtly clicking his neck side to side with the unexpected freedom.

'Nah… That's not your vibe. You want to go the distance. Runner, yeah? Or cyclist? Both? It's both, am I right?' Zach lifted his arm and brought it down in a swing of triumph coupled with a flick of the hand that clicked his fingers together with a bang. 'Nailed it! I got you, bro. Come here, come here.'

Zach raised an arm as if to wrap it around Addison's shoulders once more, but Addison stepped forward and out of reach before he could.

Now that he'd been in his presence for a bit, Addison couldn't shake the impression Zach was like an overgrown puppy whose favourite human had just got home from work and he wanted to show off what he'd been up to all day. He had serious Staffordshire Bull Terrier energy. He had the bulk and the mean look of Staffies, that was obvious. But he also had all their boundless love and affection that had to be shared immediately with anyone and everyone or he'd just burst.

Addison took a stab that he was about to be led to the 'Endurance' wall, and took himself over there before he could be aggressively side-hugged over. The alarmingly personalised doorbell had thrown him off balance for a good couple of minutes, but Addison knew he had to regain some control of this interaction or he'd never get what he came for. The first step was to not allow himself to be manhandled around the store.

Zach eagerly followed Addison's lead, clearly having mistaken his evasion for enthusiasm.

'I need something easy for when I'm out and about,' Addison said, an idea forming. 'My regular muesli bars aren't cutting it anymore.'

'I hear that. So you're not in the gym most of the time?'

'No, I'm usually outside, weather permitting. Fresh air and all that. What about these protein bars?'

'Yeah, man. They might be what you're after. Just what you need when you're on the move. We've got a few options here…' He pulled box after box off the shelves, each one accompanied with a slew of details, not that Addison managed to catch much of it. He let the guy talk while he considered how he might manhandle the conversation as he himself had been manhandled around the shop.

'Perfect,' Addison said, selecting a box at random. 'Based on what you've said, I think I might give these a go first.'

'Awesome.'

'I've got a way to go.' Addison paused, pretending to consider whether or not he was going to say anything further. 'But, well, I'm thinking of working up to a triathlon.'

'Yeah, I can see that, man. Good on you. Go for it!' Zach treated him to another back slap to emphasise his enthusiasm.

'Thanks, Zach. Probably not your regular triathlon though, you know?'

'What d'you mean?'

'I prefer to get outdoors, get amongst nature. It's where I'm at my best.' Possibly his biggest, most blatant fib to date. Addison usually preferred to keep his story close to the truth, which made it easier to keep things straight later on. But he didn't see how he could broach the topics he needed to without going out on a bit of a limb. Zach didn't need to know that Addison's body seemed rather allergic to nature, nor that his most recent foray into the wilds ended in literal death. 'With the ranges, the river and the gorge all on my doorstep, I'm thinking of taking on a cross triathlon.'

'Oh, yeah? Off road?' Zach nodded his approval. 'Hard core.'

'Yeah, it's been at the back of my mind for a while, but I've never had the guts.'

'True? What made you want to give it a shot?'

'This guy I met a few times,' Addison said, which was more or less true. Zach didn't need to know the meetings were nominally *dates*. 'It's pretty cool what he's done. Not that I could ever compare, of course, but he inspired me to maybe see if I could give it a go.'

'Oh, yeah? Would I know him? What's his name?'

'I met him back in Wellington, but he spent a bit of time up around here.' Then, Addison was sure to look Zach dead in the face when he said, 'Dominic Campbell. Have you heard of him?'

Zach's general puppy dog demeanour dropped. His lips drew into a line, Adam's apple bobbing up and down as he broke eye contact. 'Ah, yeah...'

Chapter 15

Zach didn't seem as if he was about to say anything further. Spooked into silence? Addison didn't want the guy clamming up and dismissing him from the shop, so he kept talking, hoping to encourage Zach to volunteer something.

'He was a bit controversial though,' Addison said with a shrug. 'Took what he wanted, no apologies. People seemed to love or hate him. I suppose it doesn't matter anymore though...'

Zach's attention was back on Addison in an instant. 'Did you hear about that then?'

He did much more than that, but he simply said, 'I did.'

Zach's shoulders immediately relaxed, and his eyes were wide with relief. 'I didn't want to be the one to tell you – that would've been tough. Sorry, man.'

'Yeah, thanks. I got quite the shock when... well, you know.' He wasn't about to finish that sentence – that would require a whole explanation he didn't want to get into. Addison shook his head instead, as if in dismay. Then, as is often the case when two people first discuss someone they'd both known, but probably not all that well, Addison pretended to find something else to say about them. 'I read that he often trained up here? In and around the Manawatū Gorge, is that right?'

'He sure did.'

'Great spot for it,' Addison said before slowly looking at the shop around him, as if the thought had just occurred. 'Did he ever come in here?'

'Oh yeah, of course.' Zach's voice was filled with obvious pride. 'We supply just about everyone around here.'

'Nice,' Addison said, before shifting into acting apprehensive. 'I hope you don't take this the wrong way, and I don't mean to suggest anything... but do you think, I don't know, these kinds of products might be *too good*?'

'What d'you mean "too good"?'

'Some of these supplements sound amazing, and must give athletes a real boost – physically and mentally. Do you think they might've led him to really push himself? Maybe even push too hard, beyond what his body could handle?'

'Nah,' Zach said, quick to respond, shaking his head and repeating his comment. 'Nah, Dom knew what he was about. He was a pro, not in danger of overdoing it like newbies might. Nah, Dom was solid.'

'Right, yeah. Of course.'

It had been a bit of a stretch, Dominic overdoing the supplements, thinking himself invincible and training recklessly. Despite that particular avenue running to a dead end, in all likelihood, Zach still might have other insights on the man. He was local, had dealt with Dominic more recently than Addison had, and in supplying him with supplements, he had some involvement in his professional life.

'Dominic was at the top of his game, no argument there,' Addison said, thoughtful as he considered the possible implications. 'But with such status comes *fame*.'

'Oh yeah, he was becoming a bit of a celebrity.'

'Do you think maybe that was the part of the job he didn't know how to handle properly? Not yet, anyway.'

'Yeah, maybe.' Zach gave a one-shoulder shrug. 'He wouldn't be the first to let a bit of fame go to his head.'

'For sure,' Addison said, nodding along. 'Did he try it on here?'

'What do you mean?'

'Oh, you know.' Addison gestured at the store around them. 'Did he come in here, swinging his minor celebrity status about to – uh – to *extract* sponsorship from you? Maybe some freebies?'

'You have met him, then.' Zach laughed, a quiet laugh that petered out and was more discomfort than amusement. 'We didn't sponsor him, not to start.'

'Really? Why's that?'

'Oh, we were already sponsoring another local athlete at the time, couldn't afford two. And Dom was asking for the big bucks. We're not a big business – not yet anyway! – so we couldn't be splashing the cash like that.'

'So you said no?'

'Had to, didn't we? But Dom didn't like that. He got a bit short with me, and the missus, not cool. But she can look after herself, so no worries there. Anyway, he told us to think about it, think about what was "best for the business".'

Addison felt his eyes widen and jaw slacken. 'He *threatened* you?'

Zach screwed his lips up, as if to communicate that he wouldn't put it quite like that. 'Dom was sharper than that. He wasn't shy about leaving bad reviews online, ranting on social media to all his followers, bad-mouthing anyone who didn't play his game. And he knew that we knew that. He had some clout, and wasn't afraid to use it. If he said something, people would listen.'

That sounded pretty threatening to Addison. 'What a racket.'

'Yeah, not the friendliest, but next time we talked Dom was able to convince us.'

'How did—'

'We came to a deal that made sense, financially, for us and for him. Sponsoring him has kept us in business, so all good.'

Zach may have been convinced, but Addison was far from it. 'Sponsoring Dominic was the cost to protect the business?'

'That's sort of where it started, sure. But he was a winner, and he got the Go All the Whey brand out there in front of heaps of eyeballs...'

'So, money well spent?'

'Got to spend money to make money, right?'

'Well, yeah. But—'

'I'm not afraid to say I spend a lot of money, and time, on my body,' Zach said, taking a step back and holding his hands open to his side, as if Addison hadn't already noticed his muscled bulk. 'In this industry – fitness, exercise, high performance – my body is my personal brand. Got to look good, that's number one.'

He lifted his arms then, spreading them wide before pulling a couple of poses and staring off into the middle distance, as if being photographed for a men's health magazine. It was on the tip of Addison's tongue to say yes, he got it, but he held back, hoping the guy was going somewhere with the impromptu modelling routine.

'Got to look good for the personal training gig – my clients expect it. And for the gym classes I run with the missus' – he pointed again to the giant image of them both on the wall – 'but everything else has got to be humming too, you get me? Online, we have to have social media and reviews – good reviews, I mean. Out there in the real world we've got the sponsorships, the billboards and the storefront – oh, and I got these printed the other day too. A bit old school, but kind of cool too, you know?'

Zach bounded over to the counter to fetch a business card. Addison dutifully looked down at it to see a photo of Zach Paine with his big arms folded, looking tough, and sporting a Go All the Whey singlet top. He had all the usual contact information included, but also an astonishing list of titles: Go All the Whey Co-founder, Gym Instructor, Personal Trainer, Fitness Coach, Health & Nutrition Mentor, Lifestyle Advisor, Brand Ambassador, and Social Media Influencer.

'You – uh – you wear a fair few hats, according to this?'

'Yeah, man. Gotta keep busy— Oh, here comes the missus now,' Zach said, looking up to the street beyond the storefront windows, his eyes glowing and a big, genuine grin on his face.

Chapter 16

Addison followed his gaze to see a tall and very athletic woman striding along the footpath in form-fitting workout clothes, gigantic drink bottle in hand, and with her long, wavy, dark brown hair streaming behind her. She moved in a way that seemed simultaneously unhurried and strikingly efficient.

'She's just been doing a core class for all the yummy mummies down at the gym,' Zach said to Addison before calling out as the shop door slid open. 'Hey, babe—'

Chahoo!

The woman burst into a torrent of curses as her eyes flew wide and her head whipped to the side. She immediately identified the small black box as the source of the alarm. Her arm shot forward and grabbed the offending device before jerking back in an instant, ripping the power cord from the wall.

It dangled from her grasp as she turned to face them, her lips already forming the first word when she spotted Addison – that is, a customer – and closed her mouth, working her jaw instead. She slowly approached her partner, eyes wild with the promise of words to come the moment they were alone together. Addison very much wanted to make that happen for her, preferring to be almost anywhere other than between a couple with an argument at the top of the to-do list.

He eased a half-step away from Zach, but couldn't outright abandon the situation without that making the whole thing worse.

Visibly measuring her words, she said in a dangerously pleasant tone, 'Zach, sweetheart, what did I say?'

'Sorry, babe.' If anything, he looked even more like a puppy dog in that moment, swapping out his excitement and energy for misery and regret. 'I thought it would be…' Zach trailed off at the scathing look he received, only to apologise again before gesturing to Addison and saying, 'This guy knew Dom Campbell.'

Whether the comment had been a haphazard attempt to shift the topic or just deflect attention away from himself Addison didn't much care, because at least it got them back on to the real reason for his visit.

The woman – who had to be Prisha, based on the floor-to-ceiling poster of her and Zach – turned her cold, hard glare on Addison. Her mouth moved with all the words still desperate to be spoken, but she forced it still and took a breath. 'I am sorry for your loss…' she said, drifting off, as if waiting for a name, asking who he was who knew Dom Campbell.

'Thanks, but "knew of" is probably closer to the truth. I'm Addison,' he said.

'Prisha,' she said with a nod, confirming Addison's minor deduction.

As if he felt like he had to explain himself, or just had an unwise desire to draw attention to himself once again, Zach said, 'We were just talking about, you know, how he wasn't always the coolest.'

Prisha looked from her partner to Addison and back again, her look one of exasperation. 'Um... why were—'

'Don't worry, Addison knows how it is,' Zach said with a nervous chuckle.

'Anyway...' Prisha said with a smile that was polite at best, looking from Addison to her partner and back again.

Addison recognised the attempted dismissal for what it was, but he still had one more question he had to ask. There might have been a better opportunity earlier, some way to seamlessly weave it into the conversation, but he'd had too many other things he wanted to know, and now his time was up. 'Anyway, no matter what we thought of him, it's quite the thing to happen,' Addison said, blowing air out of his cheeks and shaking his head. 'And right on Milverton's doorstep too.'

'It's been a bit like that around here recently,' Prisha said, eyebrow raised.

He ignored whatever it was she might have been trying to imply and focused on the final question he had to ask. 'Had – uh – had Dominic been in recently? Into the shop, I mean. Considering you sponsor him, you know. On the weekend, maybe, while he was up here?'

'No,' Prisha said, the one-word answer broadcasting once more that the conversation had come to an end.

For the recipient of such an abrupt response, the socially acceptable thing to do would be to make their excuses and leave. Again, Addison recognised it, and again, he chose to ignore it.

Luckily, he didn't have to do anything about it as Zach came to his rescue. 'Nah, hadn't seen Dom for weeks. He picked up a whole lot of stock a little while back, would've kept him going for months. Not anymore though, I guess.'

Addison made the appropriate noises of mild sorrow, and said as if it were of no consequence, 'So, when did you hear about his death?'

'On Saturday, just after it happened,' Zach said, eyes wide as he no doubt recalled the shock.

'Really? So soon? Did you hear about it from someone in town?' The question Addison really wanted to ask was *Were you up on the edge of Douglas Glade?* But he doubted *that* would get him to the answers he wanted.

'Nah,' Zach said. 'We were just finishing up a class when we heard all about it, weren't we, babe?'

Prisha sighed, as if resigned that this wasn't going to be wrapped up on her preferred schedule. 'Yes.'

'Someone from class heard from someone who heard from someone else who knew the guy flying the chopper.'

'Wow, right, OK. Crazy...' Addison said, shaking his head in apparent wonder. 'What kind of class was it, by the way?' He'd passed off the interest as friendly chat, hoping to mask the fact he was probing for any discrepancies, any evidence of a lie.

'Group fitness class at the gym, just around the corner,' Zach said. 'We double-team a weights class – low weights, high reps – every Saturday morning. I look after the guys' form, Prisha looks after the girls'. Good bunch. We had a solid twenty or so, didn't we?'

Prisha nodded.

'And between the two of us up on stage, everyone has something nice to look at.' Zach winked and smiled at that. 'Motivate, inspire, all that.'

Right. As far as alibis went, you didn't get much better

than having *twenty* people to vouch for you. And it would be easy enough to check. The only thing Addison was left suspecting was that Zach and Prisha's bodies were built on much more than one weekly general fitness class.

'You want to join? You should come,' Zach said with a slap on Addison's back. 'The first one's on us, just tell them I sent you and they'll let you in—' Zach cut himself short and turned to his partner. 'Oh, babe! I forgot to tell you – I meant to say, but everyone was too busy trying to get details about what happened—'

'You forgot to tell me what?'

Zach's eyes lit up in that way that says they've got something good. 'Dom struck again!'

Prisha didn't say anything, but her look of impatience conveyed it all.

'A review. Someone at the gym told me that Dom left another one. A real shocker, to hear them tell it. Just last week,' Zach said.

'Who?'

'Dale, I think. Or was it Brian? I can't remember.'

Lips held tight, Prisha breathed out through her nose. 'Who did Dom leave the review for?'

'Oh! Halswell's. Laid into them big time. That could've been us.' Zach shook his head. 'We dodged a bullet there. Apparently Julie was *fuming*.'

Prisha didn't respond immediately, looking thoughtful. 'Halswell's has been around forever – one bad review won't do any real damage. Julie knows that, she'll calm down.'

'He's dead now anyway.' Zach shrugged. 'Hard to stay angry at someone when they're dead.'

Addison had to agree, but he also couldn't help wondering at the timing of it all. On the other hand, a bad online review for your business hardly met anyone's reasonable threshold for murder, if such a thing even existed. 'Still, bad reviews are a bit of a kick in the shin, aren't they?'

'Well, yes,' Prisha said.

Addison turned to Zach, as casually as he could manage. 'Last week, was it?'

'Sure was. It's fresh, all right.' Zach flashed his eyes then drew his lips into a line. 'But yeah, Dom won't be leaving any more stinkers now, will he?'

'No, he won't,' Addison said. He truly didn't believe a bad review was cause for murder, but it did highlight Dominic's tendency to shoot his mouth, the arrogance to say what he pleased without considering the impact on others.

'What's that line about dead guys not being able to talk anymore?' Zach said. 'Dead, something…'

Addison's attention had been drifting, but at that comment he snapped back to the conversation. 'Dead men tell no tales.'

Zach repeated his elaborate arm swing, hand flick, finger click combo from earlier, resulting in a loud bang of triumph. 'That's the one, bro.'

After a pause, Prisha tried again. 'Anyway…'

'Yeah, sorry for holding you up, mate. Let me put those through for you,' Zach said, reaching out for the box in Addison's hand. 'And don't forget to come on Saturday.'

Addison made noncommittal noises about joining the group fitness class as he paid for the protein bars, his mind already miles away.

If someone has said something bad about you or your business, you might be angered, inclined to exact some kind of revenge. Addison didn't know what form such revenge might take, but he thought it safe to assume the proportional response to a bad review was not *murder*.

Putting aside the possibility it was just a terrible accident, Addison had only been considering Dominic's death as a response to something that had already happened... But what if it was the other way around?

What if someone hadn't done or said anything bad, not yet anyway? Could you be motivated to murder based on what someone *might* do or say? And killing them ensured they never would. They would take whatever it was to their grave.

Addison absently thanked Zach and Prisha as he left their shop. He had only one thing on his mind, that old saying...

Dead men tell no tales.

Chapter 17

It was indicative of how wrapped up in his own thoughts Addison was that he'd already walked past Lynne's Cafe before he realised he still hadn't had his first coffee of the day. Then he made the mistake of checking the time. He glanced up at the stone clock tower in the centre of the square as he turned to backtrack, and after a few quick calculations, realised he had precisely zero time.

If he were back in the capital, he would've had plenty of time. When it came to running simple errands, such as picking up coffee, Wellington offered efficiency and anonymity. Milverton, on the other hand, offered neither. It was small enough that everyone knew everyone else, and was always up for a chat – or near enough anyway. Which was nice, friendly, wonderful – top marks for community. But it also meant just popping in and out of anywhere with the minimum of fuss was a fantasy. And so, when Addison had a schedule to keep, such interactions had to be factored in.

He might have the time to squeeze in one more round of chat, but certainly not two. Going into Lynne's Cafe, he could anticipate the proprietress herself, and chances were good Addison would run into someone else too. He couldn't afford that when he knew, even if he skipped the coffee stop, he still had at least one round of guaranteed chat.

His current remote working arrangement, coupled with the lack of internet at Harper House, meant there was no other way. He had to get to the library, find a suitable working space, and get himself online. Only then could he get to work.

And the only way to get there was via the Milverton Visitor Centre.

Situated as it was in the library's spacious foyer, it made good use of the impressive old building and was convenient for visitors to town and locals alike. When so many older buildings were in danger of being knocked down for redevelopment, or blocked off to the public due to costly earthquake strengthening requirements, Milverton's library and visitor centre was one proud civic building earning its keep.

An asset, for sure, but it came with unintended consequences. Namely, there were always people about. Anyone stepping through the front doors couldn't expect to go undetected. Not least by the eagle-eyed septuagenarian often stationed at the visitor centre desk.

Mabel Zhou wasn't a whole lot taller than the desk herself, but from her position amongst the display stands of postcards, bookmarks, and fridge magnets, she spied all entering or passing through her domain.

'Addison!' Mabel said as she bustled around to intercept him with the agility of someone half her age. Decked out in her usual activewear, and with a cardigan over the top – today's a peachy apricot colour. Mabel had her finger on Milverton's pulse, and despite their obvious differences, was quickly developing into a close friend and confidant of Addison's. 'My dear, there you are.'

'Here I am,' Addison said for want of anything else to say, a forced cheeriness in his voice.

'Perfect timing – I've just started brewing a pot of tea. I'll grab an extra mug.'

'No need, thanks, Mabel. I've got to clock on, get some work done,' Addison said, lifting a shoulder to emphasise his laptop bag, and nodding through to the library proper.

'Don't be absurd, you can linger for a quick cuppa.'

He had factored in this very eventuality, and knew he had some time left before his absence online might be noted. It'd be fine, so long as it didn't extend to a second cuppa. And truth be told, he would rather like to have a quick catch-up with his friend. Addison acquiesced.

'Good,' she said with a quick nod before briefly ducking out back to retrieve another mug. 'I have hardly seen you lately.' Mabel's expression made her concern clear, which was backed up by her grey-white bob jostling from side to side in disbelief. 'And now *this*? Awful. Terrible. Shocking.'

'It was a shock, all right.'

'What must you be thinking of our quaint little town?'

Addison considered the question properly. He'd been in the supposed 'quaint little town' for barely a handful of weeks, so still tended to hold an outsider's perspective, but he'd also had more than a few peeks behind the curtain. He may have been more familiar with the town than your average tourist or visitor, but certainly much less so than Mabel – a Milvertonian of many decades. 'I'm thinking,' he said, 'I'm thinking Milverton might only be quaint at first glance.'

'We do rather sell that story though, don't we?'

Addison glanced at the rack of postcards, and conceded that many were undeniably quaint, with their picturesque images of the square, rose gardens, craft markets, and the like. But then there were others with dramatic, awe-inspiring scenery – the mountain ranges, the forest, the river, the gorge – and more adventure-tourism-style shots of kayaking, white-water rafting, rock climbing, abseiling, hiking, and mountain biking. 'Anyone who spends more than a few minutes around here will realise there's a fair bit going on in Milverton.'

Mabel murmured her agreement, following his gaze. 'And a little more besides.'

Addison winced as the deadly scenes he'd recently witnessed leapt to the front of his mind.

'I don't think we'll be putting any of *that* on a postcard though, will we?' Mabel said.

'No.' Addison's small spurt of laughter was one of dark amusement. 'Probably for the best Milverton doesn't advertise the string of sudden and unexpected corpses.'

'It's all rather kicked off recently.'

'Well, yes—'

'Since your arrival, in fact,' Mabel said, lips pursed and one eyebrow raised.

Addison's eyes widened and he began stumbling over a response when Mabel placed a hand on his forearm to cut him off.

'I am sorry,' she said, a smile now playing on her lips. 'I just couldn't help myself. Too soon, though, perhaps?'

'Perhaps,' Addison said, his tone void of any amusement.

'As someone new to town, though, nobody can accuse you of not *getting involved* now, can they?'

119

'There is that.' Addison sighed the sigh of the long suffering. 'I'd rather be a bit *less* involved, if I'm honest.'

'Can't even go for a nice walk without stumbling over a dead body.' Mabel tutted, shaking her head. 'What is the place coming to?'

Addison considered his new friend and had the sneaking suspicion Mabel's frustration had less to do with the tragedy or the impact on her town's reputation, and more to do with the fact that she hadn't been the one to make the discovery or break the news.

'Mabel,' Addison said slowly.

'Addison,' Mabel said, just as slowly in return.

'Are you maybe a little miffed you didn't stumble across the body yourself?'

Mabel's jaw slackened for a moment before she clasped it tight again. 'Of course not,' she said, turning away from Addison and bustling back to her station. With the desk between them, Mabel clasped one hand in the other and pursed her lips. She looked at Addison, blinking once before shaking her head. 'You mustn't be so... so *ghoulish*.'

Addison bit his lip and shrugged. 'It must have been a close-run thing. You and the Riverside Runners would've crossed paths with him too, just as Jake and I did.' Addison thought back to his ill-fated date and all the people on the trail that morning. 'It's not implausible to suggest you might have come across him there on the forest floor.'

Mabel gave Addison a long, stern look, before her features softened into something more like sheepishness. 'It is rather terrible of me – quite morbid, in fact – but I admit it may have crossed my mind...'

Addison was warming up a nice, big told-you-so for his friend – only fair considering how many he'd received himself – when she went on. 'But I would never – *never* – wish something so dreadful on anyone.'

'Even if they were, by all accounts, a bit of a pillock?'

'*Language*, Addison. But yes, even so.' Mabel's eyes narrowed. 'I see you've been thinking about the logistics of that morning, everyone's movements…'

'No, no. Just – uh – absent-minded ponderings—'

'Hah!' Mabel's short, sharp laugh cut him off, her gaze sharpening on him as she lowered her voice. 'Are you *investigating*, Addison?'

The denial was on the tip of his tongue. But he knew that wouldn't fly, not with Mabel – she would see right through him. And if he was going to find any success in his amateur sleuthing, he'd likely need her help. 'I'm keeping my mind open to the possibilities.'

'And your ears?'

'Keeping those open too.'

'And your mouth?

Addison goldfished for a moment, then cleared his throat. 'I might have asked a few questions.'

'You shock me, dear.'

'Something is *off*.'

Mabel considered the comment. 'And you won't be able to let it go until you get to the bottom of it?'

'Well, yeah.'

'I can understand that, especially considering you were the one to discover the body.'

'Exactly.'

'I don't suppose the fact he's your ex has anything to do with it?'

'What? How do you… He's not my ex.'

'Really?'

'We went on a few dates, that's it.'

'Still,' Mabel said with a shrug, 'you weren't exactly strangers, were you?'

'No, we weren't.'

Mabel nodded slowly, then jolted as she remembered their brewing tea. She slid the teapot between them – wrapped in its bright orange knitted tea cosy with pompom on top – lifted the lid briefly and nodded, apparently satisfied it had brewed sufficiently. Mabel spooned two sugars into her mug, poured tea into both, added a splash of milk, and gave each a quick stir before returning her attention to Addison.

'Tell me everything.'

Addison gave Mabel the heavily edited version of his history with Dominic, then briefly recapped what he'd been up to since he'd last seen her, sipping his tea all the while.

He touched on the quick trip back to Wellington, organising the electrician to run the fibre-optic cable up to Harper House, having the front door and back porch window latch fixed, signing the estate inheritance paperwork, and his potential new job working for the mayor of Milverton.

'Oh, yes! How is that progressing? Have you been given the contract yet? You know how the council can get bogged down with things sometimes. Do I need to have a word with Harriet?'

Mabel was already reaching for the phone when Addison had to concede the issue was with him.

'What do you mean?'

'I haven't said yes yet.'

Mabel tutted, rolling her eyes. 'Addison, are we still here, truly?

'I haven't had the space to think it through properly, and now this has happened...' Addison let out a long, slow breath. 'My mind has been a little preoccupied.'

'I can imagine,' Mabel said, sipping her tea, looking thoughtful. 'Another reason to get to the bottom of this Dominic Campbell situation, isn't it?'

'Yes, the sooner I can—'

'It all dovetails quite nicely though, don't you think?'

'What? Figuring out what happened to Dominic, and taking on a role with the mayor to help promote Milverton?'

'It's not one or the other, is it? They're both working towards the same goal.'

'Making Milverton a desirable place to live or to visit?' Addison said. 'To spend your time and your money?'

'Yes, welcome to the conversation, dear.'

'Oh, come on.'

'Clearing up this latest drama, uncovering what happened in Douglas Glade. That would be an excellent first step in repairing the hammering Milverton's image has been taking lately. I'm sure the mayor would appreciate some assistance on that front. Almost like she needs a marketing consultant from the big city to come help?'

'It's a bit of a stretch, but I can see what you're saying, Mabel.'

'You're already doing the job, practically. Might as well get paid for it.'

'I hear you, I hear you.' Addison smiled despite himself – she made a good case. 'Anyway,' he said, finishing the last of his tea, 'I'd better get to work. Thank you for the tea. We can pick this up later?'

'I feel like we've barely skimmed the surface. But OK, what about over lunch? What are you doing today?'

'I thought I might go and check out Halswell's, actually.'

Mabel tilted her head. 'Another date, is it?'

'No, I—'

'You were in there shopping *very* recently.'

'I'm not—'

'Three nice new shirts, I seem to recall. And three pairs of briefs.' She raised an eyebrow, a smirk on her lips.

'I'm hoping to catch Julie Halswell, if you must know, to ask about an online review.'

'Oh, I did hear about that. Yes, and you might as well get a haircut while you're in there. Pretty sure Julie has her barber on the chair on Mondays.'

Addison couldn't help reaching a hand to touch his hair. He knew she was right, had been meaning to sort it out for a few weeks now. 'I might do that.'

'Actually, how about we pick this up Wednesday afternoon, after work? How does that suit you?'

'Yeah? I don't think I have anything on.'

'Wonderful. We're going car shopping.'

'Car shopping?'

Mabel frowned. 'Maybe you did hit your head after all? Or just had that brain of yours rattled around a bit too much?'

'No, no. Right, of course. Your little red car isn't in such good shape after our last adventure.'

'Understated as ever, Mr Harper,' Mabel said, patting his arm. 'The poor girl has been written off, she's destined for the scrap heap.'

'Hence car shopping.'

'I do wonder about you sometimes, dear,' Mabel said, smiling while shaking her head. 'Anyway, Sergeant Murphy, your *beau*—'

'Jake is not my *beau*.'

'He was very helpful providing the police report to the insurers, and they've been surprisingly responsive. Perhaps they just didn't want to go toe to toe with me?'

'Your reputation precedes you,' Addison said with a smile.

'The car yards are open later on Wednesdays, apparently, extended hours.'

'That's all fine, but... I know nothing about cars – you know that, right? I don't even have my licence.'

'Yes, yes. But I'm a little old lady, and you are a *male*.' Mabel held up her hand to halt Addison's protest. 'I know, I know. It's rubbish. I just cannot be bothered dealing with these salesy types, trying it on with granny.'

'They wouldn't dare.'

'Oh, they would. I can look after myself, you know that,' Mabel said. 'But it would be good to have backup.'

'You're pre-empting a sexism and ageism combo?'

Mabel nodded. 'You can just stand there and look imposing.'

Addison doubted his effectiveness on that front, but considering he was a large part of the reason she needed a new car, he reckoned perhaps he owed her this.

***

As was often the case, Addison found his generous time allocation had been all but devoured by the various residents of Milverton. It was a work day, and the time when Addison ought to start working was very much upon him. There was so much going on, and he could've easily just thrown in the towel, but he knew it was important to maintain his current employment, at least until he'd settled on what he was doing next.

The inheritance from his great-uncle Herbert was significant, Addison knew, involving Harper House and other properties and assets from around the district, but not a whole lot of spare cash. From what he could see, the various assets paid their own way as far as upkeep, and a little more besides, though not enough that he could draw a decent income to live on. So, if he wanted to use his great-uncle's assets to pay for the groceries, he'd have to start selling them. He wasn't ready to bite that bullet, and he wasn't sure he would ever be. It wasn't even an option, at least not right away – with paperwork signed, things were in motion, but it all took *time*.

Even if quitting work outright was an option, he didn't think he'd ever take it – Addison didn't envision himself living as a landlord of leisure.

Moral of the story: he had to keep working. Whether that was sticking to his current role based back in Wellington or taking up the new job offer in Milverton. He knew he'd have to give the decision proper consideration, and he'd have to do it soon. Addison recognised the privileged position he found himself in and was determined not to squander it, knowing he'd hate for one of the options to disappear before he could make his choice.

He had to keep his current role ticking over so he could keep his job into the future, or at least until he could hand in his notice. To put it bluntly, he didn't want to get fired before he could quit.

It was true that Addison had flirted with a couple of deadlines, but he was yet to cross any, despite everything going on during his time in Milverton. And he'd called in a few favours from work colleagues, but he'd built them up for just such an occasion. If not now, then when?

Addison plugged into his burgeoning inbox, addressing the easiest and most urgent emails, tagging anything else important for attention later, and deleting the rest. He took a couple of calls, progressed the main project he was working on, and otherwise just hopped from one fire to the next.

The alarming tedium devoured the day and he reached lunchtime without hardly realising. He was proficient at his job, but recognised it was often almost an out-of-body experience these days. Going through the motions on auto-pilot for a few hours. Mabel was right – he needed to give the mayor's proposal serious consideration, or who knew where he might end up?

If he didn't take this chance, would a few hours on auto-pilot soon grow into a few decades?

Chapter 18

It was hard enough admitting to himself, let alone anyone else, that another reason Addison was seriously considering making the move to Milverton permanent had just stepped out onto the street in front of him.

As much as Addison liked to think all his decisions were logical – that is, made using his brain alone – he had to admit other organs had a say in the matter too...

His heart was the organ to which he was referring, of course. Decisions about the man made using his head and his heart, nothing else.

The man in question emerged from the Milverton Police Station with a frown across his brow, engrossed in something on his phone. His distraction did afford Addison a moment to appreciate him in uniform, blue from tip to toe and back up again – up those legs, around that waist, over that chest, and across those broad shoulders. The uniform fit so well and in all the right places – a sight Addison didn't think he'd ever tire of.

The casual shorts and T-shirt the man had worn for their bush walk had been made with thinner and more flexible fabric, designed for exercise, unafraid of leaving a bit of leg and a bit of arm on display. This uniform couldn't have been more different – stiff and unyielding, buttoned up, with only the skin of his hands, neck and face exposed. Yet, somehow, it was all the more enticing for it.

Sergeant Jake Murphy pocketed his phone and pulled out a set of keys, only then looking up. His expression softened at the sight of Addison, a slight smile lifting his lips as he approached, only coming to a halt when they were a pace apart. 'It's nice to see you. I'm sorry we had to cut things short.'

'Me too,' Addison said, with genuine regret. 'Kind of a mood-killer though, wasn't it?'

Jake made a noise that sounded like he wanted to laugh and agree while simultaneously recognising such a reaction was beyond what was considered acceptable or appropriate for him in his role as sergeant. 'I wanted to call,' he said instead, 'but I haven't had a moment—'

'Oh no, it's fine.' Addison waved away the explanation. 'I'm sure you've had plenty to sort out.'

Jake murmured his agreement, looking at Addison for a long while, before glancing back at the police station, then the street beyond.

'What's happened?' Addison said, thrown by how unsettled Jake seemed to be.

The sergeant shook his head, his gaze slowly returning to Addison. 'It's about Mr Campbell...' he said, trailing off as he took in and let out a long, slow breath.

Addison desperately wanted to ask what it was, but knew his prompting would not expedite the explanation. If anything, it'd cause the man to reconsider saying anything further at all. Instead, Addison pulled on his best concerned and receptive face, one which communicated that he was listening without saying a word.

Jake drew his lips into a line. 'Things aren't entirely stacking up—'

Despite the very best of intentions, Addison opened his mouth to ask what that meant, but Jake had come to know Addison too well, recognising the signs and pre-empting the immediate questions.

'—but I can't go into any real detail. Not yet, anyway.'

Addison knew it, he *knew* it. There was more to this whole situation with Dominic.

'I know that you...' Jake said. 'I know that you knew him.'

Jake paused, breaking eye contact for a moment. That statement was nothing new – Addison had told Jake himself, after all – but the words seemed more loaded than Addison thought they had any right to be. Did he detect a note of jealousy? Maybe, maybe not. Something to keep an eye on.

'I understand how it must feel to have come across him like that, and to have lingering questions. But I hope you can understand that we have it all under control?'

Addison nodded.

Jake, apparently requiring verbal confirmation, raised an eyebrow.

'Yes, of course.'

'Good,' Jake said. 'And by "we" I mean the police department.'

Addison glanced up at the station, then back to Jake. 'Absolutely.'

Jake waited a moment until he was sure he had Addison's attention before he said, 'And you understand that you are not a member of the police department?'

'Yes, yes. I know that.'

'So you'll leave this – a possible *murder* case – up to us?'

Addison could see what Jake was doing in drawing out commitments and removing any room for convenient misunderstandings. Such treatment would typically irk him, but Addison couldn't begrudge the man for it, considering his recent track record. And in this particular situation, he knew the answer Jake was looking for, but also knew that was not an answer he could provide. He may not have been able to respond in the affirmative – not in good conscience, anyway – but neither could he lie by responding in the negative – that would only lead to trouble. Instead, Addison opted for the third option, favoured by politicians the world over – he would ask and answer his own question instead. 'Will I leave the police investigation up to the police?' Addison said. 'Yes, I will.'

Sergeant Murphy narrowed his eyes, clearly suspicious, and about ready to object.

Before he could identify the gaps in Addison's statement and extend the ban to include, just as an example, any other, non-police investigations, Addison leapt back in. 'The whole thing has just thrown me a bit,' he said. 'I think it's as you say, I knew Dominic so it feels more personal somehow.'

Addison had to say something to shift the conversation away from its focus on his sleuthing tendencies, but reminding Jake of his previous involvement with Dominic was a low blow. Such a salvo was liable to push the Jake he was coming to know back behind his walls of professionalism, leaving only the cool and efficient Sergeant Murphy in his place. He would hate to see Jake retreat like that, not when he was only just making inroads past the tough exterior to the soft and squishy bits inside.

There was a slight change in his face, but Addison was

relieved to see Jake remained – wary, sure, but present. 'I'm sorry, I can understand that,' he said, nodding. 'Hopefully we'll be in a position to resolve this situation soon, give everyone some closure.'

Addison almost confessed then and there, unprepared for the impact of his skirting around the truth and the misdirection. The guilt he felt at the blatant emotional manipulation was like a rock in his gut.

They were both all over the place, clearly ill at ease with each other. If Jake was holding back as much as Addison was, he shouldn't be surprised.

'Anyway,' Jake said, nodding towards the police station. 'Was that what you were here for?'

'Huh?'

'To get more information about Mr Campbell?'

'No,' Addison said much too quickly and insistently. His immediate instinct was defensiveness, his guilt-addled subconscious on edge. Yes, he was out during his lunch break, perhaps with the goal of asking a few questions about Dominic. But it wasn't why he was *here* – that is, outside the police station. It just so happened that the police station was situated on the most direct route between the library and his actual destination: Halswell & Company. But he'd be lying if he said he hadn't considered – perhaps even hoped? – when he'd closed his laptop and set out that he might encounter Milverton's top cop.

When Addison hadn't volunteered any further explanation, Jake tried again. 'Were you here to see me?'

'No.' Addison's response came out once again with more force than he would've preferred. He cleared his throat. 'A happy coincidence,' he said, smiling, comfortable in that truth. 'Just popped out over my lunch break. Was on my way to get a haircut.' Mabel had put the idea in his head, and his mouth had clearly run with it. His hair had already been getting in his eyes weeks ago and was now longer still.

'Oh,' Jake said, jaw slack as his eyes drifted up and then to each side of Addison's face. He lingered for a moment, as if he wanted to say something but couldn't quite decide what, before eventually returning his gaze to meet Addison's. He cleared his throat and said, 'Did you want to do something one evening this week?'

Addison was too surprised at the unexpected question – and relieved to hear dating remained on the table – that he barely considered the outing might be an excuse for Jake to keep an eye on him. If that's what he wanted, he could look all he liked.

He may have been surprised, but was pleased to find he had apparently retained his wits, and responded with more nonchalance than he felt. 'Pick up where we left off?'

Jake sucked in some air through his teeth. 'We won't have enough daylight for a walk after work, not for another month or so.'

'Oh, I didn't mean—' The small smile tugging at the corner of Jake's mouth cut Addison short. He paused and regrouped, then said that was fine by him. 'I've had my fill of nature lately anyway. What were you thinking?'

'Dinner?'

That was much more Addison's speed. 'I could do dinner.'

'How's Wednesday?'

Not good. He'd already committed to car shopping with Mabel on Wednesday. His face must've communicated as much because Jake's tentatively growing smile faltered.

'It doesn't have to be—'

'No, no. Wednesday's great,' Addison said. He could do both – accompany Mabel to a car dealership, then head out for dinner with Jake.

Jake waited for a beat, giving Addison the chance to think it through and change his mind if he wanted. 'You're sure?'

'Yep. And you organised last time, so this time it's my turn.'

'You don't have to do that,' Jake said. 'I asked you—'

'No, no.' Addison held up a hand. He had no idea what he was going to organise or where he was going to take him but he just knew he couldn't leave Jake making all the decisions.

What were his options? He had to think quick.

Grab some fish and chips and have a picnic in the square? That'd be nice and relaxed... Too relaxed? Possibly. Probably.

Also, much too open – the square didn't have the kind of privacy Addison was looking for, the kind of *intimacy*...

Besides, the last picnic hadn't exactly been a wild success.

No, he wasn't going to do any form of takeaways – too easy, too disposable. He wanted somewhere *proper*, somewhere that said *This is a date*.

What about the pub? The food at The Langston was very good, and Addison already knew Jake liked it there too. But then so did his constables, and practically everyone else in Milverton... No, the risk someone would invite themselves to join their table for a drink was just too high. Absolutely not the vibe Addison was going for.

There was the restaurant Jake had taken him to the weekend before... It was ideal, but no, they couldn't do the same place twice in a row. And Addison didn't know about other local restaurants – any might serve for their purposes, but he didn't *know*. He'd be taking a stab in the dark and hoping for the best. Much too much would be left up to chance, and Addison could not abide such a situation.

Even if the dinner went perfectly, he didn't want to risk a repeat of last time, with him falling asleep on the drive home. The only surefire way to remove that risk was to remove the drive home altogether.

Only one option remained. Addison looked up at Jake and with more confidence than he felt, he said, 'Come over to Harper House for dinner. I'll cook.'

Chapter 19

The moment they parted, Addison's mind flooded with self-recrimination.

What had he just committed himself to? He might be a capable baker, but he was a notoriously terrible cook.

Addison took a deep breath in, knowing that if he allowed it, he'd spend the next two days worrying himself into a puddle of paralysis. He would not dwell on it. There would be plenty of time for that later, so he could afford to park the issue for now. He had to trust he'd come up with *something* in the meantime, but not right that minute. His destination was already in sight, and he didn't have time to wallow.

He slowly released the breath, looking up at the handsome building before him. A contemporary of the civic buildings fronting the square, this was one of the town's original structures, diligently maintained throughout the many decades – no cheap construction thrown up on a budget. It had been home to Halswell & Company since 1949, according to the signage.

His reasoning for visiting may have been thin at best, but it was all he had. With nothing else for it, Addison stepped inside.

The low light and dark decor gave the shop a hushed and indulgent air, with heavy timber shelving, racks, and display tables stacked with menswear, hiking gear, camping equipment, fishing rods, and bicycles. And then there was the taxidermied, and impressively antlered, deer's head on the side wall – not so much Addison's style, but it fitted in well up there. Even with so much *stuff*, the high ceilings kept the space from feeling too closed in and claustrophobic.

Then there were the industrial-style light fittings, brushed metal, exposed pipework, and the faint scents of leather and oil which lent the shop a decidedly masculine vibe. But he wasn't there looking for anything on the shelves – he was looking for information, and a haircut.

Addison passed a shop assistant and a few other shoppers on his way to the far corner where he'd remembered seeing the barber's chair.

The barber was tall and lean, of similar age to Addison, with dark hair that was as long as Addison's, or even longer, its wildness in stark contrast to his well-groomed moustache. He had a random assortment of individual and small, seemingly unrelated tattoos up each arm, and sported a navy apron with thin vertical white stripes that looked more like something a butcher might wear than a barber. He leant against a bench lined with combs, clippers, razors, and a mirror which was propped up against the wall. In one hand he held a small cup of espresso – which he sipped – and in the other a tatty paperback – which he read, his eyes never leaving the page.

Addison called out a tentative greeting as he approached. The barber slowly raised his gaze, as if he couldn't fathom someone interrupting his reading. But the moment he caught sight of Addison, he snapped the book shut – without even marking his place, Addison couldn't help but notice – cocked his head, and smiled.

Downing the last of his coffee, he set his cup and book aside, then pushed off the bench.

'Were you looking for me?' he said, his voice light and playful.

Addison hated to stereotype, but by the look of the guy, he had to be the barber on duty today. 'I was hoping to get a haircut.'

A smile slowly spread across the face of the man in the butcher's apron. 'And I was hoping to *give you one*,' he said, and in such a way that left no doubt in the mind about what he was referring to – like the verbal equivalent of a waggled eyebrow.

Addison blanched at the shamelessly suggestive tone, told himself the barber meant he was hoping to give Addison a haircut and that was all. Because he was a barber and that's what barbers did. Still, Addison couldn't shake the feeling he'd stepped into some full-service massage parlour, and that he'd somehow signalled he'd like the works, happy ending included. 'Just a haircut, please.'

'Absolutely. Sit, sit,' the barber said, still smiling as he gestured to his chair. 'I will take *very* good care of you.'

Addison grimaced – that was what he was worried about. As he stepped over and settled himself down into the chair, he reasoned the barber would be like this with everyone. It was just their ideas about the boundaries of friendliness didn't quite match. From Addison's perspective, the barber had burst out of the friendly client interaction zone, stormed across no man's land, and thrust deep into flirtation territory.

With a flourish, the barber draped the black cape over Addison's front, tied a strip of paper towel around his neck, and fixed the cape in place. 'Not too tight, is it?' he said, hands resting lightly on Addison's neck.

'No,' Addison said, clearing his throat. 'It's fine.'

'Good, that's good. I want you to be comfortable.'

Addison was anything but. Still, he was here for a purpose. Two purposes, in fact. He needed a haircut and he needed information.

No sooner had he reminded himself of this than the thought evaporated. The barber was running his fingers through Addison's wavy, loose curls – a surprisingly intimate act. 'You don't want me to cut this, do you?' he said, voice incredulous. 'I'd kill for thick, luscious locks like this.'

'Yeah,' Addison said, mentally grasping onto at least the need for the haircut. 'It's getting in my eyes.'

'Just a trim then, hmm? A little tidy up?'

'Please.'

'Nothing too drastic, or you won't need to come back for months. No, we can't have that.' He continued to run his fingers through Addison's hair, inspecting from every direction. Finally he ran both hands up the back of Addison's head, through his hair from the base to the crown, then kneaded his scalp, each fingertip applying firm pressure, pulsing one, two, three times.

Addison blanked for a second, coming back to his senses a moment later with his jaw slack and body slumped in the chair. He also caught the tail end of a groan of pleasure, only realising when it was already too late that it was him making the noise.

'Now, now. Can't be making sounds like that or you

might give a guy the wrong idea. Or the right idea.' The barber's hands were on Addison's shoulders then, kneading them once for emphasis, a glint in his eyes. 'And seeing as we're getting to know each other so well, what should I call you?'

'Addison,' he said, pulling on his bravest grimace of a smile.

'Very nice to meet you, Addison,' the barber said. 'OK, let's sort you out.' He pulled away and moved around to the bench, with his back to Addison, busying himself with his equipment.

Addison shook himself, relieved to be out of the barber's direct focus, if only for a moment.

'I'm Seb, by the way,' he said when he turned back and started spraying Addison's hair with his little mist bottle. 'Not Sebastian. *Never* Sebastian.'

The barber – Seb, not Sebastian – didn't say anything further, just kept spraying. But Addison sensed he wanted to keep talking.

Considering Seb had already fit one barber stereotype with the assorted tattoos up his arms, Addison wondered if he might fit another. Barbers – and hairdressers, for that matter – were renowned for their small talk. Armed with a skill that few professions had mastered so completely, they could chatter away all day no matter who was in their chair, often carrying much of the conversation themselves.

Addison wondered if perhaps Seb required a little prompting to make it clear he was a receptive audience. The barber didn't seem to need any prompting in their interaction so far, the opposite in fact. But if Addison engaged, then the occasional nudge later on to steer the conversation wouldn't seem so out of place…

'Why not Sebastian then?'

'Well,' Seb said immediately and with great drama – it seems he had been waiting for Addison to ask. 'I dropped the "astian" – all those extra syllables – back in primary school. Had to get a bit of distance from that ridiculous red crab.'

Addison took a second to catch up to what Seb was talking about. '*The Little Mermaid*?'

'What else?' Seb said with a grunt, squirting yet more water. 'Walt Disney has a lot to answer for.'

Again, Seb didn't appear as if he would volunteer what the animator had to answer for. 'What's so bad about—'

'I'll tell you what's so bad. My bully – a girl by the name of Gretchen Thorpe – she hit puberty before anyone else, towered over all of us, and the tyrant took full advantage. Well, when the teachers weren't looking, she'd start singing "Under the Sea" and making crab hands at me.' Seb made pincer movements with his free hand to illustrate the point. 'Soon half the school was singing that ridiculous song at me, and with terrible Jamaican accents too.'

'Children can be awful.'

'Oh, they can be. Teenagers though, they can be so much worse. But by the time we hit high school I had grown a bit, and more importantly, had learnt how to play the game.' Seb paused with his spraying, caught Addison's eye in the mirror, and smiled something sinister.

'*The Teenaged Mermaid*,' Addison said. '*Revenge of the Crab*?'

Seb laughed. 'You know it,' he said, beaming as he returned to his spraying. 'Socially, I was on the rise, but Gretchen had passed her peak, not that she recognised that yet. She tried to revive Sebastian and his musical number under the sea, but updated for her pubescent audience. Can you guess how that went?'

Addison had no clue, and he said as much.

'She sang about crabs *under the pants*, accompanied with the appropriate scratching gestures.'

Addison let out an involuntary 'Eww.'

'*Eww* is right, but I knew better than to take the bait. Instead, I kept my mouth shut and feigned the confusion that everyone else was feeling. Most of our class had only ever known me as Seb, and *The Little Mermaid* wasn't as fresh in everyone's minds as it had once been, so nobody made the connection between me, Seb, and Sebastian the singing cartoon crab. And worse for Gretchen, her attempted taunt backfired big time. Forever after, itchy bits were associated with Gretchen, and to seal the deal, one of our classmates bestowed her with the nickname Crabby Panties.'

'You're right,' Addison said with a grimace. 'Teenagers are so much worse.'

'Indeed.' Seb laughed and shook his head. 'Poor girl. I almost felt bad for her, but she only had herself to blame.'

With Addison's hair more than sufficiently wetted, Seb moved on to cutting, all while maintaining a steady stream of light banter and gossip.

In the course of his amateur sleuthing, Addison had grown accustomed to easing unsuspecting interviewees into the questioning he'd intended from the start. Seb needed no such warming up. As far as preliminaries went, this guy did it all, simultaneously acting as interviewer, interviewee, and barber.

Who said men couldn't multitask? Admittedly, Addison often struggled. But Seb was a master. The only encouragement he needed from Addison was the occasional murmur of agreement or tut of mutual disapproval.

Addison realised he'd allowed his mind to wander when he found himself picturing Seb as Sebastian the crab, with the barber wielding a comb in one hand and a pair of scissors in the other, cutting and chatting away.

The uncharitable thought brought Addison back to the task at hand. Seb had been snip-snip-snipping for a few minutes already, and Addison reckoned he'd better start steering the conversation or he'd have one task successfully completed – the haircut – before he'd even started the other more important one – acquiring information.

Chapter 20

'What brings you to Milverton?' Addison said after the apparent conclusion of one of Seb's stories but before he could launch into the next. 'I hear you're only here a couple of days a week. Is that right?'

'You are well informed. The rest of the week I'm in Wellington, but Mondays and Tuesdays I'm right here – usually, anyway. I try to keep it consistent, so my Milvertonians know when to come in. It has been a bit quiet today...' Seb trailed off, glancing around the rest of the shop, as if he might have missed a sudden surge in customers.

'And you stay overnight in Milverton?'

Seb returned his focus to Addison, a smile growing. 'Are you offering to keep me company tonight?'

'Oh—' Addison realised his error the moment he'd made it, and felt the familiar surge of blood rushing to his face.

'We could make it a weekly engagement?'

'No, no—'

'The nights can get quite chilly.'

Addison wanted to say he already had someone else in mind for any future chilly nights, to make it clear he had no

144

intention of offering Seb such company. But he knew that would only lead to more questions and he found he did not want to discuss Jake with this uncomfortably forward barber. Addison cleared his throat while simultaneously willing the redness to take leave of his cheeks. 'I was just interested in how it all, you know, how it all fits together, splitting up your working week?' All things considered, Addison was rather pleased with his response.

Seb sighed, then shook his head, his smile still present, though a little less effusive than it had been a moment earlier. 'I love it, truly, coming up here. So good to get out of the city, have a bit of a break and some fresh air. Lately though,' Seb said, shaking his head, 'it feels even more chaotic here than in the city, what with everything going on.'

Those goings-on were precisely what Addison had come to get more information about. This was his opportunity.

'I do love it though, secretly,' Seb said, then lowered his voice, leaning a little closer to Addison's ear. 'I love hearing all the gossip and scandal, what everyone's up to.'

'Oh, yeah? What have you heard?' Addison didn't want to lead the witness, so to speak, not if he didn't have to. 'What's everyone up to?'

'I heard that a certain someone and a certain sergeant are getting up to a certain something.' Seb paused with the cutting, one hand on his hip and the other holding the scissors out at a jaunty angle while he pinned Addison with a look via the mirror, one eyebrow raised.

So he already knew, and yet insisted on continuing with his shameless flirtation? This guy was infuriating.

Apparently Addison's lack of immediate response was all the confirmation Seb required. 'Sergeant Jake Murphy,

145

gorgeous man.' He shook his head in disbelief. '*Gorgeous* man. I've had my eye on him for months – months! – and then you come swooping in before I could even catch his attention. I could just…' Seb bit his lip and snapped the scissors shut, flipped them around so the point of the blades protruded from his closed fist and stabbed at the air.

The motion was a good foot away from Addison's neck, but he couldn't help clenching every muscle and tendon in response.

'I'm having you on. Relax,' Seb said with a chuckle and a quick squeeze of Addison's shoulder before returning to cutting his hair, as if he hadn't just pseudo-stabbed him in the neck. 'I'm happy for you and Jake. True, I would be happier if it was *me* and Jake we were talking about. But I wouldn't want to get between you two. Or maybe I would?' Seb cocked his neck, as if picturing it. 'You let me know.' And then he winked. He *actually* winked.

Addison was a wreck – a ball of nerves, with heart beating and blood rushing down, then up to his face, then back down again. He'd gone from being blatantly propositioned to jealously threatened then right back again, all while trapped in the barber's chair.

He did not want to talk about this and needed to change the topic, get back on solid ground. It was getting clammy under the cape draped across his front and around his neck. Addison cleared his throat and redirected the conversation. 'You mentioned before you're usually back in Wellington over the weekend. Was that the case for this weekend just gone?'

'Oh, spoilsport,' Seb said, giving Addison's shoulder another quick squeeze. 'Yes, I was. I missed all the drama, again!'

OK, here goes. 'You heard about Dominic Campbell then?'

'Did I ever! It's all Julie has been able to talk about since I got in this morning.'

'What did she—'

'Don't know much yet, but it's terrible, isn't it?' Seb sighed, shaking his head. 'Good-looking guy. Super fit too – though that was his job, wasn't it? And a nice head of hair.'

'You met him?'

'I did one better: I cut his hair a couple of times, in this very chair. He came in here a bunch for supplies, not usually when I was working, but you hear things.'

Addison waited for him to go on, but apparently he needed prompting again. 'What things?' he said slowly.

'Well, you didn't hear it from me.' Seb made a show of looking around the space for anyone else who might overhear. 'Julie doesn't want word getting out, giving people ideas, you understand? But, well, Dominic had come in here and ripped off the shop something shocking. He'd stocked up on all his outdoor gear, then returned it a few weeks later saying it was faulty, demanding a full refund. There was nothing wrong with any of it – he'd just thrashed it, used it to death. Thousands of dollars' worth. Daylight robbery is what Julie reckons. Not that that man of yours could do anything about it.'

Addison wanted to say he didn't own Jake. He also felt an almost overwhelming urge to defend him. But then he caught Seb's expression and realised the barber was goading him. That realisation took him precious seconds, so he was still working on what he wanted to ask next when Seb went on.

'Dominic didn't strike me as the kind of guy with many

147

friends. Fans, maybe. But not friends,' Seb said, pulling various lengths of Addison's hair taut, and making only the occasional cut. 'Just the way he spoke about things, oblivious and completely selfish. He didn't realise how much he was screwing others over. No respect.' Seb's eyes went wide and he scoffed at himself. 'Oh my Gaga, listen to me. "No respect"? I sound like some crotchety old grouch twice my age.'

'What kind of things was he—'

'Speaking of, Hugo Li. You met him?'

'What? No, I—'

'He's old – well, not that old, but *older*, I guess. And he's not normally a grouch, too much of a salesman for that. But I had him in my chair only last week, and boy was he fired up. Telling me about some mega-triathlete or something who'd taken a car from his lot for a test drive, but didn't return it until right on closing time. He'd treated the car like a rental for the day, and didn't pay a cent for the pleasure. Returned it filthy too. Sounding familiar? Can you guess who that might have been?'

'Dominic.'

'You bet your sweet—'

'There's certainly a pattern of behaviour emerging,' Addison said, making a mental note to see if he could find out more about this Hugo Li.

Seb made noises of agreement that left no doubt how he felt about it. 'There's only so much of that you can put out into the world. Something – or *someone* – was bound to get him one of these days.'

'You seem sure of that?'

'Well, he is dead, isn't he?' Seb shrugged, as if it was obvious.

'True.' Addison had to concede the other guy had him there. In fact, for the majority of this conversation Seb had been keeping him on his toes, or on the back foot, or both. To push the podiatric analogies beyond where most might consider acceptable, Addison needed to re-establish his own footing, while simultaneously wrong-footing Seb. 'So, was it you, then?' Addison said. 'Did you *get him*?'

'Me? Hah! You won't catch me dragging myself up into the bush, let alone someone else. Do I look like someone who goes *off-road*?' Seb stepped back and gestured by running a hand up and down his front.

'I guess not?' Addison had thought the same of himself, city boy through and through, at least until lured well beyond the town limits with the promise of a picnic and a day with the sergeant.

'No,' Seb said, returning his attention to Addison's hair. 'I've got all the *opportunity* I need right here in this chair.'

'How's that?'

'Oh, I marvel at the power we wield. All these sharp objects, so close to so many important body parts. One little slip... We demand such trust from our customers.'

Well, if that didn't make someone wildly uncomfortable, Addison didn't know what would. More than a little unsettled, Addison decided his best bet was to play for a laugh. 'What, you'd go full Sweeney Todd on him?'

'Exactly!' Seb laughed, a touch too maniacally for Addison's liking. 'Scissors, razors, clippers – all these cutting implements around people's throats all day, every day. But if that's all it took, if I popped off every time someone said something a bit off-colour then Mrs Lovett wouldn't be able to keep up.' Seb laughed again, snapping his scissors to demonstrate, his message reinforced by their sharp, quick sound.

Addison wondered how he could have ever seen this man as a musical, cartoonish crab. Instead, he now had a murderous barber and cannibalistic pie-maker in his head, which once again had things heating up under the cape with all the trapped, nervous energy.

Seb dropped his head so it was level with Addison's, hovering just over his right shoulder, and pinned him with a glare in the mirror as he spoke, his voice low and menacing. 'Seb Naylor: the demon barber of Milverton.' And then he was back up again with a smile. 'It's no Fleet Street, but it's got a certain ring to it, doesn't it? I'll have to talk to Julie about making space in here somewhere for a pie shop.'

Addison rallied, reassuring himself the barber just loved a bit of theatre, especially when he had a captive audience. As Seb had said, if he wanted someone dead, then he'd have no trouble. And Addison had been there for quarter of an hour by now, with the man's hands and sharp implements in close proximity, and yet he remained very much alive and well.

'Maybe over in that other corner?' Addison said. 'Shuffle a few fishing rods over, and lean that kayak somewhere else – plenty of space for a pie oven and serving counter.'

'I think you're onto a winner,' Seb said, beaming. 'Now, how do we feel about this length?'

Addison had been so distracted by the various unsettling comments and sort-of threats to life that he'd almost forgotten he was getting a haircut. 'Yeah,' he said, jostling his head to confirm his hair wasn't liable to stab him in the eyes anymore. And now it'd been cut, he could concede it had been starting to look a little scruffy before. 'It's looking good.'

'"Good"?' Seb had his hand on his hip. 'Is that all I get?'

'It's looking great, thanks,' Addison said, trying to inject more enthusiasm in his voice.

'Don't hurt yourself.' Seb rolled his eyes. 'And don't worry, I'm almost done.'

With his haircut approaching completion, that was one task practically in the bag. But of greater importance, had he gathered any useful information? Or just reinforced what he already knew? At least that meant he knew Dominic was consistent – an equal-opportunities ingrate. Seb's boss had reason to think ill of Dominic based on their altercation. Addison already knew that, and Seb had confirmed as much. He'd also provided a little more detail, but given Addison nothing more that would shift Julie Halswell up or down his list of suspects, such as it wasn't.

Seb was running lengths of hair through his fingers, making the occasional judicious little snip, when he abruptly turned to something out of Addison's line of sight.

'Ah! Speak of the devil and she shall appear.'

Chapter 21

'Do you want this sandwich or not, Seb?' The devil in question was a woman in her late forties, with shoulder-length, dark brown hair, held back by a pair of yellow sunglasses sitting on top of her head. She wore a white blouse, light blue, high-waisted jeans, and a look of mild exasperation.

'That depends on what—'

'BLT on ciabatta from Lynne's, minus the bacon, plus the halloumi, as you very specifically requested.'

'I do love halloumi.'

'Grilled rubber, hideous stuff,' she said. 'I don't know how you eat it.'

'I could say the same about that roast beef and mustard of yours.'

She gave him a long look, responded with the most deadpan 'Moo' Addison had ever heard, then jostled the small brown paper bag as if to ask *Do you want it or not?*

'Moo to you too. Just pop mine over there – please, thank you, you're amazing. I'm just finishing off Addison here. Addison, this is the boss. Boss, Addison.'

'Also known as Julie. Nice to meet you, Addison,' she

said, lifting her free hand in acknowledgement.

'Julie *Halswell*, owner and operator of Halswell & Company,' Seb said, as if that wasn't already quite clear.

Julie ignored him and faced Addison. 'You were in here a week or two ago?'

'Yeah, I grabbed a few shirts, and – uh – other things.' By 'other things' he meant underpants, but he didn't want to draw attention or give Seb any excuse.

'Right. Yes, of course, that's great.' But her attention had already shifted to her sandwich, protruding from the brown paper bag. She took her first bite as she moved over to the shop's main counter, still just within Addison's line of sight.

Seb paused in his work, once more looking absently around the store. Where barbers typically turned over customers within quarter of an hour – half an hour at the absolute maximum – Seb seemed uninterested in sticking to such a schedule, having already sailed past the half-hour mark. Normally such tortoise-like speed would irk Addison, but in this instance it gave him plenty of opportunity to sneak in a few pertinent questions. At least when Seb wasn't busy kidnapping the conversation.

'Jules,' he said, 'you know how your granddad ran this place selling menswear and outdoor gear, right? Then your old man added bike repairs and a barber's chair, for which I am grateful, of course.'

Elbows now resting on the counter, Julie murmured her acknowledgement as she chewed, and gestured for Seb to hurry up and get to the point.

'I've got your next business expansion idea.'

'Oh, yes?' Julie said, taking another bite before slowly looking around the crowded shop, as if asking where such an expansion might go. 'What did you have in mind?'

'Pie shop. Then you wouldn't need to head out for lunch.'

Julie paused her chewing to raise an eyebrow, which Addison interpreted as either: *What a ridiculous idea* or *You're going to need to give me more than that.*

'Well,' Seb said, leaning forward from behind the chair and clamping a forearm across Addison's chest. 'Addison here reckons I could' – he snapped open his scissor blades as far as they'd go and drew them through in the air in front of his throat – 'plenty of filling for all the pies.'

'Oh, Seb. Don't be so grotesque. I'm eating here,' Julie said, dismissing Seb and his idea with her free hand. 'And you're terrorising poor Addison – he's gone as white as that halloumi in your sad little sandwich.'

Addison cleared his throat, glad he still had a throat to clear. The blades may have been nowhere near his neck, but he reckoned he'd involuntarily play-acted the murder victim enough for one day. 'It's fine.' It wasn't, but it's what you said, wasn't it?

'And how, dare I ask, did such a thought come up?'

'Oh, you know.' Seb shrugged. 'Just chatting, about Dominic Campbell among other things. It's like lotto, isn't it?'

'To be honest, Seb,' Julie said. 'I'm struggling to make the connection.'

'Everyone has ideas about what they'd do if they won the lottery, right? Same goes with murder, and disposing of the body – everyone reckons they'd know how to get away with it.'

Julie shook her head and sighed. 'I suppose with your – uh – your *entrepreneurial* approach, Dominic might've been good for *something*, recoup some of his costs.'

Addison didn't think he'd ever been caught in such a grisly, morbid conversation, but at least it was somewhat illuminating. 'I heard he was taking advantage of a fair few people and businesses around town?'

Julie scoffed. 'That's putting it lightly.'

'Hit you here too, is that right?' Addison said, and received a reprimanding prod in the shoulder and flash of the eyes from Seb for it.

Julie didn't notice Seb's reaction, only sighing and setting down the remainder of her sandwich, as if she didn't want to sully it with such talk. 'Dominic came in here badmouthing my stock, trying to tell me I'd sold him shoddy stuff. The quality of the kit wasn't the issue though, *he* was. I've never seen someone mistreat their gear so badly. He demanded a full cash refund, which we are not required to give. We're not required to offer replacements either – not when they're the one who has destroyed the gear – but I did in the end, just to get rid of him. He made a bit of a scene, but eventually accepted. Good riddance, right?'

'Sure,' Addison said. 'Did he—'

'Do you know what popped up the next day?'

Addison had a sneaking suspicion that he might have an idea. 'A bad online review?'

'Absolutely *scathing*. And all nonsense, of course – doesn't bear repeating.' Julie blew out her cheeks, vibrating with agitation just thinking about it. 'And then – then! – if that wasn't enough... You won't believe this – Seb, I don't think I've told you yet either – just last week he had the gall to come back and try to return the gear again.'

'*Again*?' Seb said. 'No, you didn't tell me that.'

'Oh, I was too angry,' Julie said, shaking her head. 'Came sweeping in here, thinking my shop was some kind of charity exchange for arrogant athletes.'

'What did you do?' Addison said, almost wondering if he was about to hear a full-on confession.

'I kicked him out, banned him from the store. Told him he wasn't welcome back. It felt good, let me tell you.'

'And he just… left? You weren't worried he was going to get violent or something? Throw a tantrum and start smashing up the shop?'

'It did cross my mind,' Julie said. 'But Zach and Kyle happened to be in here at the time, picking up some things. They can be pretty intimidating when they want to be.' Julie shrugged. 'So I kind of had backup.'

Seb murmured his agreement. 'Those guys are looking extra ripped these days – Kyle especially, but Zach's not too far off either.'

'Zach?' Addison said, ignoring Seb's wistful tone. 'Do you mean Zach Paine?'

'Yeah, from the supplement store around the corner. And Kyle Thompson. Dominic started getting loud, so Zach and Kyle made their presence known – just stood there, looking imposing, didn't say anything – then Dominic gave them both a dirty look, smirked, and left without another word.'

Addison frowned, his mind racing. He'd spent his entire haircut getting next to nothing, then all at once he'd been flooded with new information. But, as before, he had to be sure who they were talking about. 'Kyle Thompson,' Addison said, racking his brain for why that name sounded so familiar, and then it came to him. 'The electrician?'

'Yeah, that's him,' Julie said. 'He's a cross triathlete too, like Dominic. Amateur though, not pro – not at Dominic's level. They have raced in the same competitions, but Kyle has never quite managed to come out on top. He is much more respectful though – buys gear and uses it, treats it well, doesn't thrash it and bring it back broken.'

Addison wondered at Kyle's unexpected appearance in Julie's story. Was there anything untoward going on there? Or was it just a coincidence? 'It's a small world' was a tired, old cliche, yet he had to concede there was some truth in it, and it only became truer when you were talking about a small town like Milverton.

Still, coincidences could be suspicious, and Addison had learnt to take notice of suspicious things. The likelihood of it being anything of consequence remained low, as it always seemed to be, but he couldn't disregard it outright.

Kyle was scheduled to do work at Harper House on Thursday, so Addison could ask a few innocuous questions without drawing attention to himself or his purpose. Another potential source of information, and he conveniently had a time and place to extract that information already lined up. Nothing put Addison at ease quite like a nice plan falling into place.

'It's hard enough running a store on the high street these days,' Julie said. 'Competing with the big department stores and online stores. Have to go hyper-local, do things the others just can't. And they will come.'

'It's great you have such supportive customers—'

'It's not by accident, of course. None of it. Have to become ingrained in the community, which is not a one-and-done kind of thing – have to keep it up or risk losing relevance.'

'Like getting your lunch from Lynne's?' Addison said. 'Showing your face, supporting other local businesses?'

'Oh, I suppose? But I was just getting a sandwich.' Julie picked hers up again and took a bite. Finishing off a mouthful, she said, 'Better example, Saturday morning, I joined the Riverside Runners for their roving gossip session, which I do every now and then. Why? It's not my favourite – they doddle along like they've got all day – but I do it because next time they're thinking about getting a new raincoat, hiking boots, things like that, where will they think to go?'

'Right here,' Seb said when Addison didn't respond immediately. He was too busy thinking about how he now had another member of Dominic's anti-fan club in the bush that morning...

'That tactic probably worked a bit too well,' Addison said, hoping the comment's vagueness would be enough to draw Julie in.

'Too well?' she said.

'Attracted customers that you would probably rather not have,' Addison said with a wince, 'like Dominic?'

Julie pursed her lips. 'Yes,' she said. 'I suppose you're right. Treating this place like his own personal wardrobe.'

'Do you think,' Addison said, as if the idea was only just occurring to him. 'Do you think, you know, considering how much Dominic pushed everyone else around...'

'That someone went and pushed him right back?'

'Yeah, literally.'

Julie considered it, or at least gave that impression, as Addison had been doing only a moment earlier.

Means, motive, opportunity – Julie had it all. Though her motive wasn't the most convincing. And she'd already volunteered that she was in the vicinity, but with so many potential witnesses around, perhaps she never had the opportunity.

'He was found in Douglas Glade, I heard. We must've

crossed paths, or been close to it.' Julie shook her head. 'Scary thought.'

Julie was genuine, or just a very good actor. Whichever it was, it'd be easy enough for Addison to check with the other Riverside Runners whether the proprietor of Halswell & Company ducked off for a time, possibly for a spot of revenge.

'Oh,' Julie said, hand to her mouth, eyes locked onto Addison as a realisation struck. 'It was *you* who discovered the body, wasn't it?'

Addison felt himself involuntarily pressing back into the chair at the question that came across more like an accusation, and he slowly inclined his head. 'Yes.'

Seb stood, mouth agape. 'You sure kept *that* quiet,' he said, with a prod to the shoulder for emphasis.

'I assumed you knew, that everyone knew,' Addison said quite honestly. 'You know how word gets about.'

'Oh, āe,' Seb said, nodding along, 'that it does.'

Julie was nodding too, her expression softening, as if sympathetic. 'That must have been—'

'—quite the shock, yes,' Addison said. 'I think it'll give me some peace of mind to know how it all happened. So hopefully we'll get a clearer picture soon.'

'Get some closure, I can understand that. I've put the issue behind me, no good comes from going on about it,' Julie said, as if she hadn't just been doing that very thing. 'And he's dead now besides, which I wouldn't wish on anyone, but there you are.' Another shrug. 'Anyway, I've got some things to sort out back. Nice to meet you, Addison.'

'You too, Julie.'

'Well, there you are,' Seb said the moment the door swung shut behind his boss, eyes flashing wide. 'Who needs

TV when you've got all this drama to look forward to each week?'

'I could do with a little less, if I'm honest.'

'At least this round had a happy ending, of sorts.'

Addison caught Seb's eye in the mirror, appalled. 'A man is dead.'

'Yeah, but, you know' – Seb made a squirrelly movement with his shoulders – 'at least he won't be here to bully or take advantage of anyone anymore.'

'There is that,' Addison said, thoughtful as he conceded the truth of the situation. He could admit he struggled to muster up much sympathy for Dominic, but to consider his death a happy ending was a step too far.

When Seb didn't respond, Addison looked up at the barber, who had long since finished cutting his hair. He'd been in no rush to wrap things up while he still had things to tease out of both Seb and Julie, but he doubted there was anything further to be gained. 'So...'

'Yes, sorry,' Seb said, shaking himself. 'I've kept you in my chair much too long – I'm sure you have things to be doing.'

Addison offered a good-natured laugh. 'That's no trouble. It was good to hear a bit more about what's been going on' – he didn't say anything about that being the primary purpose for his visit – 'and to meet you and Julie.'

Seb smiled. 'One last thing before you go.' He picked up a small mirror and held it behind Addison's head, moving it slowly from side to side. 'How do you like it from behind?'

Addison's eyes darted up and caught the smirk on Seb's face. 'Wouldn't you like to know?'

Seb's smile widened. 'Touché,' he said as he replaced the small mirror, unfastened the cape and swished it aside.

'Perhaps you'll let me know next time.'

It was Addison's turn to offer only an enigmatic expression in response. He knew that would either intrigue or infuriate the barber, but he hoped for the latter – only fair after all the verbal jabs he'd been subjected to.

After the wild and unpredictable ride that had been his visit to Halswell & Company, Addison left feeling a little more in control. More important than that, he left having learnt a few things about Dominic's movements and interactions in the days and weeks leading up to his death. He still didn't know exactly what went down that day, but he was one step closer to finding out.

Chapter 22

Two days later, after a full day of work, Addison logged off and packed up his laptop, leaving his temporary workstation at the library with a smidge more confidence about the upcoming endeavour than he'd had even an hour earlier.

He'd never bought a car before, nor accompanied someone on such an expedition. So, he did what all self-respecting millennials would do: he looked it up online.

The search – 'what to watch out for when buying a car' – brought up a bunch of checklists. This was good, Addison thought, at least until the first result's number one item suggested he 'Select a good make and model' which was no help at all. If he already knew what was 'good' then he wouldn't be asking the internet.

Next up: new or used? He didn't know what Mabel was looking for, what her budget was, or how much cars should cost anyway. Presumably more than a bike, but less than a house, which left a rather large price range.

One key piece of advice – for buying used cars at least – was getting a pre-purchase inspection. Outsourcing to an expert, seeking professional advice – this Addison could understand. He didn't know what to look for, but a mechanic did.

A second useful recommendation was that you should take any potential purchase for a test drive. This was another suggestion Addison could get on board with – get to know the car a little, see if you like how it feels, get comfortable with each other. Committing to a car without going for a spin first would be like getting married to someone without... well, you know. No judgement on anyone who preferred to approach things that way, but Addison would never gamble on such potential incompatibility, much too risky.

Without quite realising, the mental preparation for his role as automotive wingman had been supplanted by thoughts of Sergeant Murphy. Addison had done his best to avoid working himself up with thoughts of everything that might or might not happen later that evening, to limited success. He was still thinking through his plans for dinner and beyond when he stepped out into the library foyer-cum-visitor centre.

'Who is this handsome man? I was supposed to be meeting someone here,' Mabel said from her post behind the visitor centre desk. 'He looks very much like you, only scruffier.'

Addison rolled his eyes, but couldn't help the smile. 'A friend very unsubtly hinted a couple of days ago that I might like to get a haircut.'

'Is that right?' Mabel said, pursing her lips and inclining her head. 'Sounds like your friend knows what she's talking about.'

'It does indeed.' Addison raised an eyebrow, and shrugged. 'If that's the case, she probably doesn't need a deputy to accompany her on a lap around the car dealerships.'

Mabel paused in the process of closing up the desk for the day, looking up at Addison with a widening smile on her face. 'And this is why we're friends.' She laughed. 'Looks very nice, by the way.'

'Thank you—'

'But you never told me you had such bright blue eyes. You've certainly kept those hidden.'

Addison didn't think it was something you tended to tell people. They were as plain as, well, as the eyes on his face. 'They've always been right there.'

'But hidden behind all that hair before.' Mabel's smile shifted to what Addison recognised as one of mischief. 'Our sergeant will be putty in the face of those baby blues.'

Addison was preparing his next retort, but didn't manage anything more than clearing his throat.

'Enough chit-chat,' Mabel said, taking pity on him. She finished closing up the desk and grabbed her things. 'Shall we do what we came for?'

'We shall.'

'You are a good sport.' Mabel patted his forearm as she led them out onto the square. 'Thank you for doing this.'

Addison hadn't thought he had a choice, but just as Mabel had shown him mercy, so would he. 'I'll be sure to point out a nice red one for you.'

'See, you get it. Off to an excellent start. Already proving yourself,' Mabel said as she led them along the edge of the square on foot.

'So, where are we headed?'

'Not far. And we're walking, for obvious reasons.' Mabel let out a little huff and shook her head. 'Thank you again for doing this, Addison.'

'Oh, no worries. I still don't see what help I'll be, but I'll do my best.'

'That is all I ask. My daughter and her husband have been very gracious ferrying me around this past week or two, but I can tell it's already wearing thin. They're both very busy, and they're used to me taking on some of the Sophia Taxi Service duties. This way,' Mabel said, turning down a street that would take them away from the square and the river, towards the hills and the main road out of town. 'I am happy to drive my granddaughter – and her friends – around to the various after-school activities. It means I get to spend more time with her, and be a part of it all.'

'That's great, she must love that.'

'She does, and long may it last. I think I'll have another few good years, maybe more, before she's not so keen to have her old nana driving her about.'

'You sell yourself short, Mabel. And you're always welcome to drive me about, if you like.'

Mabel tutted and rolled her eyes. 'Anyway, since our little incident the other weekend, Sophia's parents have had to pick her up and drop her off when I would usually pitch in. Not only that, but now they're driving *me* around too, and I'm no Miss Daisy.'

'More like Miss-Behave-y.'

'That's enough cheek from you, young man,' Mabel said with a laugh and a backhanded slap on the shoulder. 'Let's just say I'm ready to have my wheels back, but my daughter and her husband are *more* than ready. I didn't want them chauffeuring me around today though. If they had their way, I'd be driving out in the first car they spotted, just to have me out of their hair.'

'This is an information-gathering mission, right?' Addison said, unsure if he was prepared to jump in Mabel's passenger seat again, not just yet anyway, if he was being honest.

'That's right. I want to do this properly, not get swept up into buying a car today and quickly realise it's something I don't want or need.'

'Get a feel for what your options are, maybe put together a shortlist, organise a test drive or two for another day, and go from there?'

'Just so. You'll be my second pair of eyes and ears.'

'So,' Addison said, 'what are we looking and listening out for then?'

'Something small and zippy for getting around town. Mostly, at least. With the occasional trip over to Palmerston North, or down to Wellington.'

'Sports car? One of those convertibles with the tops that fold back?'

Mabel gave Addison a withering look. 'I'm not some bloke having his mid-life crisis. No, I need something waterproof, and easy to get in and out of. Red—'

'Because red cars go faster.'

'Correct,' Mabel said with a nod. 'But not burgundy or coral or any of those muddy red colours that you see around. I want a proper fire engine red.'

'Have you thought about if you'll get a hybrid, or fully electric car?' Another consideration that had cropped up during Addison's quick search.

'I did wonder. I think something like that might suit what I need it for, you know?'

'You're no long-distance trucker, Mabel.'

'That's right. And besides, it's the way things seem to be going, isn't it?'

'I have been seeing a lot more around lately. You have to wonder how much longer they'll still be selling petrols and diesels.'

'Yes, and this might be just the nudge I need to take the leap,' Mabel said, looking up, thoughtful. After a moment she lifted her hand towards the ranges that formed the backdrop above Milverton's rooftops, the large blades of the distant wind turbines sweeping in endless rotations. 'I do like the thought of seeing those every day and thinking *that* is what's powering my little red machine.'

'So...' Addison said, thinking over Mabel's criteria. 'You're really just looking for an updated version of what you had before?'

'I think so. That served me well. At least until we parked it in someone's front garden.'

'At speed.'

'Yes,' Mabel said with a sigh. 'Probably best we make sure we find one with airbags as well.'

'I'm pretty sure those are standard these days.'

'Good, good. We have to think about these things. I want to be sure I'm choosing the right one.'

Addison absently murmured his agreement. 'Choose the right...'

'I want to *investigate* – make sure I'm coming to the right conclusion.' Addison was still nodding along with what Mabel was saying when she turned to face him, one eyebrow raised. 'And speaking of... how is *your* investigation going?'

That brought Addison out of his distracted thoughts. 'What—'

167

'You said you were keeping your – what was it? – your mind, ears, and mouth open to the possibilities around Dominic Campbell's death. What have you uncovered?'

'Oh, this and that.' Addison shrugged. 'A whole lot of nothing really.'

'I'm sure you have more than that.'

'Nothing to get excited about. Nothing I didn't really already know.'

'That Mr Campbell was not the most upstanding gent?'

Addison laughed. 'Yeah, pretty much.'

'I'm sure you have more than you realise. Go on, from the top.'

What did he have to lose? He'd relied on Mabel's insights and knowledge of Milverton before, and she might spot a connection or a potential lead that he'd missed.

Addison briefly recapped his meeting with Zach and Prisha, how they had initially rejected a sponsorship deal with Dominic, a decision which they later reversed. The cross triathlete represented a threat of backlash. Not great for business, but also not nearly the end of the world. Dominic may have built a profile in the outdoor endurance sports community, but he was far from a household name, and didn't have the clout to ruin a business on his say so. Zach and Prisha may have been peeved, but that was far from the threshold required for murder. And as he'd already found, they had an alibi.

'Is it worth following that up?'

'There were twenty-ish people in the fitness class, or so they said. I doubt they'd volunteer that information if they couldn't back it up. It'd be too easy for me to catch them in a lie. At this stage I'm inclined to take their word for it, but they invited me to come along to one of their classes, so I

168

can always check if I think it becomes relevant.'

'That's fair,' Mabel said. 'You don't really want word getting back to them that you're on their case.'

'Exactly. Don't want to go ruffling feathers if I can avoid it,' Addison said. 'Anyway, it was pretty much nothing, what I got from Zach and Prisha. And a box of protein bars – I had to justify being there somehow. The only other thing was the potential whiff of discontent at Halswell's. Next to nothing, but it wasn't nothing.'

'Which is why you were there, of course,' Mabel said. 'Ah! Hold that thought. We're here.'

Chapter 23

Addison had noted the parade of blue, red, and white flags lining the street on their approach, the text alternating between 'Cars' and 'Sale'. The colour scheme continued with bunting strung across the yard, ends fixed at points around the perimeter and all strung up to meet at one, much taller pole in the centre. It gave the entire place the feeling of a big top circus tent.

'I wonder if they sell clown cars.'

'Addison,' Mabel said with a tut, though she did a terrible job hiding her smile. 'Don't be such a snob.'

'I'm almost disappointed there isn't one of those inflatable hand wavy guys.'

'Behave.' She batted him on the arm. 'We're here to look at vehicles, not comment on the decor.'

'Yes, boss,' Addison said, smiling now himself.

Still, he couldn't help noticing the gigantic sign above the glass-fronted shop to the rear of the car yard. It featured a funky cartoon-style car with oversized wheels racing off the left-hand side. Tyre marks trailed behind, serving to underline the big, bold text, which was also severely slanted, as if it too was travelling at great speed. It read 'Vroom

Vroom Vehicles'.

Addison could feel the bone-deep cringe already surging through him, but he tamped it down before an appalled groan or other such snootiness could escape. The name felt more like something you'd expect from a toddler's picture book, the type with nice thick cardboard pages that were built to survive the occasional vigorous chewing.

His cringe-tamping efforts were aided by the confusion that came hot on the heels of his first impression. What appeared to be an old barn door had been tacked onto the huge sign, partially hanging off the right side, with more text picked out in rough brush strokes in what appeared to be an afterthought.

Addison couldn't help himself that time – he had to ask. 'Vroom Vroom Vehicles... and Vintage Clothing?'

'Oh, yeah,' Mabel said, apparently unfazed. 'That's a whole other story. Another time.'

Addison shook his head, returning to the task at hand. A clear path led directly from the street to the shop, with immaculately clean vehicles – prices scrawled across their windscreens – to either side. Signage indicated used cars were to the left, and new to the right.

They started on the left, which included a selection of small and medium-sized vehicles – some petrol-powered, others electric, a bunch somewhere in between, and plenty with some kind of aftermarket modifications.

'I'm seeing a lot of tinted windows and – uh – other bells and whistles,' Addison said, making it clear he really didn't have a clue what he was talking about.

'I think we've found where the boy racers come to shop,' Mabel said. 'What do you think of this one?'

Addison may not have had his driver's licence, but he

understood the basics, though that was about it. Cars had four wheels – at least, unless you were Mr Bean's archenemy – and they often had a spare one squirrelled away somewhere. Addison understood this was in case you got a flat tyre, and that you would call someone in a van to come and swap it over for you as required. Cars also tended to come with one more, rather important wheel, which was required to steer the thing. Again, straightforward enough. Addison had been on the bumper cars at Rainbow's End, so appreciated the basic principles of steering. Though, unlike at the theme park, in real life the aim of the game was to *not* bump into anyone else.

Addison had nothing worthwhile to contribute, and wasn't about to embarrass them both by trying to come up with something on the spot. 'What do *you* think, Mabel? That's what matters here.'

It was red – excellent start. It had four doors, but was still small, about what Addison had been imagining based on her previous car. Mabel scanned the information sheet in the window before abruptly shaking her head. 'No, this thing has as much mileage on the clock as I do.'

'And you're still tearing up the place.'

'You're sweet, dear.' Mabel chuckled. 'Oh, did I mention the insurance had already come through?'

'You said something about it.'

'The full amount, and quickly too. Practically unheard of' – Mabel shook her head – 'but I wasn't about to look a gift horse in the mouth.'

'Too right.'

'I was considering buying used, but no, I think I'm better off getting something new. And the budget ought to stretch that far,' Mabel said, steering them to the new vehicles on

172

the other side of the car yard. 'I've paid more than my fair share in insurance over the years. I'm almost glad to be getting some of it back.'

They'd been wandering amongst the new vehicles for barely a minute when the first salesperson approached. Addison let Mabel do the talking, just stood there as a deterrent in case they got any ideas about taking a little old lady for a ride, as Mabel put it. The first of the 'Vroom Pit Crew', as their name badges identified them, was happy to leave them to it. 'I'll just be in the showroom if you need me.'

The second, who appeared shortly afterwards, kept trying to engage Addison, as if he was in charge of this endeavour. Addison repeatedly deferred to Mabel, who'd soon had enough of the salesman and so sent him on his way.

A third was making a beeline for them when Mabel hooked her arm through Addison's and marched them in the opposite direction, right off the yard.

'No good?' Addison said.

Mabel confirmed. 'No good.'

'I was worried they were going to keep flinging salespeople at us until you bought something.'

'I had a similar thought,' Mabel said. 'But they didn't have anything like what I wanted anyway. Practically all the new vehicles were just oversized SUVs.'

'Not to mention they only seemed to come in various greys.'

'Steel.'

'Cloud.'

'Fog.'

'Slate.'

'Charcoal.'

'Really,' Addison said, 'how many ways can you jazz up "grey"?'

'I wouldn't have been surprised if they had all fifty shades,' Mabel said, cracking a cheeky smile.

Addison let out a surprised burst of laughter. 'Still, all that grey just gets washed out against the grey of the concrete.'

'Yes, practically invisible,' Mabel said. 'No wonder they had all that bunting flapping about. Give the place a bit of colour.'

'So, where next, boss?'

'Not far. Just around the order.' They'd cleared the alternating 'Cars' and 'Sale' flags lining the street when Mabel said, 'Anyway, Halswell's, you were saying?'

Right, yes, what else had he learnt? That Dominic's behaviour continued to be consistent? No surprises there. Seb didn't think much of the cross triathlete. He cost Julie Halswell a pretty penny, then left a bad online review for her trouble. Addison plucked out the most salient points to relay to Mabel, skipping past any mention of Seb's thoughts of himself, the sergeant, or Sweeney Todd. With Mabel up to date, it was time to solicit some information for his own purposes.

'Was Julie with you and the other Riverside Runners the entire time on Saturday?'

Mabel fixed Addison with a quizzical look. 'Are you asking if she could have slipped away at all?'

'Unlikely, I know,' Addison said. 'But yes, I am.'

'No, no. No stone left unturned. Very good.' Mabel paused to replay the excursion through in her mind. 'No, nothing stands out. We do keep together. Don't want to lose anyone. It's dangerous to go wandering off in the bush by yourself. No big bad wildlife to worry about, not really. But one wrong step and you twist your ankle on a tree root, or go tumbling down a steep slope, and it might be too late for anyone to help.'

Addison couldn't help thinking back to Dominic. He was an experienced athlete, training on a well-used loop track, and passing through a nice picnic spot. It would be hard to argue that any of that screamed mortal danger, yet that is what he found. It didn't matter how nice Douglas Glade was, it didn't change the fact Dominic had been discovered there, very much dead. He was alone when Addison had last seen him alive. Was he also alone a little later when he suffered a terrible accident and died before anyone arrived to help? Or was he only alone until reaching Douglas Glade, where someone had been lying in wait with ill intent, ready to 'help' Dominic along on his supposed accident?

'I suppose that doesn't help,' Mabel said when Addison didn't respond. 'I'm sorry.'

'No, no. I didn't expect to strike with that one. But it was worth looking into.'

'So you could cross Julie off your list with conviction?'

'Something like that,' Addison said, still not sure if he was convinced of anything when it came to this whole situation.

'Maybe it was just a terrible accident after all?'

'Still a possibility.' Addison blew out his cheeks. 'But the more I look into it – that is, the more people I talk to who have dealt with Dominic recently – the less I believe it.'

'And you have been busy – Sandra and Ariana, Zach and Prisha, Seb and Julie – I swear, I leave you for five minutes—'

175

'Two days, Mabel. It's been a full two days since we spoke.'

'Yes, yes. Five minutes? Two days? They're practically the same thing when you're my age – you'll see.'

'Oh, come now, Mabel—'

'Don't worry, I have plenty of mileage left in me,' Mabel said, flapping a dismissive hand. 'But maybe this investigation of yours doesn't? Are you at a bit of a dead end?'

'Not quite...'

'Is that so? How very intriguing. Do tell.'

Addison thought back over all they'd discussed back at Halswell & Company. 'Nothing groundbreaking, but I did get another couple of names to follow up.'

Mabel waited for a beat before saying, 'Are you going to make me keep asking, Addison?'

'Sorry.' Addison laughed, consciously shifting more mental capacity towards verbalising his thoughts, instead of just thinking them. 'Uh... There was Hugo Li and Kyle Thompson.'

'Hugo Li, you don't say?'

'Why's that?'

'You're about to find out.'

Chapter 24

The structure Addison and Mabel approached was a long, cream-coloured weatherboard building with red corrugated iron roofing and red trim around the windows. A wide awning ran its entire length on the far side, with 'MILVERTON' spelled out in block capitals on the end. Beyond that the platform level stepped down to the ballast, sleepers, and tracks of the railway.

Milverton Station looked like it was overdue for a waterblast and a lick of paint, probably a good weeding around the edges too.

'I don't think just anyone can buy a train, Mabel.'

'I'm not buying a train, Addison.'

'Yeah, they don't meet the brief – trains aren't known for being small or zippy.'

'You are quite ridiculous sometimes,' Mabel said, though her chuckle made her amusement clear. 'The station's been out of regular use for twenty, twenty-five years now, something like that.'

'Yeah, not looking its finest, is it?'

'Only the Vintage Railway Society are using it these days, for their special outings. I took Sophia once – a day trip with lunch and afternoon tea on an old steam train. But that's not why we're here.' Mabel twirled her hand in a triumphant flourish. '*This* is why we are here.'

Just beyond the station building itself was what appeared to be the old station car park, taken over by the simply and sedately named 'Milverton Motors'.

'Right,' Addison said, quite unsure what it was about this particular dealership that had got Mabel excited.

The vehicles did appear to be all new, with some hybrid and fully electric cars on offer, and even a range of colours that weren't some shade of grey.

'I think this might have just what we're looking for,' Mabel said, leading Addison onto the car yard. 'For both of us.'

'We're not shopping for me.'

'Addison, for a bright young thing, you can be rather dense sometimes,' Mabel said, shaking her head. 'It's a wonder you've unravelled any mysteries at all.'

Addison was beginning to wonder the same thing, as he remained completely at sea. He blamed the tedium of his workday for putting the lion's share of his brain cells to sleep, and was in the process of swallowing his indignation and asking for clarification when a man appeared across the yard, immediately making his way over to them. He was in his mid to late fifties and wore a shirt in small chequered squares of various shades of blues and pinks, with a lightweight puffer vest in charcoal grey over the top. Navy trousers led down to shiny black leather shoes with pointy toes. Back up top was an equally shiny, dyed black head of hair, and a gleaming set of white teeth on full display.

'Mrs Zhou,' the man said, still half the yard away, his voice booming to fill the space between. 'I did wonder if I might see you here soon.'

'Did you just?' Mabel, in contrast, kept her voice at a regular conversational volume. 'Well, wonder no more.'

Addison himself had still been wondering why Mabel was so enthused to present Milverton Motors, that is, until he spotted the man's name tag – Hugo Li – and it all became apparent.

'I heard about your recent automotive adventure, Mrs Zhou,' the car salesman said. 'I hope you are doing OK?'

'Yes, I am quite well. Now' – Mabel levelled a finger at his chest – 'I may have known you since you barely came up to my elbow, and I may have distinct memories of you tearing up my back garden with all the neighbourhood kids, but you're a fully grown man now, so just "Mabel" will be fine.'

'Mabel, then,' he said with a smile and a nod, then turned to Addison and thrust out his hand. 'Hugo Li.'

'Ah yes,' Mabel said, before Addison could get in there. 'This is my co-driver, Addison Harper.'

'Is that right?' Hugo said, eyes widening.

Addison snorted. 'I don't think I'll be making a habit of it.'

'No, and that's probably for the best. Quite the chase you two had. And I am glad you both appear to be all in one piece. A shame the same can't be said for your little red car, Mabel.'

'Which is why we're here, I'm afraid. I find myself in need of a replacement, perhaps a little sooner than I'd anticipated.'

'Yes, indeed,' Hugo said, clasping his hands in front of him, then quite literally rubbing them together. 'Yes, indeed… I would be very happy to find something for you.

Actually, I have a brand-new model, just in, which I think will be perfect for your needs.'

Mabel raised an eyebrow as the man bustled away, encouraging them to follow. Under her breath so only Addison could hear, she said, 'Didn't I tell you? Hasn't asked me a thing, and the man already thinks he knows what my *needs* are.'

'I'm sure you'll set him straight.'

Mabel tutted. 'That's why I have you here.'

'Not my strong suit,' Addison said, 'if I'm being honest.'

'What isn't?'

'Setting people straight.'

Mabel gave him a sidelong glance, but then picked up his meaning, chuckling as Hugo came to a halt.

'How about this? Gorgeous, stunning. And it gets you up nice and high – a queen on her throne – you can look down on everyone.'

Without a word Mabel strode over to stand directly in front of the SUV, her head barely clearing the front end. 'Everyone, except children of course, and adults like myself who have not been bestowed with great height. I will be able to see everyone, except those crossing directly in front of my vehicle?'

Hugo barely skipped a beat before changing his tune. 'I hear what you're saying. Let me run you through all the safety features, and you can judge for yourself—'

'I already have, Hugo. Moving on.'

'Something smaller, perhaps? I have just the ticket. And this one's fully electric.'

Addison had to give the guy a little credit: he had recognised a lost cause and immediately pivoted.

'Sounds like we're heading in the right direction,' Mabel

said, clearly having similar thoughts.

'Perfect for your next car chase,' Hugo said, with a flash of the eyes.

'Like Addison said before, I am not planning to make a habit of it.'

'As you say,' Hugo said. 'It was a thrill though, wasn't it?'

Mabel pursed her lips before conceding that it was.

'OK, are you ready for this?' Hugo said, inviting them to share his enthusiasm.

'Let's see what you have for me, then.' Mabel's response was more measured, dubious that this man would have what she was looking for, considering he hadn't even asked.

And so it was. The vehicle was red and rather compact, but based on Addison's understanding of what Mabel was looking for, that's all that could be said for this particular offering. Hugo stood before a two-seater open-top sports car.

Mabel looked around, as if he couldn't possibly be suggesting such a thing, but the neighbouring cars were not any more likely candidates. 'That?' she said, her voice thick with doubt.

'That's right. This is—'

'Where do you imagine I'm going to drive that?'

'Perfect for the open road. I can just see you cruising along, the wind in your hair. You'll be down in the capital for dinner and a show in no time, or up to Hawke's Bay for a nice day sampling the wineries.'

Mabel looked slowly from the salesman to the car and back again. 'That all sounds lovely, but—'

'Doesn't it just? You could—'

'But,' Mabel said, hand slightly raised, clearly

unimpressed, 'I would say that ninety-five percent of the time I'll just be pootling in and around Milverton so I'm looking for more of a runabout.'

'Oh, yes. And this will be perfect for that, but with just a dash of added glamour.'

'How glamorous do you expect I'll be when I am sopping wet? Milverton and her surrounds aren't lush and green by accident. We get our fair share of rain.'

'Of course,' Hugo said, apparently undeterred. 'That's where this clever little feature comes in.' He flashed his pearly whites as he leant into the vehicle and pushed a button on the dashboard. Still smiling, he stepped back as a compartment behind the headrests opened up and folds of metal struts and black fabric levered out like some kind of self-erecting garden gazebo.

Addison watched as the retractable top extended across the front seats, or more accurately, the only seats. Hugo beamed for the entire ten or fifteen seconds, as if he was pulling off the cleverest trick. Meanwhile, Addison was mentally withdrawing the credit he'd recently bestowed on the man. It appeared his earlier perceptiveness may have been a fluke.

'Yes, very clever,' Mabel said, not wowed in the slightest. 'Where do you suggest I put my granddaughter and her friends?'

'That's what parents are for, aren't they? Ferrying their own children about town. Glamorous ladies such as yourself mustn't concern themselves with such things. You should be enjoying your golden years, and this is just the car for the job.'

Addison winced multiple times through the man's unsolicited and ill-advised comments, and could confirm based on Mabel's reaction that they had gone down like a cup of warm sick. He caught the briefest creasing of the salesman's eyebrows before the full wattage of his smile returned.

'Plenty of storage for such a small vehicle too. Think of all the shopping you could —'

'You could barely fit a loaf of bread and a bottle of milk in there, let alone "all the shopping". Where am I supposed to put my groceries? No, I don't see why we're still wasting everyone's time talking about this.' Mabel shook her head, tutting as she did so. 'I'm going to pop to the loo. And when I return' – she raised a pointed finger – 'can I look forward to some more sensible suggestions?'

Hugo's grin remained firmly in place, but Addison could see the strain in it now. 'Of course,' he said, hitting the button to retract the top again.

'Good,' Mabel said with a nod. She glanced one way, then the other, only to find herself surrounded by sleek shining metal in all directions. 'Where's the loo?'

'Ah, just on the end of the station building. I can show —'

'No, I'm sure I'll manage, thank you.' Mabel turned away, giving Addison a subtle nod as she did so.

Chapter 25

Mabel was right, of course. There was no way Addison would get anything out of Hugo with her present. The man had his own ideas about what was and was not appropriate for a little old lady, and as ridiculous as it sounded, talk of murder was unlikely to meet his criteria. This was Addison's chance, and he had to make it count.

'That Mrs Zhou is one tough customer,' Hugo said, watching Mabel go.

'You're not wrong. She knows what she wants.'

'Yes, that's the trouble. But we need to help her see what she *needs*.'

This guy, unbelievable. 'And what's that?' Addison said, not that he wanted to know, but he was going to have to roll with the conversation to get the information he needed.

'Well...' Hugo said the word in such a way that implied he meant *everything*, but recognised he wouldn't get away with that. And so he said, 'When it comes to cars, she needs to leave it up to us.'

Addison had the uncomfortable impression that he understood precisely what this man was saying without actually using the words. Mabel had, once again, been right.

Whether this salesman was offering sexism, ageism, or some unholy combination of the two, the outcome was much the same.

Addison, with just a few decades under his belt – and other things besides – was apparently better equipped to buy a car. Never mind that he had never driven, outside a fairground attraction at least.

Despite the strong desire, this was not the time nor place to introduce this man to the twenty-first century. Perhaps once this was all over he could revisit the man's prejudices, but right now he had a job to do.

'Do people normally come here with a strong idea of what they want already?'

Hugo beamed. 'They do indeed, they do indeed. Some don't, of course, but they usually do. And those who do, they're wrong more often than not. They think they want the same as what they had before, but the newer version, maybe updated with a few extras.'

'But they don't?'

'Right again, Mr Addison. Of course they don't know that they don't know what they want.'

'Until you show them?'

Addison didn't think Hugo had any more bright, white teeth to reveal, but he somehow widened his smile, showing off even more of them. 'See, you get it.'

Addison was conscious he couldn't let this conversation drag on – Mabel would be back any minute. Though, in Addison's mind, the greater danger was the longer it went on, the higher the likelihood that gaps in his knowledge would be exposed. Gaps that Hugo could drive an oversized SUV right through.

He may not have known a thing about cars, but he knew

Hugo's type and he knew how to push that type of man's buttons. This situation called for the double whammy of pumping him up with an ego boost paired with inviting him to mansplain. 'You're the professional,' Addison said. 'You know these vehicles – and the business of buying and selling them – inside and out. So once you've shown customers what they need, it's a done deal, surely?'

Hugo guffawed, shaking his head, his smile widening. 'If only! You'd think so, wouldn't you? But no.'

'Oh, really?' Addison was laying it on thick, but he didn't have time to ease the conversation into place. With Hugo, though, it didn't seem to matter. 'So, what does it take to convince them then?' Addison said. 'A test drive or something?'

Hugo's response this time was a satisfied nod, as if commending a worthy apprentice. 'You catch on quickly, Mr Addison.'

Hoping to solidify his position in the man's esteem, Addison said, 'I've heard people joke that the fastest car you can drive is a rental.'

'Oh, yes. People are a bit more "freewheeling", shall we say, when they're driving someone else's car.'

Addison gave Hugo his best impression of a knowing chuckle. 'Does the same thinking apply when people are test-driving cars?' He gestured to the vehicles around them – all buffed to a high shine, and not a scratch or dent on them.

Hugo pinched his lips together. 'I would not be surprised, Mr Addison.'

'That must be a worry though, mustn't it?'

'Sure, sure,' Hugo said, shrugging his shoulders in a way that suggested he'd at least mostly reconciled himself to the situation. 'But I like to think I get a higher class of customer here at Milverton Motors.'

'Oh, I can see that. Your offering is a step up from others I've seen.'

Hugo nodded, drawing his chin into his neck. 'I appreciate your saying so, Mr Addison.'

'No worries at all,' Addison said, as if the comment was nothing. 'Still, everyone likes to put their foot down every now and then, surely?' Addison knew the thrill of heading down a smooth, steep slope on his bike, picking up some serious pace. And he had to assume the same could be said for hurtling along the road in a tonne or three of metal.

'As I say, I wouldn't be surprised,' Hugo said, nodding to Addison's words. 'But they usually have me in the passenger seat, so I expect their foot may not be as heavy on the gas as it might have been otherwise.'

Addison picked up on something the car salesman said. 'You said "usually"?'

'That's right. Some customers prefer to take the vehicles for a spin *unsupervised*, I guess you'd say. I don't let just anyone take them out without me. I take it case by case, of course, size them up first. Sometimes it's what needs to be done. Last thing I want is to have a buyer thinking I'm nannying them – fastest way to kill a sale.'

'You must be a pretty good judge of character then?'

'Oh, absolutely. You've got to be. Can't have some hoon taking off for a joyride.'

'Right, yeah. Of course.' Addison paused, as if thinking something over. 'You've been in this game a while now, Hugo, I hope you don't mind me saying?'

'Not at all.'

'Even someone as sharp as yourself has to have had one

or two dodgy drivers slip through the cracks?'

Hugo had been nodding along, happy to be told once again how clever he was. Now that he had him all buttered up, Addison hoped it'd be enough for Hugo to concede that even someone such as him could have the occasional slip-up.

'You got me there, Mr Addison,' Hugo said, with his attempt at a self-deprecating chuckle. 'My track record is *pretty* impressive, but you're right, there has been the odd, let's say "misjudgement" on my part, through the years.'

'Happens to the best of us,' Addison said with a chuckle of his own. 'Any shockers recently?' He had one very specific shocker in mind and had to trust Dominic made as unfavourable an impression as Addison suspected he would have.

Hugo shook his head. 'Funny you say that. If you'd have asked me a couple of weeks ago, I would've said no. Had a good, clean run. Months without any sort of trouble. But just the other week, had one "customer" take one of our latest hatchbacks – gorgeous vehicle, will have to show Mrs Zhou once she's back – anyway, he took it out for a test drive. So far, so good...'

'Sure.'

'No speeding fines, or any actual damage. Not a worry, right?'

'Right.'

'Wrong,' Hugo said. 'The exercise get-up he was wearing should've clued me in. Who goes car shopping in their running gear?'

This was promising – Addison could feel Hugo warming up to a rant. He nodded, encouraging the man to continue.

'He was going on about his cousin – her and her wife, I

think, something like that. Anyway, didn't have anything good to say about them. "If it's not one thing, it's another. Doesn't she realise how important my career is? But family, what can you do?" And so on, and so forth. I don't know what their car being with a mechanic had to do with anything. All I heard was that he needed to buy a new car. And his talk of competitions and sponsorships and all that, well, it sounded like he had money to burn.' Hugo shook his head.

'No good?'

'Oh, he had no interest in buying, not that I could see that at the time. No, I thought he was about ready to sign on the dotted line. And we were busy on the lot that morning, so I let him head out by himself for a test drive.'

When Hugo didn't immediately carry on, Addison jumped in. 'And it didn't end up going so well?'

The car salesman laughed. 'You could say that. I normally expect them back within a quarter of an hour, maybe twenty minutes, half an hour tops. But he was gone *all day*. He wasn't answering his phone, and I was about ready to call the cops, tell them I had a stolen vehicle for them to look into. But then he pulls back in, not that I recognised the vehicle right away. It was *filthy*,' Hugo said, but with a few additional words to appropriately describe the state of the vehicle. 'Covered in mud, dust, pollen, and bird droppings.' Again, Hugo opted for a more colourful and forceful description that he would never have used in Mabel's presence.

'What had he done?' Addison said, hoping he appeared appropriately appalled when he was in fact mentally rubbing his hands together.

'He'd clearly taken it on unsealed roads, through a good

few muddy puddles, and then parked it under a tree for good measure.' Hugo shook his head. 'Anyway, the arrogant sod threw me the keys, said he'd be in touch, then just walked off. Would you believe it?'

Addison absolutely could believe it. But that wasn't the response Hugo was looking for. Instead, he followed Hugo's lead in shaking his head. 'Some people.'

'You know it. Mind you,' Hugo said, 'it's not the car being returned in a right state that gets me. The team had the car washed and cleaned up, ready to put back on the yard the next day. No, it's that I didn't have the car here to show to anyone else. Someone who wasn't mucking me about.'

'So, you missed out on the commission from him, but also potentially others as well?'

'You know it. To say I was *frustrated* does not do it justice.'

And embarrassed, professionally speaking, Addison suspected. Not that he saw any merit in shining a spotlight on that. 'So, what did you do?'

'Live and learn.' Hugo scoffed. 'What can you do? We blacklisted him, of course.'

'Of course.'

'Not that we need to worry about *that* anymore.'

Addison frowned in confusion, hoping Hugo would take the bait that was his feigned ignorance.

'Well, I don't think there's any harm naming the guy now he's dead,' Hugo said, without even a whiff of the grief that accompanied unexpected deaths, even when they weren't everyone's favourite person. 'Dominic Campbell... I was right here when I heard the news, actually. I'd been cursing his name all week, ever since he did me dirty – just quietly, to myself, you know?'

'You're a high-profile guy, can't be going around bad-mouthing people.'

'That's right. People wouldn't want to work with me, for fear they'd be next.'

Addison nodded. Then, before the conversation could wander off in whatever direction came to Hugo next, he said, 'So, did you say you were here at the dealership when you heard about Dominic Campbell?'

'Oh yes, one of my customers mentioned it. They'd heard about it from someone who knew someone at the medical centre or the mortuary or something.'

Addison quietly watched the man, searching for the lie in his words, but didn't see it. 'That must've been quite the shock?'

'You bet it was. Of course, you make all the right noises in the moment, no matter how you feel about the person, don't you?'

'Mm, yes. "Terrible, awful, gone too soon." All that?'

'You know it,' Hugo said. 'But I didn't have too long to think about it all, if I'm honest. Back to the job at hand, closing the deal, selling the car.'

Addison nodded along as if he was on board. 'No point letting the guy lose more potential sales for you, even from beyond the grave.'

'Exactly right!' Hugo smiled, shaking his head. 'Mr Addison, I said it before, I'll say it again, you know how it is.'

Addison smiled, then frowned as if a thought had just come to him. 'Remind me, what day did you say all this was?' Hugo hadn't specified the day, but Addison took the chance to probe again for any hint of a lie.

'Saturday morning, it was,' Hugo said without batting an eye. 'Saturdays are busy for us – after a hard week of working, people are looking to do a hard weekend of spending. We had customers back to back all morning – sold two of those, one of those' – Hugo pointed to a blue medium-sized SUV and a bronze hatchback before patting the red sportscar he'd been unsuccessful in foisting on Mabel – 'and even landed an order for one of these, but next year's model.'

'Nice work. And good thing Dominic wasn't here to mess things up again.'

'Isn't that the truth.'

'Did your customer say what happened? With Dominic's death, I mean. '

'Nah, they didn't,' Hugo said. 'And nobody I've heard from since seems to know for sure what caused his death... but I do.'

Addison's mind had already started to drift off in the face of another dead end, but homed right back in at the man's bombshell of a statement. 'You do?'

Hugo nodded, his face at maximum smugness. 'Bad karma,' he said, raising a hand to forestall any objection. 'I know that's all a bit woo-woo, but my wife swears by it. She says if you put that much bad energy out into the world, it'll come back to get you, one way or the other.' Hugo shrugged. 'And I'm inclined to believe her.'

The surge in excitement at the prospect of a breakthrough was immediately followed by an equally sharp drop. Karma felt much too passive to Addison, as if it allowed someone to abdicate from any responsibility. That it was all up to the universe at large.

You've made a habit of prodding each and every beast

you encounter? Of course one is going to take against such treatment, enough to do something about it. Addison just needed to know who Dominic had prodded that little bit too hard, or one too many times.

Addison pulled on a weak smile, valiantly trying to mask his disappointment. 'What goes around comes around.' The trite remark was the best he could manage under the circumstances, not that Hugo noticed.

'That's the one,' he said, nodding as if that was all sorted then.

Not that it mattered anymore, but Hugo didn't seem to have noticed that this conversation had been very purposefully steered towards the unexpected death of Dominic Campbell. He also did not know that this had been an interview, nor that he had been a potential suspect. Finally, he did not appear to be aware that he had been slowly and subtly reoriented so that Addison would spot Mabel upon her return from the bathroom.

And spot her he did. If the car yard was his stage then Mabel was ready in the wings and had been waiting for her cue for a minute or so now. Keeping his focus on Hugo, Addison raised a hand and rubbed his neck, just behind his jaw, as if dealing with a slight itch. Then, as he withdrew his hand and dropped it back to his side, he ever-so-briefly extended his thumb.

Mabel understood the signal immediately, which in this instance indicated that Addison had everything he needed from this man – which turned out to be practically nothing – and it was past time they wrapped this circus up.

In a matter of seconds Mabel had rejoined their little gathering, thanked Mr Li for his time, assured him that she had much to consider and would get back to him if she had any questions.

Hugo was still recovering from her whirlwind return and didn't manage anything beyond handing over his business card before Mabel swept off again with Addison in tow.

Chapter 26

'Quite retro back there,' Mabel said.

'Sorry, what?' He'd been feeling good about how he'd navigated the questioning, keeping it seemingly unobtrusive yet still asking what he needed to. But any feeling of success was tempered by the lack of any actual results. Addison remained a little distracted by such thoughts, but doubted that was to blame for his struggle to make the connection between a yard full of brand-new vehicles and Mabel's 'retro' label.

'The facilities, I mean,' Mabel said. 'Very retro. Those bathrooms and Harper House were probably last renovated around the same time. They were nice and tidy though, clean.'

'That's the important bit.'

'Oh, the hand dryers though – utterly pointless. You know the ones?'

OK, they really were discussing the bathrooms then, Addison couldn't help but think. Though, considering they were still within earshot of anyone wandering around Milverton Motors, probably for the best. 'The hand dryers that just, I don't know, gently *waft* warm air at your hands?'

'Exactly. They do little more than move the water droplets around,' Mabel said.

'I normally give up after a few seconds and dry my hands on the sides of my trousers.'

'Mm. I've never had the patience to stand there long enough to actually dry my hands.' Mabel held up her hands before them, not a drop of water to be seen. 'But today was the day, apparently.'

'Wins all around.'

'Finding new firsts each and every day – that's a win in my book.'

'Hear, hear,' Addison said, raising an imaginary toast.

'Though, some firsts are more exciting than others,' Mabel said. 'And I've had a fair few of those too since I first met you, Mr Harper.'

Addison could've said the same thing about Mabel, and Milverton in general.

They'd made it off the car yard and were walking back past the tired old Milverton Station when Mabel glanced back over her shoulder.

'So,' Addison said, just as bored as Mabel by the small talk, and judging they ought to be safely out of earshot.

'That Hugo, didn't listen to a word I said, did he?'

'He did not.'

'Just wanted to sell me the biggest or most expensive thing he had. Completely impractical. That SUV? Might as well be a monster truck.'

'I could see you in one of those, if I'm honest.'

Mabel thought on it for a moment, and smiled. 'Would be fun, wouldn't it?'

'A real crusher. Can you imagine? That sports car wouldn't last a second under those giant tyres.'

Mabel laughed, as if to say that's where it deserved to be, then shook her head. 'Treated me like his old mother. Haven't seen him for years, and he thinks he can condescend to me like that.'

'It was... embarrassing.'

'That's by the by.' Mabel shook her head, glad to be done with the interaction. 'Now, Dominic Campbell. What did Hugo have to say for himself once I'd toddled off?'

'Not much, really.' Addison sighed. 'He was here all Saturday morning, bragged about doing swift trade. Easy enough to look into, if we think we need to.'

'Any insights on Mr Campbell's death then?'

'He basically put it down to bad karma,' Addison said with a shrug.

Mabel considered this, probably with more sincerity than it warranted. 'I wouldn't be too quick to dismiss something like that.'

'Well, yes, but you can't make arrests based on "something like that", can you?'

'Don't you go doing those bunny ears with your fingers at me,' Mabel said, mimicking Addison's air quotes.

'Ah. I'm sorry, Mabel. I guess I'm just annoyed that we didn't find anything worthwhile.'

'That's OK. If everything was straightforward every time, where would the fun be in that?'

Addison couldn't help the small smile. 'You're probably right. Still, I just do not believe we can blame general bad vibes,' Addison said. 'When bad people do bad things, someone else is bound to do bad things right back soon enough.'

'Yes, you are probably right on that one. And we just need to find out who that "someone else" is,' Mabel said, air quoting back at Addison.

Addison laughed. 'Yeah, that's the tricky bit.'

'If someone's going to get to the bottom of it, it's you.' Mabel gave him a reassuring pat on the arm. 'But we are not going to figure all that out right this minute,' she said with emphasis, as if to draw a line under the discussion, at least for now. 'Let me treat you to some dinner, as thanks for your help this afternoon. It's still early, but we can have a little tipple first and you can fill me in on everything else that you've learnt. Drink, dinner, debrief.'

'I was happy to help, not that I think I did much, if anything at all. And I would've been very happy to join you now but, uh… I'd better head off actually.'

'Oh, what are you up to?'

'I've got Jake coming over for dinner.'

Mabel flung an arm out in front of Addison, drawing them both to a halt. 'You what?'

'I'm cooking.'

'You distracted me with talk of sudden death and suspicious circumstances when you've been sitting on this bombshell.' Mabel batted him on the arm. 'What are you cooking?'

'Roast chicken, roast potato, veggies.'

'Nice, hearty. Classic,' Mabel said, nodding her approval, which lasted barely a moment before switching to expressions of her disapproval – a quick succession of tutting, huffing, and scoffing. 'And you let me drag you around car yards when you've got a chook to get in the oven? My dear, this is *much* too important. We've wasted enough time. Do you have everything you need?'

'Yes, I picked up groceries yesterday.'

'OK, good…' Mabel slowly raised a finger, her mind

whirring as she stared off into the distance before her attention snapped back to Addison. 'Right, you wait there, I'll be back in *one* minute.'

'I really ought to go—'

'Just...' Mabel held up a hand then gestured to a nearby bench seat before pulling on a smile that seemed to say, 'Trust me,' and power-walked back the way they'd just come.

Addison took the seat and glanced at the time – it had just gone half past five. He'd said to Jake to come around 'from seven' – just under an hour and a half away. Minus maybe fifteen minutes for the walk back to Harper House. Nobody expected to be served the moment they stepped through the door. It'd be fine as long as he had things prepared and in the oven by then.

Addison took a deep breath in and slowly let it out. He had time... Provided Mabel was back soon from whatever she was doing – what was she doing? Actually, what was *he* doing? Why was he waiting? Mabel must realise he couldn't hang around all evening?

He'd already lost a minute, and now that he'd done his little calculation, he realised he probably couldn't afford to lose another. Mabel would understand.

Addison hopped up from the bench and was making one quick guilty glance back the way he'd come when a blur of red shot out of a driveway. With a short, sharp screech it swung onto the road then closed the distance with Addison in a matter of seconds. Once the tyres had recovered from the abrupt manoeuvre, the high-pitched hum of the motor was the only audible indication that the machine was on the move.

Hair already in disarray, Mabel beamed from behind the

steering wheel as she pulled up alongside Addison.

'What are—'

'Come on then, get in.'

Addison knew better than to argue, settling into the form-hugging leather passenger seat and barely securing his seatbelt before Mabel put her foot down.

'Sorry it took so long,' Mabel said, speaking up to be heard over the rush of the air. 'That Hugo wasted precious seconds talking nonsense about paperwork, then I had to find the buttons to boost the seat.'

'You told him you wanted to take it for a test drive after all?'

Mabel's smile widened. 'I did. And it means we can get you home at least ten minutes earlier.'

It may have been peak traffic time for Milverton, but considering the population of the town, that didn't amount to a whole lot. And Mabel was on fire, slipping into the flow of other vehicles without delay.

In what felt like seconds, they'd hit the edge of town and swung through the gates of Harper House and under the avenue of mature trees. Mabel flew up the gravel driveway and around the turning circle, pulling to a seatbelt-jolting halt at the front door.

Addison looked over at Mabel, pulling his face into an attempt at a grimace of gratitude. 'Thanks for the ride,' he said, though in truth he was less grateful for the ride and more that they – and the car – had made it in one piece.

'It is the least I can do after you spent your afternoon as my automotive wingman. Now, out you get,' Mabel said, waving her hand as if to shoo him from the car. 'We can't have you serving the sergeant undercooked chicken.'

Chapter 27

Addison waved Mabel farewell and caught her flicking up a bit of gravel as she tore up the driveway in the red sports car. He closed the front door and decided that as he did so, he was closing down his investigation into Dominic's suspicious death, at least for the night.

He remained determined to get to the bottom of the situation, to remove any lingering suspicion in anyone's mind that he had anything to do with it.

Right now though, he didn't have any time to stew about the fact his investigation was at a dead end. Not for the first time, he also had to concede that he may be at a dead end because there wasn't anything to investigate and he was just chasing nothings. And was he disappointed about that?

It wasn't like Dominic could get any more dead, so Addison's pursuit of the truth – which nobody had asked for – could wait until tomorrow. He didn't have the luxury of investigating Dominic's death or his own thoughts on the matter, not when he had a dinner to prepare and a man to entertain. All going well, he hoped that would keep him occupied for the rest of the evening and well into the night.

Temporarily pausing his investigation was all the more

important considering his date. Addison told himself he didn't want to inflict work chat on Jake when the man was off the clock, but really, he'd rather the sergeant didn't know he was sticking his nose in where it didn't belong once more.

With that settled, Addison stepped inside and found himself looking around, assessing the place with fresh eyes, as a new visitor might. Of course, Jake had been to Harper House before, but he'd never visited with anything like romantic intent, and he'd also never been upstairs.

Addison couldn't help noticing anew just how much *stuff* his great-uncle Herbert had owned. Not that there was anything to be done about it, not in that moment. It'd take more than a couple of minutes to sort through the decades of his relative's life in this house, and Addison knew he didn't want to rush it, either. He was sure to uncover many clues about the man's life and character, but that would have to keep for another day.

Right now, he had a dinner to cook.

Addison was as prepared as he could be, and he hoped for the best, but he had a backup plan – of course he did. That plan consisted of a shortlist of local restaurants and takeaway shops who did delivery, along with a few likely dishes from each. There were a number of good options, though some dropped off the shortlist when he checked whether they'd deliver beyond town limits. Still, if it all went pear-shaped in the kitchen, he was reassured that hot food could be at the door within the hour.

He should've just skipped dinner and invited Jake over for dessert. Addison knew his baking repertoire was strong, could whip up any number of baked delights, no worries.

But inviting someone over to the house later in the

evening, nominally for dessert... Well, that sent an entirely different message.

Not that Addison objected to that – not at all – but dinner came with at least a smidgen of plausible deniability. After the meal, either party could initiate farewells at any point and for any reason – 'This was great, we should do this again sometime' or 'I'd better be off, have to get up early' or 'Thanks for dinner, I'll see you around' – and that would be OK.

So, they would have to see how the evening went, and if Jake was still around later, then Addison had something else in mind for *dessert*.

He shook his head – he was getting ahead of himself. They had to get through dinner first, and that wasn't a given. Addison may have had confidence when it came to baking, but cooking was another thing entirely. Too much vagueness. 'Two medium onions' – who's to say how big 'medium' is? 'Heat the oil over a low-to-moderate heat' – well, which is it, low or moderate? 'Cut into large chunks' – again, how big are we talking here? It's all just feeling it out, judging by eye...

The only way Addison could deal with such ambiguity was to do one thing at a time. He knew better than to attempt to have multiple things on the go – something boiling or frying on the stovetop, something else grilling or baking in the oven, all while he was slicing and dicing something on the bench.

The last thing he wanted to do was poison the sergeant with undercooked chicken, as Mabel had so helpfully reminded him.

Addison had over an hour, which he reckoned ought to be enough time to get at least the messiest parts out of the way before Jake arrived.

He pulled the chicken out first – giving it the best chance to get to room temperature before it needed to go in the oven – followed by all the ingredients and implements he needed from the fridge, pantry, cupboards, and drawers. A quick stocktake of everything scattered across the bench confirmed he had all he needed.

Addison was patting down the chicken with paper towels when he caught sight of Keith. The orange ball of fur was at the threshold, alert, observing the frantic goings-on in the kitchen. On a typical day, Keith enjoyed the run of the house and could depend on getting what he wanted when he wanted it. And despite the fact it was rapidly approaching the feline's regularly appointed dining time, Keith held back. He had arrived, assessed the situation, and apparently determined that the new human seemed to have more than enough going on. With great magnanimity, he remained in place. Addison had to assume the cat was waiting for a break in the storm to present itself. Should that not happen, and Keith had deemed it had gone on long enough, Addison was sure the cat would make his demands known.

Addison stuffed the chook with a lemon – he'd heard something somewhere about that helping to keep the meat from drying out – rubbed butter over the skin, seasoned it, set it on a few sticks of celery laid out in a roasting tin, then added a bit of water to the bottom.

Next up were the potatoes – peeled, cut up, parboiled, then roughed up, which supposedly helped with the crunchiness when cooked. Then a few carrots and an onion, all peeled and chopped. Addison arranged the vegetables on a baking tray, oiled and seasoned the lot, and set it aside.

The beans and broccoli were ready for steaming, but he wouldn't do that until he was ready to serve dinner. And the gravy – well, he was cheating there. Maybe one day he'd do it properly, but tonight it was packet gravy, just add boiling water. But again, not till later.

And then there was the cheese board, which he assembled, ready to bring out after dinner. He'd gone for a local Camembert and a Havarti – that is, one soft and one a bit firmer – a quince paste, a relish, a couple of cured meats, and some crackers.

Done.

Ready.

Summarising everything so succinctly made the process sound relaxed and efficient. It was anything but, and involved much back and forth, rinsing implements to use them again on something else, tapping his phone screen whenever it started to dim so he could read or re-read the next instruction, and emitting a few alarmed curses each time he nicked his fingers with the potato peeler or a knife. But overall, things had gone better than Addison had feared. He hadn't burnt himself, lost a finger, or even forgotten to buy any key ingredients. Anxious and mistrustful, the usual Addison would scrutinise his apparent good fortune until he uncovered the cracks he knew must be there. But tonight, Addison was determined to have a nice time and enjoy the good fortune for as long as it lasted.

Everything was ready.

'All right, Keith,' Addison said. 'Ready for dinner?'

Keith glanced up, seeming to communicate with his posture and demeanour that he was past ready, thank you very much. A quick flick of the tail added that his food had best be served without further ridiculous, rhetorical questions, or Addison could expect reprisals to be swift and without mercy.

However, such haughtiness evaporated the moment Addison scooped dry biscuits into one of the cat's bowls and heaped the feline's favoured canned concoction into another. Keith was soon in there with purrs turned up to the max – live, laugh, love; forgive and forget; all that.

With the chicken ready to go and Keith in kitty culinary heaven, Addison still had time to jump through the shower and freshen up ready for his date.

He was back downstairs, all cleaned up, dressed and ready to go with a whole minute to spare. He found the place to be eerily quiet, with only the occasional creak to break the silence. Addison flicked the TV on in the lounge and set the volume low, thinking any lapses in conversation might not kill the mood so quickly if there was at least some background noise.

With that sorted, Addison decided to do one last check in the kitchen, and maybe pour himself a wine while he was there. He was weighing up whether he felt like a red or a white when he stepped through and spotted the uncooked chicken still sitting in its roasting tin on the kitchen bench. After one short, sharp curse, Addison told himself it was OK.

Careful not to get anything on his new shirt, he slid the raw chicken into the pre-heated oven, set the timer, and stood back. Dinner would just be a little later than he'd originally intended, but that was fine – Jake wouldn't be any the wiser.

What else had he forgotten?

A quick scan of the kitchen brought up no obvious candidates. Another time check: seven on the dot. He'd said to come around 'from seven,' so he should expect Jake any time. And in the meantime he reckoned he deserved a wine.

Addison was reaching for a glass when he heard a knock on the front door.

Chapter 28

Addison breathed in and out before unlocking and opening the front door.

Sergeant Jake Murphy stood on the threshold looking more handsome than Addison had ever seen him. Addison could appreciate the man in his uniform – as he had done on a number of occasions, in fact – but tonight his simple shirt, trousers, and lightweight jacket left no doubt that he was here not as Milverton's sergeant, but in a personal capacity, as Jake. And Jake was here specifically for Addison.

This was a date, with a man.

A very attractive man.

Whose gaze drifted up, a look of uncertainty on his face. 'You've had a haircut.' The words were said mildly, but as if it were part question, part accusation.

'Oh, yeah.' Addison had forgotten he hadn't seen Jake since before his time in Seb's chair. He smiled, a little self-conscious. 'Gay powers restored.'

Jake frowned but laughed at the same time. 'What?'

Addison shrugged. 'It's just what you say after getting a haircut, isn't it?'

'Sure, why not?' Jake said, shaking his head for a

moment before gesturing to the open door. 'I'm glad to see you've had this fixed, by the way. Sorry about that, again.'

'I think I can forgive you for that one,' Addison said with a smile. 'I'm alive because of it, after all.'

An apprehensive expression flicked across Jake's face. Addison had to hope it wasn't his being alive that was the cause, but perhaps how close he'd come to *not* being alive? It lasted only a moment before Jake rallied, lifting his arms to present a bottle of wine in each hand – one red and one white. 'I didn't know what we were having, so I brought both.'

Addison's attention had drifted. He didn't know about the wine, but he did know what – or more accurately *who* – he'd quite like to be having. He'd barely had the thought before he forced himself to rein it in. 'We're having chicken,' Addison said, clearing his throat. 'But that doesn't mean we have to have the white. Anyway, come in, come in – why are we still standing out here? Take those into the lounge, and I'll grab something to put them in.'

After a quick detour to the kitchen, Addison joined Jake in the lounge. Jake had taken a seat on the forest-green three-seater couch, perched in the same spot as he had last time. Thankfully, compared to last time, he was looking much less concerned and much more relaxed.

With the wine glasses in one hand and the cheese board held up in the other, Addison felt as if he had to explain himself. 'I'd intended to have this later, but dinner will be a little while away, so thought I'd bring it out now, in case you were getting hungry?'

'I'm all right at the minute,' Jake said, eyes fixed on Addison, before the corner of his mouth lifted ever so slightly. 'But I wouldn't pass up a snack.'

The glasses clinked in Addison's hand at the man's words and attention. He cleared his throat for the second time in a minute. The colour may have been rising in his cheeks at the hint of suggestion in Jake's comment, but he was encouraged to hear they were apparently of one mind.

Without further incident, Addison set down the cheese platter on the coffee table and handed over the glassware as he went to take a seat on the couch.

He had never had cause to consider the logistics of sitting on furniture designed to accommodate more than one person. The unspoken, unconscious etiquette of a three-seater couch required the first sitter to pick a side, which Jake had done. Sitting in the middle was just not an option.

The same was true for the second sitter, because again, to sit in the middle would be unbalanced and quite frankly unhinged. So, Addison was obligated to sit on the *other* side of the couch. The result, however, was a vast gulf between Jake and Addison, which Addison did not appreciate. The clue was in the name, with three-seaters being suitable for three. So when there were only two, each party was afforded plentiful personal space – *too much* personal space, in Addison's opinion.

He consoled himself with the fact the night was still young, and he had reason to get up and down a few times yet, which would allow for some subtle repositioning, as and when the situation called for it.

'They're both quite fruity,' Jake said, 'according to the woman at the wine shop.'

Addison was proud of himself for letting the man finish speaking and not immediately voicing the first thing that leapt to mind. 'Good to know,' he said with a smile and a nod.

'The – uh – the red is a Hawke's Bay Syrah, which she described as "big and bold". And the white is a Marlborough pinot gris, more "smooth and subtle". What are you feeling this evening?'

This guy, and some of the subtly suggestive things coming out of his mouth... Addison could play along, was happy to do so, in fact. 'Let's ease ourselves in with smooth and subtle, shall we? And then once we're well lubricated, we can go for big and bold.'

In his role as Milverton's sergeant, Jake regularly had to maintain a straight face in the most trying of situations, as was the case in that moment. But the flash of his eyes as they locked onto Addison's own betrayed the war within – appalled, amused, aroused, or some combination of the three – and revealed that Addison had brought him to the brink. Jake broke eye contact, reached for the pinot gris and busied himself sorting out the wine.

Addison didn't fare much better under Jake's intense gaze, only relaxing once Jake had shifted his attention elsewhere. And the moment it had, Addison became aware of the absurdity of the situation...

A light current affairs programme playing quietly on the TV in the background. His great-uncle's things surrounding them, the most prominent of which was the oversized and overloaded knick-knacks cabinet. Then there were the overhead lights, probably bright enough to serve in a hospital operating theatre – all the better to behold the many colours, swirls, flowers, and spots of the garish sixties-era carpet.

Together, it presented a wildly unromantic and unseductive setting for their date.

Addison was mentally adding a two-seater couch and

lamps with dimmers to his future renovation shopping list when he noticed the cat sitting stock-still in the doorway, attention locked onto Jake, like a sharp-eyed and rather disgruntled supervisor.

Jake had just finished pouring their glasses and was in the process of handing one over when he caught Addison's strange look, following his gaze to land on the bristling ball of fur glaring right back at him.

'Keith,' Jake said with a nod by way of greeting.

The cat did not acknowledge that he'd been addressed, only continued his glare, unnerving in its intensity.

'He's just keeping an eye on you,' Addison said. So often scrutinised by others in recent weeks, he was enjoying not being on the receiving end this time.

He should've known better than to revel because the comment drew Jake's attention immediately back to him. Jake's expression shifted into something that looked decidedly disrespectful, slowly raising one eyebrow. 'Is he making sure I don't try anything?'

Addison unconsciously shifted himself slightly on the couch, though more in anticipation than awkwardness. He was rather hoping that Jake Murphy *would* try something.

Couldn't Guard Cat Keith see his services were not required? It was very thoughtful and well-meant, but Addison did not need his virtue defended. If he were in a position to be issuing orders, his next would be 'Stand down, Keith, stand down.' Instead, he said to Jake, 'I don't know what that cat's doing.'

'I think he might be acting as our very own feline chaperone.'

Perhaps that was for the best, at least before Addison had served dinner. He didn't want to get carried away and forget about the food in the oven. Still, he hoped Keith would chill out soon, or better yet, get bored and wander off in search of something else to torture. 'Let's hope he's not very good at his job.'

A smile slowly grew on Jake's lips and, without a word, he raised his glass in a toast.

Addison smiled right back and clinked his glass against Jake's.

Chapter 29

In Addison's experience, dates often started off with a little tension or uncertainty, some nervousness perhaps. They could take a while to get into their groove, and some dates never did manage it, but he and Jake had pulled it off before they'd even taken their first sip of wine.

Conversation was easy, relaxed, with plenty of light chat and more than a few hints of flirtation.

Jake mentioned he'd had a school friend called Keith, and they both agreed the name was much too old for someone so young. Something better suited to a middle-aged accountant who dared not leave the house without checking the weather forecast yet always packed an umbrella anyway.

They moved on to childhood friends and pets, their experience growing up in Auckland, family, siblings, and moving to Milverton, barely skimming the surface of each subject before jumping on to the next. Possible topics branched off at every step, but they could only pursue one at a time.

On the one hand, the approach frustrated Addison's desire to dive deep into every topic and satisfy his curiosity.

On the other, it delighted him that he still had so much to uncover about Sergeant Jake Murphy, and hopefully plenty of time and opportunity to do just that.

One area of particular interest to Addison was Jake's relocation from Auckland – a big bustling city – to Milverton – a quaint little town. Had he been drawn in by something good? Pushed away by something bad? Was it personal or professional? Was the topic a perfectly light and pleasant one, or was he entering heavy territory? Or was it some complicated mix of the whole lot, as was Addison's situation? There was only one way to find out...

'So,' he said, 'what was it that brought—'

Addison had only half-asked his question when the couch started bleating. It took him a second to realise his phone had slipped between the cushions, then another to rummage around one-handed and fish it out. He silenced the alarm and set down his wine glass, which he'd apparently drained without realising.

'I just have to put the potatoes in,' Addison said, getting up from the couch. 'Sorry, back in a sec.'

'Did you need a—'

'No, no. They're ready to go, just need to slot them in the oven, thanks.'

Addison had been so engrossed in his date – the man himself, the chat, the wine, the cheese board – that the feline sentry on duty had slipped his mind. Keith tracked Addison's progress across the room from his position in the doorway, but didn't move as his resident Harper passed by. The behaviour was decidedly *odd*, but other than Keith's strange, lurking presence, he wasn't actually doing anything. If it was some form of protest, at least it was a peaceful, silent one.

Figuring out the cat was a job for another day, and his focus would be better utilised on preparing dinner and entertaining his guest. Addison ducked down in front of the oven to peer through the glass, not that he knew what he was looking out for precisely. The oven was still on, at temperature, and the roast appeared to be roasting.

The urge to have a quick little check was almost overwhelming, but the chicken wasn't due to be done for a while yet. And he dared not fuss, or he might ruin something which had previously been going perfectly well. This was one aspect of baking that probably translated over into cooking.

Addison turned his attention to the tray of potatoes on the bench, adding another dash of oil, and a few extra crunches of salt, because why not. That's what cooks did, added things just because they felt like it. And Addison was feeling bold.

Heat rushed and steam billowed from the oven as he cracked the door open, filling the air with the delicious scent of roasting chicken. Addison quickly slotted the tray of potatoes inside and closed the door again, pleased that despite the initial delay, things seemed to be going to plan.

A quick check of the instructions on his phone confirmed that was all he needed to do for now. Addison returned to the lounge feeling quietly confident. He didn't notice Keith's absence from the doorway until he'd stepped through and spotted him perched on the arm of the couch. He remained motionless, his glare fixed on Jake.

Baffled, Addison couldn't help but laugh. 'I suppose he's taken it upon himself to keep an even closer eye on you?'

'He's taken to higher ground,' Jake said. 'Keith is quite the strategist.'

'All the better for launching his attack,' Addison said, smiling as he reclaimed his seat on the couch, now sitting between the suspicious cat and the bemused sergeant.

'Watch out,' Jake said, 'you might get caught in the crossfire there.'

'You can stand down now, Keith. I'm quite capable of looking after myself.' Addison smiled, reaching out to give the cat a reassuring pat but stopped his hand in midair when he abruptly found himself the target of Keith's attention. The cat slowly, silently exposed his teeth. Addison got the message, withdrawing his hand. And the moment he did, the cat's glare shifted immediately back to Jake.

'You *will* be protected,' Jake said, a wry smile on his face, 'whether you like it or not.'

'So it would seem.'

'I didn't mean to take more decisions away from you, but I went ahead and filled you up.'

'You filled me up?' Addison said, eyes widening as he cleared his throat, quite sure he'd have noticed if Jake had done such a thing.

'Yeah, I topped—'

'You topped?' Addison's eyes widened yet further, at least until he noticed, rather too late, Jake gesturing towards his refilled wine glass. That made *much* more sense, and really shouldn't have taken him so long to comprehend. 'You topped up my glass. Yes, you did, thank you.' Addison took a sip to show his appreciation, and to give his mouth something to do so it didn't incriminate him further.

He needn't have worried, as they slipped back into comfortable chat without any trouble or further embarrassment. On the whole, he was happy to go wherever the conversation led them.

Though Addison did have an inkling that the direction was not entirely spontaneous. On one occasion, Addison felt like they had been moving towards what brought Jake to Milverton in the first place, when suddenly they weren't. Addison let the chat run for a while before reclaiming the conversational reins, attempting to gently tug them back towards the topic. Other than mentioning he'd been in Milverton for a few years now, Jake didn't offer anything new. And before Addison knew it, Jake had flipped the conversation back onto something else.

Curious.

It didn't feel to Addison like the about-turns were done in a secretive, squirrelly kind of way, just that when it came to whatever had happened at that time, Jake wasn't entirely forthcoming. Addison suspected he wouldn't find any joy in pushing the subject further, and had to trust Jake would volunteer the information when he was good and ready.

They sipped their wine, snacked on cheese and crackers, attempted to ignore their chaperone, and otherwise continued getting to know each other. With everything that had gone on lately, it almost felt like they were covering the basics you'd usually knock out on a first date.

They'd moved on to chatting about some of the local characters when Addison saw he'd already sipped his way through another half a glass without noticing. He set it down to avoid absent-mindedly sipping, lest he drink too much and nod off before bed time – he refused to allow that to happen, not again.

Despite Addison's best efforts, they'd barely made a dent in the cheese board by the time the alarm on his phone rang again. 'That's my cue to finish off dinner,' Addison said, levering himself up from the couch. 'It shouldn't be too long. You can stay here with the snacks, or come—'

'I'll join you, I think,' Jake said, gesturing towards Keith with a subtle nod of the head as he stood up.

'Yes, probably best I don't leave you alone with him.'

'Who knows what he might do next,' Jake said. 'Should I bring the cheese board through?'

'Nah, leave it there for now. We can pick at it after dinner if we're still hungry.'

Addison moved through into the kitchen, shifting the tea towel aside to peek through the oven door. The potatoes were well on their way, and the chicken was presumably just about there too. A quick glance at the instructions on his phone – still facing the oven, his back to Jake – confirmed he had to crank up the heat for the last little bit to crisp up the skin.

Addison moved on to steaming the greens. He didn't love broccoli or beans – they were fine, but they were no roast potato, were they? His mother said you always needed something green on your plate, and despite being a grownup he couldn't bring himself to serve a meal without at least a token tuft of greenery. And this was something he could happily manage without a recipe's guidance, but also, more importantly, with the distraction of a hot man in his kitchen.

Jake had tactfully positioned himself at a distance that was out of the way, yet close enough to continue the conversation over the water boiling and the extractor fan's whirring. He leant, with his weight on one foot, hip resting against the side of the bench, and wine glass in hand. 'Are you sure you don't want a hand with anything?'

'No, no, you just stand there,' Addison said, cutting himself off before the second half of the sentence slipped out. You had to know someone very well before telling them to stand there and look pretty could be taken as a light and polite *No, thank you*, instead of the wildly condescending instruction that it seemed at face value.

In truth, the only thing left to do was the gravy, and he didn't need help mixing a packet of premade gravy powder into a jug of boiling water. He would rather his dinner date didn't witness that culinary shortcut at all.

Addison glanced over his shoulder as he stirred, listening to Jake, and couldn't help noticing that Keith was once again in attendance, though seemingly content to observe silently from the doorway. What was he going to do about that cat? Tonight, nothing. But he'd have to have a word.

Addison shook his head and smiled, transferring the gravy from the mixing jug into a cow-shaped ceramic pitcher he'd found in the cupboard. He suspected it was intended for serving milk at the breakfast table or over afternoon tea, but Addison had repurposed it as tonight's gravy boat.

With that done, he was ready.

Addison pulled on oven mitts, slid two dinner plates onto the oven's bottom rack, then pulled out the sizzling chicken and roast vegetables, bringing a rush of steamy deliciousness into the kitchen with it.

'That smells amazing,' Jake said.

Addison had to agree. 'Fingers crossed,' he said, though in truth he was struggling to be humble about it, proud that his cooking hadn't turned into a disaster as it so often did. This whole thing was going so well... suspiciously well. He kept waiting for the other shoe to drop – food poisoning was still a possibility, as was a red wine spill, among many other potential catastrophes – yet he remained determined not to self-sabotage.

Once more with his back partially turned to Jake, he cut into the thickest bit of the chicken and was relieved to see the juices running clear. He hoped that meant he could take food poisoning off the table.

Addison pulled the warmed dinner plates from the oven, plated up the food, and took it through to the dining room. Jake following with the second bottle of wine and the glasses.

Chapter 30

The dining room had multiple doors leading off, with Harper House's ever-present wood panelling lining the walls, and an impressive fireplace halfway along one side. The space itself was dominated by the large dining table, with five seats to either side and one at each end, comfortably seating twelve, and the chandelier hanging over the centre of the table.

Addison had never had an occasion to use the dining room, typically opting to eat at the kitchen bench or from his lap on the couch. He'd barely even been in the room, sometimes passing through, that was about it. But tonight seemed like the occasion for it. And despite the psychedelic carpet, the room more closely matched the mood Addison had been hoping for with its dimmed lights and lack of knick-knacks.

'This looks great, by the way,' Jake said of the food, taking the place set at the table opposite Addison.

'It turned out better than I'd hoped, if I'm honest.'

'Yeah, I thought you said that you didn't cook?'

'I don't, not really, at least not for guests. The best I can usually manage is *edible*.'

Jake took up his fork, speared a broccoli floret, put it in his mouth, chewed, swallowed, and set his fork down again. 'Can confirm, definitely edible.'

Addison watched the spectacle and smiled. 'Back in Wellington, my housemate and I tend to share dinner-cooking duties during the week when it's just us. But she takes the lead if we ever have people coming over.'

'But I take it you took the lead tonight?' Jake said, making a show of glancing towards the doors that led into the dining room, as if he expected to spot a mystery chef. Instead, he spotted the ball of orange fur that had been shadowing him throughout the evening. As they'd settled themselves for dinner, Keith had taken up position on the chair at the head of the table, with only his head clearing the table top. 'Or, do I have Keith to thank for this meal?'

Addison gave the cat his most incredulous face. 'Really, buddy?'

Keith didn't acknowledge him, just looked to Jake, to Addison, then back to Jake, where his gaze lingered for a moment before he hopped off the chair and exited the room, his tail twitching in the air as he left them to their dinner.

'He's a character, that one,' Jake said.

'He sure is.' Addison shook his head. 'Anyway, let's eat.'

Conversation took a back seat for a minute, at least until they'd had a few mouthfuls each. Addison approached his plate with purpose, checking each item in turn: the chicken completely cooked without being overdone; the greens just right, retaining a little of their crunch, yet far from wet and soggy; the carrots sweet and tasty; and the roast potatoes crisp and crunchy on the outside, light and fluffy on the inside. The humble potato really was dinnertime's unsung hero.

The wine Jake had brought was very nice too. They'd moved on to the red, and Addison made a mental note to keep an eye out for it in future.

Satisfied the food and wine appeared to be in order, Addison could focus once more on his date.

They took their time, chatting between mouthfuls. They talked about places they'd visited, movies they'd seen, books they'd read. One particularly rich seam of conversation involved the baffling things their colleagues had done. Then, for Addison it was his clients, and for Sergeant Jake Murphy it was members of the public.

Considering Dominic's untimely death hadn't come up once that evening, Addison had to assume Jake was avoiding the topic as studiously as he himself was. But that was a small price to pay in order to switch off from his amateur investigation, relax, and properly enjoy himself.

However, Addison hadn't factored in his instinctive curiosity, which apparently needed a new topic to latch onto – that is, Sergeant Jake Murphy himself. He wasn't taking a break from his little investigation to jump right over into interrogating his date. Addison had to consciously restrain himself, stuffing in a few mouthfuls of the obligatory greenery as negative reinforcement.

Otherwise, Addison kept it cool, and was pleased to see Jake had finished every last thing on his plate. That pleasure lasted for all of a second before he worried he hadn't served up enough.

They were both guys, but Jake was taller and broader and all those good things. And he probably had a calorie intake to match. The sergeant didn't maintain a chest like that with half portions.

'Did you want more?' Addison said, already reaching for

Jake's plate. 'There's some of everything left.'

'Oh, no, that was plenty, thanks.'

'OK, great.' But it wasn't great. With that anxiety calmed, another flashed up to take its place. Had he finished his plate... out of politeness? No, Addison may not have had great confidence in his own cooking, but he recognised good and bad food. Tonight's efforts certainly weren't going to earn him any Michelin stars, but he didn't think anyone could argue it wasn't a decent, solid meal.

As if reading his mind, Jake said unprompted, 'It was delicious.' Then he paused, thoughtful, before adding, 'I haven't had someone cook for me in, well, in a fair while.'

Addison wanted to ask, *oh* how he wanted to ask. It was on the tip of his tongue, but then Jake cleared his throat. 'Shall I take these dishes through?'

'Ah, no, no. I'll take the plates.' Addison led them back through to the kitchen, telling himself there was no rush. He had all the time in the world to get to know this man, but the thought was cut short when he spotted the ceramic cow on the bench.

He'd forgotten the gravy.

The realisation prompted another mini panic, but then he consoled himself with the fact dinner had been plenty juicy enough without it. Gravy was a culinary crutch, but in this case hadn't been needed to swoop in and rehydrate any desiccated chicken.

Considering the makeshift gravy boat again, only then did he realise the contents of the cow poured from its mouth, as if it was barfing up the brown liquid. Still, better than coming out the other end, he supposed. Not that either end was appetising in the slightest and would be almost enough to put someone off their dinner.

All up, it was probably for the best that he forgot the gravy. He might have to retire the ceramic cow, put her out to pasture, so to speak, or at least to the back of the cupboard.

Addison stacked the dishes on top of each other and shunted them to one end of the bench. He hated to leave the mess, but the idea of slamming the brakes on their date to do dishes, that was worse.

He then quickly shifted the extra cooked food into a container and slotted it in the fridge, cautiously optimistic that he wouldn't have time to do so later that evening. He was also conscious he didn't want to leave the food on the bench overnight and run the risk of Keith getting into it.

A responsible thought, but it appeared it may have already been too late.

Replenished glasses in hand, Addison and Jake stepped back through to the lounge to find the cheese board with a distinct lack of cheese. It had also been stripped of the remaining cured meats. All that remained on the board were a handful of crackers and a small jar of quince paste with suspicious teeth marks in it.

Addison found he was too contented after dinner and a few wines to be annoyed or angry about the situation. 'I wonder what's happened here.'

Jake surveyed the scene. 'It looks to me as if a crime has been committed.'

'The Great Cheese Heist of Harper House,' Addison said as he moved around the coffee table only to discover the small dish of relish had been overturned on the carpet. If not for the dish, he might have missed the relish, lost as it was in the carpet's colourful patterns. And once he'd scooped it up, any stain that might be there appeared to vanish from sight.

He had to concede, the carpet had that advantage at least.

'And here he is now,' Jake said as Keith appeared in the doorway. 'The culprit returns to the scene of the crime.'

Addison tutted. 'Couldn't help himself.'

Keith appeared unrepentant, despite the rather incriminating clump of relish snagged in his left eyebrow.

'You could have at least cleaned up the evidence, Keith.'

With the worst of the carnage cleared, Jake settled onto the couch, picking a spot not quite at the end like before, but also not in the middle. He managed to come down at about the one-third mark. Addison did likewise, his thigh barely a hand's width from Jake's. Cosy, without being presumptuous. Besides, they'd just eaten – couldn't be getting carried away before their food had settled.

Conversation resumed, drinks were sipped, and knees occasionally brushed each other. Things were becoming increasingly cosy on the couch, which Keith apparently objected to. Without warning, their feline chaperone imposed himself once more, jumping up and settling himself directly between the two men.

Addison appreciated the thought behind the cat putting his body on the line, presumably to protect his new human, but this was one step too far. He was about to relocate the cat to literally anywhere else, when he caught sight of a familiar face on the TV and gasped.

Chapter 31

'That's Sandra,' Addison said, shocked to recognise Dominic's cousin. He lurched forward, unintentionally dislodging Keith, who let out a brief snarl in protest but nonetheless took himself elsewhere.

The image on the TV cut to a pre-recorded segment of the reporter speaking to the camera with the Manawatū Gorge in the background. Addison grabbed the remote and turned the volume up.

'—cousin lives near where Mr Campbell's body was discovered. On his way to becoming a household name, the professional athlete was already a well-known figure in New Zealand's sporting scene. We spoke earlier to Ms Campbell, who said her cousin was a regular visitor to Milverton, which he often used as a base while training on the local trails and rivers. His sudden death has once again rocked the quiet town, which has seen more than its fair share of troubles in recent weeks.'

Then the image cut back to the late-night news presenter in the studio, already moving on to the next story. Addison turned the volume back down. 'Sorry,' he said. 'I had to hear what they were saying.'

Jake's smile was one of understanding. 'That is fair enough.'

'I really was hoping you could have the whole night off.'

'No, no. That's all right. The job can sometimes be...' Jake lifted his glass, moving it in a circular, all-encompassing motion.

Addison nodded. He understood, with his own clients' demands infiltrating well beyond his nominal work hours. And Jake's work was on a whole other level, with his clients effectively being the public. And the public expected him to be answerable at all times.

Addison tried, unsuccessfully, more than once to go back to what they were talking about before.

'Addison,' Jake said. 'I know we're only just getting to know each other, but I see your curiosity, which is part of what drew me to you.' He paused for a moment, as if to make sure Addison was hearing him, before he continued. 'And I think I already know enough to recognise that you won't be able to focus on anything else until you've asked your questions.'

Much of what Jake said had left Addison lost for words – he didn't know what to think.

'And selfishly,' Jake said, 'I'd prefer we address your questions now, so I don't have you distracted *later*.'

Now Addison absolutely knew what to think about *that*. He reddened, considering all the things he wouldn't want to get distracted from, and he recognised that Jake spoke the truth. His overwhelming curiosity was liable to rear its head at the most inopportune moment... In *that* case, he'd be doing Jake a favour, and it was best to minimise that risk.

Jake raised an eyebrow, as if to say *Come on.*

'Um.' Addison winced. 'So, uh, have the police been

looking into Dominic's death?'

'Yes, we have been doing some background on Mr Campbell, and what was going on in the lead-up to last Saturday. We are yet to rule anything out.'

Jake's response was a masterclass in saying next to nothing. But even just the fact that Dominic's case wasn't already closed suggested the situation was not a clear-cut accidental death. Jake got nowhere near admitting the police were treating the case as a likely homicide, but they were clearly convinced it was at least suspicious.

Addison knew he wouldn't get anywhere trying to pin down specifics, so decided to keep his enquiries as open as possible, leaving it up to Jake to answer how he saw fit. 'And what have you found?'

Jake considered the question, sipped his wine, his eyebrows slowly drawing together. 'That your ex was not a nice guy.'

'He wasn't my—'

The look of concern from Jake cut Addison off mid-objection, as if he was searching the past for anything he should be worried about there.

'He was— We weren't—' Addison took a breath. 'Yes, Dominic was a piece of work. And I cottoned on to that pretty quick, no damage done.' He shrugged a shoulder, making his emotional detachment clear.

The line of Jake's shoulders slowly settled in response, visibly relaxing. 'OK.'

'How's Sandra doing with all this, though?' Addison said, tipping his wine glass to the TV where her face had appeared only moments earlier. 'She wasn't his biggest fan, but family is family. And they clearly saw a bit of each other.'

Jake's look sharpened, as if Addison had just admitted to the amateur sleuthing which he was absolutely not supposed to be doing.

Addison kept his cool. 'I met Sandra at the police station, while we were in the waiting area.' He hadn't been actively prying into Dominic's death at that point, just talking. So what he said was truthful – perhaps a little too selective to be considered completely transparent, but truthful nonetheless.

'Of course,' Jake said. 'That's right.'

'What did she have to say?'

'When I talked to her at the station?'

'Yeah.'

Jake thought about it for a second before saying, 'Just that things had been a bit, well, *strained* between them lately.'

'Dominic being Dominic?'

'Yeah, and that he'd damaged her car.'

That was new information. Addison's mind was already whirring, the comment triggering another that Hugo had made – something about how Sandra's car had been at the mechanic's.

'Oh, did he hit something?'

Jake shook his head. 'Nah, he'd taken Sandra's car up some pretty rough roads in the ranges. You'd need a four-wheel drive with good clearance to manage those. Sounds like he bottomed it out a few times, did some damage underneath, suspension, that kind of thing.'

'I bet Sandra wasn't best pleased.'

'She was not, said he had to sort out his own transport when he was in town from then on.'

That would explain Dominic's visit to Hugo's car yard.

Again, not that Addison was reasonably in possession of that information. But, if that information would help the police, saying nothing would effectively be obstructing a police investigation... wouldn't it? Addison battled with himself for all of a second, but knew he had to say something. 'So, Dominic—'

'Turns out he stopped by Milverton Motors the next time he was in town, helped himself to a vehicle for the day. Mr Li was not impressed by the length of the "test drive", nor by the state Mr Campbell returned the car in.'

'That sounds like Dominic, all right,' Addison said. It also sounded like Jake already had all the information that Addison had. 'How did he get to the gorge on Saturday, by the way? He'd lost borrowing privileges from his cousin, and I presume he wasn't going to be handed the keys for another "test drive"...' He didn't know if Dominic's transport to the trails had any relevance to the situation, but everything added to the overall picture. 'Did he sort out a rental car? I suppose he could've hit up another car yard, maybe one in Palmerston North? Or he could've cycled there I guess – the gorge is just out of town, and he was more than fit enough to manage a bit of extra exercise. Did he take his bike?'

Jake raised an eyebrow at Addison's rambling stream of consciousness, but answered him anyway. 'Mr Campbell took his cousin's car.'

'But I thought—'

'She'd banned him from using it again? She had.'

'And wasn't it in getting fixed?'

Jake nodded. 'The mechanic had finished the work and she'd just got it back.'

Addison's mouth hung open, quite speechless. The

audacity of the guy. 'And he took it again, presumably without asking?'

Jake's eyes flashed in the affirmative.

'Wow.'

'He didn't take it off-roading this time, just to the gorge car park at the start of the trails.'

'Still,' Addison said, 'not cool.' An understatement, but he was beyond being surprised at Dominic's shameless, selfish antics. Being inconsiderate was not illegal, but it did nothing to win people over. Sandra, Zach, Prisha, Julie, and Hugo all had reason not to be on Team Dominic, but nothing truly murder-worthy. At least, that was his working theory. However, he did wonder if he had written off Sandra too soon. She had been used by her cousin repeatedly and over extended periods. Had something finally tipped her over the edge?

Absently, Addison sipped his wine only to find his glass empty, which brought him crashing back to the room. Here he was, mind a million miles away, meanwhile what he wanted was right there sitting on the couch beside him. He realised he would much rather the evening involved a little less of his mind wandering, and perhaps a little more mutual hand wandering.

'Sorry,' Addison said, shaking his head, hoping to distract from the heat in his cheeks. 'Again! You're off the clock, and here I am going on. Making you think about work.'

'It's fine, truly,' Jake said, giving him a reassuring smile. 'I have a hard time denying your curiosity, Addison. Like I said before, it's part of what drew me to you. You are inquisitive and perceptive, and I find that very attractive, even if it might get you into trouble sometimes.'

233

Addison nodded, speechless once more as he swallowed the lump in his throat, but was duly reassured that he hadn't gone and spoilt the night with his excessive curiosity.

He picked up the bottle, hoping to distract himself, only to find there wasn't a whole lot of wine left. He poured the remainder, giving them each barely a mouthful. 'Good thing we have backups,' Addison said, nodding through towards the kitchen. He was about to get up and retrieve further refreshment when he noticed, out of the corner of his eye, the lump of orange fur parked on the first step leading upstairs. 'I had wondered where he'd got to.'

'He's been sitting there for a while now,' Jake said, clearly amused.

'Feeling very pleased with himself, I'll bet. The smug little terror,' Addison said. 'Anyway, shall I grab another bottle, or—'

Jake had knocked back the last of his wine and pinned Addison with a look. 'Or,' he said, drawing out the word, setting his empty glass down, not taking his eyes off Addison for even a moment as he slowly leant in.

Addison was very willing to take the hint, closing the gap and pressing his lips to Jake's. Jake pressed right back, shifting closer on the couch. Addison was attempting to do the same when Jake suddenly broke contact, smiling as his gaze roved around Addison's face.

'Or we could head upstairs,' Jake said, 'if you like?'

Before the kiss, Addison had been about to ask if Jake wanted a soft drink or some water instead of another wine, something about being responsible with it being a weeknight, work tomorrow, etcetera. But Jake's alternative was so much more appealing and had wiped all other thoughts from his mind.

Addison murmured, as if considering the suggestion. As if minimising the time and distance between the first and hoped-for second stage of their date hadn't been a significant factor in his decision to host rather than going out. 'It is *well* past my bedtime,' Addison said. 'Which I expect is what Keith is trying to communicate by sitting himself there on the step.'

'In that case,' Jake said, clapping his hands on his thighs and nodding once in that universal time-to-go-then gesture. 'Thank you for dinner – it was delicious. And now I'd better head off and let you boys get some rest.'

Addison's building anticipation dropped abruptly at the words, but then he caught Jake's lip twitching up in the corner.

'You wouldn't want to leave before...' Addison said, his imagination already jumping ahead to consider the possibilities. 'You wouldn't want to leave before *dessert*.'

Jake's eyes shifted from a look of amusement to one of hunger. 'You're right, I wouldn't want to miss that.'

Addison downed his last mouthful of wine, set the glass aside, and pushed himself up off the couch before extending a hand to Jake. 'Are you coming?'

Jake accepted the offered hand and moved right up into Addison's personal space, smiling like the cat that got the cream. 'I sure hope so.'

Chapter 32

Addison couldn't remember the last time he'd had such a good sleep. He woke slowly, unaccountably blissful, rubbing the sleep from his eyes.

The low light suggested it might be just about time to get up. And the birdsong outside was all that featured on the morning's soundtrack, louder even than the sounds of the city he was accustomed to, but infinitely more pleasant.

He didn't really have a commute these days, which meant he had plenty of time to get in a run, or he could just take his time getting ready. He opted for the slower morning routine, keen to extend the inexplicable serenity he was experiencing.

Addison slowly shifted his leg over, confused when he found no obstruction, the familiar lump at the foot of his bed notably absent. Where was Keith?

Finally, his sluggish brain brought the events of last night to his attention.

His date with Jake. Wine and cheese, dinner and *dessert…*

Addison felt a smile tugging at his lips. He had enjoyed himself very much last night, and had reason to believe that

Jake had too.

He'd already decided to take his time this morning, and he had a few ideas for how they might fill that time. He reached a hand out to the other side of the bed only to find it empty. Addison was alone in the bed, which he already knew, of course, his foot having established as much. The growing smile shifted to a frown.

Jake had been right there when he'd fallen asleep, and now he wasn't. When had he left? Had he waited for Addison to doze off, then untangled himself and ducked out? Or had he slunk out before first light without a word?

Had Jake been hit with regret? They'd played at flirtation, had their fun, and that was that. Addison spiralled for all of a heartbeat before staging a self-intervention.

Jake had work today, Addison knew that, and he would've wanted to get back to his place, clean himself up before heading in to the station. Addison told himself this was the most likely scenario, and not just wishful thinking on his part.

He grabbed his phone, but found no message from Jake.

No farewell, no message – after what he thought had been a successful evening, this was like a little jab to the gut.

He was back to speculating with next to no information, wondering if another half an hour of sleep might make him feel better, when he heard crashing sounds from downstairs.

Eyes wide open, he bolted upright, straining to pick up anything else.

He heard a sliding noise, wood against wood, followed by a soft clunk. Was that a sash window? They were latched closed, or they should be. Or the front door? Surely Jake wouldn't have left it unlocked on his way out.

Who was in the house?

Addison's eyes darted around the room, barely able to see anything in the low light. He did a quick mental stocktake of the room's contents. Nothing even remotely weapon-like sprung to mind. How was he supposed to confront an intruder without a weapon? Clobber them with a bedside lamp? Ridiculous. What else? Hide and hope they didn't find him? Head downstairs and ask them nicely to leave?

No, the immediate surge of panic had scrambled any chance of logical thought, but he knew what he needed to do. He had to be sensible about this and call for backup. He reached for his phone, willing his shaking hand not to fumble or make any other noise that might draw the intruder's attention.

He had to swallow his pride and ask for help. He knew that if he didn't, and something happened, Jake would have something to say about that. The sergeant answered on the second ring.

'Morn—'

'There's someone in the house,' Addison said, his voice a whisper, desperate not to be discovered. 'They're—'

'It's me,' Jake said.

'What?'

'I am the someone in the house.'

'What? I thought you'd left?'

'No, I'm downstairs, in the kitchen.'

'Ah.' Addison pulled the phone away from his ear and screamed his mortification soundlessly into the pillow, took a breath, and put the phone back to his ear. 'I'll be down in a minute,' he said as calmly as he could manage, then immediately ended the call.

Addison dropped his head back into the pillow, then

again a couple more times for good measure. So much for investigative instincts.

There still wasn't a whole lot of light in the bedroom. But if he'd taken even a second to look around, he might have noticed the clothes that were not his, scattered wherever they'd landed the night before.

Addison pulled on some grey sweatpants and the shirt from last night, doing up a couple of buttons to hold it in place. He splashed his face, rinsed his mouth, and dealt with the worst of his bedhead before venturing downstairs to face the man he'd just made a fool of himself in front of, again.

Addison found Jake at the stove, wearing nothing but briefs and a T-shirt, his back to the open doorway.

Jake hadn't noticed Addison's presence yet, but Addison had sure noticed his. He watched as the T-shirt pulled taut across Jake's shoulders, bunching and shifting as he moved his arms. Not just that, but the man was cooking breakfast. Here he'd been thinking Jake had slipped away without a word. Instead, the complete opposite was true.

Watching him, Addison felt an uncomfortable pressure in his chest and lightness in his stomach. The strange sensation had come on in a rush, and was one he didn't recognise…

He shook himself, reasoning it must just be hunger, or at least something hunger-adjacent. It had been a good few seconds of Addison standing there before he caught himself staring, and decided he'd best announce his arrival before *someone else* caught him staring too. 'Morning,' he said, his voice coming out a little huskier than he'd anticipated.

'Ah,' Jake said, turning around, spatula in hand and a slightly concerned look on his face. 'Good morning, again.'

'Sorry about calling—'

Jake held up a hand to stop the apology. 'No, no, that was the right thing to do.'

A moment ago Addison had been captivated by Jake's back and shoulders, but now they faced each other across the room, his attention had shifted to the man's chest.

'Sorry, I couldn't find my shirt in the dark,' Jake said, tugging at the hem. 'And this one was on top of the laundry hamper by the door.'

It was a size too small, but that was absolutely fine, and Addison said as much. He hadn't had his first coffee yet, so it was nice not to have to use his imagination – or his memory, now that he thought about it – to know what was underneath.

Jake lifted the pan. 'I hope you're OK with scrambled eggs?'

Addison had many things he wanted to say in response, but settled for a simple, 'Yes, that sounds great.'

His eyes had apparently stolen all the processing power for his senses, and the moment Jake drew his attention to the food, his ears and nose engaged. The sizzling sounds and savoury smells of a cooked breakfast, and was that—

'Did you want to finish off the coffees?' Jake said, buttering the toast. 'These eggs are almost done.'

Something to do. Yes, good. He was getting the milk from the fridge when he remembered the other thing he was yet to do – the dishes. He'd been so distracted by the man at the stove that he hadn't even noticed the stack of dirty dinner dishes, but a quick check of the benchtop confirmed they'd vanished. Not only was Jake cooking him breakfast, but he'd done last night's dishes. Addison wanted to protest, apologise for being such a terrible host, but it was done now, nothing he could do about that. And telling him off would be no way to reward his efforts. Instead, he would have to show his appreciation some other way.

Addison was busy considering what form such appreciation might take while he added milk to their coffees. It was then he spotted the surly ginger lump lurking in the corner.

Keith had led the way upstairs last night, and had already been kneading his chosen spot in preparation when Addison and Jake entered the bedroom.

'Oh, mate,' Addison had said. The confusion on the feline's face as he was relocated from the foot of the bed out onto the landing was like a dagger to the heart. But he'd promised to make it up to Keith, and then any feelings of guilt were forgotten the moment Addison had closed the bedroom door behind them.

Keith, it seemed, had not forgotten nor forgiven his eviction. The looks he'd levelled in Jake's direction last night were nothing compared to the death stare now. And it appeared he held Addison at least partially responsible, as the look occasionally transferred to him before returning to Jake.

Addison didn't know how to address the animosity coming off the cat in waves, and feared Keith's eventual retribution. He filled the cat's food bowls with a bit more than usual – a tentative peace offering – but otherwise left the cat to hopefully cool down in his own time.

'Shall we have that out on the back porch?' Addison said as Jake portioned out the scrambled eggs.

Jake seemed unsure. 'I'm not really dressed for it,' he said, looking down at himself in briefs and the slightly too-small T-shirt.

'That's a benefit of being semi-rural, not in the middle of the city. No neighbours. Come on, it's nice.' Addison loaded the breakfast plates and coffees onto a tray and nodded for Jake to open the kitchen door that led outside.

Chapter 33

Addison had enjoyed breakfast out on the back porch more than a few times, and was pleased to see the morning sun flooding the space, taking the edge off the chill in the air.

They settled into the wicker chairs, not saying a word, just enjoying the sun, the outlook over the garden behind the house, the morning birdsong, the breakfast, and each other's company.

Addison realised he could get used to this, with Jake. Not just the man cooking, though that was very nice, but having Jake in his life – this solid, sorted, purposeful, caring, and very handsome man. The thought filled Addison with warmth as he allowed his mind to wander, fantasising about such domesticity.

'Thanks for cooking breakfast *and* for doing all those dishes,' Addison said. Then, despite telling himself he wouldn't, he couldn't help adding, 'You really shouldn't have.'

'That was my pleasure, and the least I could do after you cooked dinner last night.'

Addison shrugged, a sheepish smile on his face. 'That was just a ploy to get you back to the house.'

Jake's eyes locked onto Addison's face for a beat before he let out a full, rich laugh. It eventually settled down to a smile, his eyes shining as they tracked down Addison's body then jumped back to his face again. He shook his head, but the smile remained fixed in place.

Addison shrugged again, but the nonchalance wasn't fooling anyone, his smile one of success.

'Anyway, I'd better put some more clothes on, then go get ready for work. I'll take these back inside,' Jake said, waving off Addison's attempted protest as he started stacking his breakfast things on the tray.

In the meantime, they'd both been too preoccupied to notice the shift in the background noise. Addison was taking a sip of his coffee when a rumbling and crunching came from the gravel track that led around the side of the house from the driveway at the front to the shed out the back. It quickly grew in volume until a small flatbed truck appeared with a lawnmower on the back and pulling a high-sided trailer behind.

The signwriting along the sides identified the early morning interloper as 'Dave's Lawn Mowing and Bush Trimming Services'. The owner and operator herself leapt from the truck when it had barely come to a halt.

Short and stocky, Dave – never Daphne – sported a polo shirt with the logo of her business, hard-wearing shorts, and a pair of chunky boots.

Addison said nothing of bypassing such niceties as knocking on the front door, just coming right around to the back and effectively letting herself in. It was wildly familiar – something only close friends or family would do – but to be fair to Dave, the front door had been out of action on her first visit. 'Uh…' he said. 'Dave, hi, what are you doing here so early?'

At first Dave seemed as surprised as Addison and Jake, her eyes darting between the two men, but then her expression settled. 'Mm, yes. I could ask the same of our sergeant here.' She raised an eyebrow, the corner of her mouth following suit. 'But I think I can figure that one out for myself.'

Heat surged up Addison's neck, across his cheeks, and out to the tips of his ears. If she'd had any whisper of doubt before, such a reaction would've sealed the deal. He was speechless, had no clue how to respond to such a statement...

Confirm that her suspicions were accurate, and tell her what they'd been up to? Absolutely not.

Reject her insinuations? Plead ignorance? His date with Jake was not something shameful or regretful, so that was very much not an option either.

Addison was still frozen with indecision when Dave saved the situation. Her expression had softened as she nodded her approval. 'Anyway, I'm glad to see you settling in, Mr Harper.' Then she turned to Jake, another nod. 'Sergeant.'

He'd been so wrapped up in his own head that he hadn't considered Jake would be having thoughts of his own. Worse, Jake was the one in the briefs and undersized T-shirt.

'Dave,' Jake said, acknowledging the greeting with a nod of his own, though his face remained unreadable.

'Right, back to business,' the mowing-business owner said, returning her focus to Addison, as if nothing were amiss. 'I was due to do your lawns and tidy up the hedges tomorrow but something came up, so I thought I'd get onto them first thing today? If not, you'll get pushed out to next week or the week after, and before you know it you won't have Harper House, you'll have Harper Jungle.'

She said it all as if reminding him of something he already knew. What was he supposed to say? She was here now. 'Yeah, uh, sure.'

Dave frowned, recognising his confusion. 'I left you a message last night?'

'Ah, sorry. I didn't see it. I was, uh…' Addison realised the moment he started that he was under no obligation to explain himself, but it'd be worse if he just trailed off to nothing. 'I was busy.'

Dave was once again the picture of amusement.

And Jake? Well, Addison had never seen the man looking quite so uncomfortable. He tried to convey his apologies with a look, not that he regretted having Jake over, not a bit. But if he was to do one thing differently, he might not have suggested they enjoy their breakfast out the back while still half-dressed. But really, how could he have known?

'Thanks for coming anyway, Dave,' Addison said, holding onto his still mostly undrunk coffee, but adding his plate, knife, and fork to the tray, hoping the gesture was enough to bring the conversation to a close. 'We'd better let you get on.'

'Yep, yep. Jolly good.' Dave raised a finger as if she'd had another thought. 'Were you still happy for me to use your great-uncle's ride-on mower?'

'Whatever you need.'

'OK, good – it's a very nice machine. Would be a shame to see it gathering dust in the shed. Then I can tidy up around the outsides with my push mower and edge trimmer.'

246

'Sure,' Addison said, his expression now less pleasant and patient smile, and more strained and please-get-on-with-it grimace. 'I defer to you on this, Dave. You're the professional.'

'Very good,' Dave said with a nod and a smile. 'I'll leave you gents to it.'

It was a shame the back porch was so solidly built. Addison would have welcomed a few rotten boards, preferably directly under his chair, giving way at that very moment. They weren't about to head upstairs for another round, especially not now Dave would be doing laps around the house.

Then again, the roar of the lawnmower would mask any other sounds that might come from inside—

Addison shook himself. Time and place, he had to remind himself. 'Sorry,' he said the moment the lawn mowing contractor was out of earshot, 'I didn't know Dave—'

'It's fine,' Jake said, attempting a reassuring smile, though the pinched expression exposed the lie in his words and the attempt at portraying amusement.

He was picking up the tray when they heard another engine coming from around the side of the house. Too soon for Dave to have started up the lawn mower, and too low pitched besides.

Addison was still puzzling over the latest unexpected noise when a signwritten white van shot into view, coming to a stop beside Dave's truck and trailer.

Chapter 34

The side of the van featured two cartoon superheroes with lightning bolt motifs on their skin-tight bodysuits flexing their biceps at either end of "Turn It On Electrical Services".

The man who jumped out looked much like his mascots, possibly even more ripped than Addison remembered. He'd already gone a couple of steps towards the house when he spotted Jake and stopped dead in his tracks.

Still only halfway to the kitchen door, Jake did likewise. He abruptly lowered the tray in an attempt to shield his dignity, but there was no hiding that he had only briefs covering his lower half. Addison wasn't exactly looking put together either, with a rumpled button-up shirt and grey sweatpants.

Meanwhile, Kyle Thompson was fully dressed in a crisp branded polo, cargo shorts, and a pair of steel-cap boots.

The electrician and the sergeant appeared to be in a battle for who was the most mortified, and Addison couldn't help taking on the feeling second hand, absorbing the atmosphere of overwhelming discomfort.

'Hi, Kyle,' Addison said, hoping to break the tension.

'I can, uh...' The electrician didn't move from the spot

but fixed his gaze on Addison, eyes determinedly not flicking over to Jake, as if not looking meant the underdressed man wouldn't be there anymore. 'I can come back another time if—'

'I was just leaving,' Jake said, voice void of any inflection or indication of his mental state. He turned from the electrician, balancing the tray on one arm while trying to open the door with his free hand.

Addison was up on his feet. 'Let me help with—'

'I've got it,' Jake said, short and sharp.

Addison had all of half a second to process being cut off so abruptly when yet another vehicle pulled in. This was another flatbed truck, this one with some kind of earthmoving equipment on the back. He hadn't even heard it approaching, but he did hear the rattling of crockery ratcheting up before Jake finally managed to get the door open and slip through. He slammed it shut behind him as the morning's third visitor climbed out of their vehicle.

Addison was stuck, desperate to go after Jake but also very conscious he now had two contractors waiting to speak to him, not to mention the other one already doing work further down the property.

Kyle Thompson had no such indecision, immediately launching into introducing the newcomer and describing the work they were there to do.

Not that Addison knew the electrician beyond their brief introduction earlier in the week, and not that his mind was wholly on the conversation, but he couldn't help thinking Kyle sounded stiff and stilted.

He had obviously made the same deductions Dave had earlier, though his response couldn't have been more different. Kyle may have seemed much less likely to explode

249

now that the briefs-clad Jake was out of sight, but still remained far from comfortable. He hadn't fled, but Addison suspected it might have been a close-run thing.

Addison's mind was almost entirely occupied by Jake, Jake's discomfort, and Jake's hasty retreat. The little mental capacity he had remaining for the situation at hand meant he didn't catch the name of the earthmoving guy or any of the finer details of the proposed work, though he at least grasped the key points. Kyle had subcontracted the guy to dig a trench along the driveway from the roadside up to the house. The electrician would lay the fibre-optic cable in the trench, connections would be made at each end, and then – voilà! – internet. Not said in those words, but that seemed to be the gist of it.

By the time Kyle had finished his little spiel, the nameless earthmoving contractor had left to start offloading his trench-digging machine.

Addison might not have anticipated Dave's arrival, but he should've known to expect the electrician. He'd been reminded of the scheduled work only a few days ago, but what with looking into Dominic's death and preparing for last night's date, something as ordinary as fibre installation couldn't compete. If he'd been up and organised a little earlier, they could have avoided such an excruciating start to the day for everyone involved.

'Sorry about all—'

Kyle held a hand up. 'None of my business. I'm here to do a job, and that's it. I shouldn't have' – he cleared his throat – 'I hadn't expected to see your… *guest.*'

As much as Addison wanted to get inside and apologise to Jake, he wanted to get away from the conversation with Kyle more. But seeing the electrician in person reminded him of Kyle Thompson coming up in conversation earlier in the week, and what he'd intended to say when he next saw the man.

Kyle looked about ready to escape the conversation himself, to excuse himself and get on with the work. Addison didn't have time – nor, at this hour, the wits, to be fair – to subtly bring the conversation around. Instead, he said, as if voicing a random thought, 'You didn't mention you were a cross triathlete.'

The electrician's face featured a parade of expressions, with confusion and suspicion being chief among them, before settling on something consciously mild. 'You were already halfway out the door, so we didn't get on to small talk.' He shrugged, as if it was no matter. 'We weren't doing the full rundown, were we,' he said, more statement than question.

Addison did know that, and he was regretting not taking a moment to come up with a better opening gambit when Kyle continued, a touch more defensively.

'I was focusing on what was relevant to the job, and that's all. I didn't think it was the time or place to go into what we get up to *after hours*.' His gaze drifted to where Jake had been sitting only a minute earlier and Addison got the message loud and clear.

On a typical day, after being *told* like that, Addison would've folded in on himself, but apparently he'd already endured his daily quota of embarrassment so the comment flew past without consequence.

'Yeah, fair,' Addison said, offering a shrug of his own. 'I guess it's just been on my mind lately – cross triathlons, that is. Not something you hear about every day. But I take it you heard about Dominic Campbell?'

Kyle's expression hardened then.

'Sorry, that was insensitive of me.' Addison waved the air as if to suggest he should ignore the question, but then he went on. 'With you both involved in the same sport, you must have known each other quite well?'

'Yes, we did.'

'He had quite the track record.'

'He did.'

'That must have been inspiring?' Addison said, hoping the more open-ended question might elicit a response of more than a few words. 'Having someone at the top of their game when they're so local?'

'He was based in Wellington,' Kyle said.

'Yeah, but he trained up here a lot, right?'

'He did.'

If Addison thought earlier had been excruciating, this was quite possibly more so. Time for a new tactic: portray himself as a sports fan, someone interested in the inner game of competition. 'Did his success give you something to look up to?' Addison said. 'Or even motivate you to beat him?'

'I haven't gone pro. I'm just an amateur. It keeps me in shape.'

'Mm it does,' Addison said before his brain could tell him not to. It felt wrong to even think such a thing, especially with Jake so close by, but nobody could deny the guy was in shape. He rushed on before Kyle could wonder at the comment. 'Must be tough being second best all the time though? Is that why you and Dominic didn't get along?' It was bold, a big swing, and Addison knew it. But he had to get this thing moving.

'What?' Kyle said, eyes wide, taking an involuntary half-step back.

'I overheard someone saying something about your run-in with him at Halswell's.'

Kyle obviously gathered himself, pulling on his mild expression from earlier. 'Oh, that.'

'Yeah, what happened there?' Addison pitched this question with a tone that suggested he was scandalised, like he was someone after the juicy gossip, not someone running an impromptu interrogation.

The electrician and amateur cross triathlete scoffed. 'Dominic thought he was untouchable, thought he owned everyone, could do what he pleased. It's why he liked coming here to Milverton, easier to throw his weight around.'

'Big dog in a small town?'

'Yes, *exactly*. Seems like he didn't stand out enough, get enough attention back in Wellington. He has no respect for Milverton, the people, or the wildlife.'

Addison had heard from more than a few people about Dominic's antics, but no mention of wildlife, and he said as much to Kyle.

'Running and biking wherever he liked, stuff the consequences. He's been disrupting birds by training on trails that are closed during nesting season, dropping his rubbish wherever he pleases, and who knows what else. I know Lars had words with him, if you know what I mean. Told him to sort his act out, but I doubt that made any impression on him.'

'Who's Lars?' Addison said when no clarification was forthcoming. 'Was he at Halswell's too?'

'What? No, this was another time. Just saying there are others Dominic wasn't fooling. Lars Blomqvist is his name.

DOC ranger up in the gorge, based out of the DOC office at the carpark there.'

'Right.' Made sense the Department of Conservation would have something to say about such things, and it might even be something worth following up. But for now... 'So, what happened at Halswell's then?'

Kyle made a sound of disgust, clearly unimpressed with the situation. 'Zach and I just happened to be in there when Dominic started going off. We didn't do anything, just stood there, making our presence obvious. That was enough to get the message across and made him pull his head in, not that he was happy about it. He's gone pro, and thinks that gives him a free pass for everything.'

'Have you ever considered going pro yourself?'

The full-time electrician and part-time athlete twitched, but then shrugged. 'Who hasn't? But no, not seriously, just a hobby to keep fit.'

Addison suspected he'd touched a sore spot, so he proceeded to do what everyone does upon making such a discovery: he prodded it.

'Keeping that fit is a huge commitment, a lot of work, and you look like you're putting in the work,' Addison said, nodding vaguely at the man's body. 'I heard that you've come close a bunch of times.' He remembered Julie Halswell saying something about it. 'That you could go pro if you went for it?' She hadn't said that, but Addison needed to see what might come out. 'Do you reckon if you did take it seriously, shot for the top, that you could be the best? Instead of Milverton's second best?'

That last was a low blow, and Addison could see it had hit home. But Kyle was fairly hit-and-miss when it came to volunteering information, so direct questions were the only way to go.

'Look what *first* best did for Dominic.' Kyle shook his head. 'I hate to think about it. If it could happen to him, it could happen to anyone, you know?'

Addison did know, and had recently been having thoughts along very similar lines.

'But Dominic pushed too hard to maintain that position, and look what happened. The trail running, mountain biking, and swimming are just to keep me fit. And sometimes I put them all together. Cross triathlons are just a hobby.'

'So, you're not going to go pro?'

'Never say never.' Kyle offered his characteristic shrug. 'But being a full-time athlete is expensive and tough on the body. I've got an electrical business to run, which will see me further into the future than a career as a professional sportsman. No, I don't have the time or money to commit to going full time, even if I wanted to.'

'Yeah, I can imagine.'

'Besides, if I did that, who would install Milverton's fibre?' Kyle said with a roll of the eyes and a short bark of a laugh.

'True,' Addison said, relieved at the levity after a rather awkward and then intense interaction. 'Right, I'd better let you get on with it then, and I'd better get into town to do some work of my own. It was Lars, wasn't it? The DOC ranger?'

'Yeah, that's him,' Kyle said, eyebrows drawing together. 'Why's that?'

'I might pop out later and see what he has to say about Dominic. I'll take my bike, I think,' Addison said, thinking aloud to himself. 'Should have time to get out to the DOC office and back over lunch. Hopefully Lars is in.'

If anything, Kyle seemed more confused. 'Why?'

'Oh, you know, closure,' Addison said. 'Dominic and I have history.' He reasoned the electrician would find out soon enough, and after the conversation they'd just had, Kyle would be wondering why Addison hadn't mentioned it. Harper House was a grand old dame, and Addison expected she might have a few more electrical jobs for Kyle Thompson in the future, so best to keep the electrician on side.

'Is that right?'

'Yeah, and things aren't exactly adding up.' Addison shook his head, huffing out a breath, frustrated at his lack of progress. 'It might have been an accident, but also maybe not.'

Kyle had just as much reason as anyone to want Dominic out of the way. He didn't like the guy, but then nobody did. As far as their sporting lives went, he seemed content with his position, not overly competitive, not scrambling for the top spot. And professionally the man was well established with his business. He was as likely or unlikely as anyone else. And here Addison was, once more, at square one – at least, that's what it felt like.

'Sure, sure,' Kyle said, nodding slowly. 'Wow, OK.'

'Anyway—'

'Yes, anyway…' Kyle shook himself. 'Yep, I'll give you a call if I need anything.'

'Sounds good.'

Addison stepped from the back porch into the kitchen, his mind shifting gear the moment he crossed the threshold, hoping while simultaneously not daring to hope that Jake would still be there.

When he saw the dirty breakfast dishes stacked next to the sink, he knew Jake had gone. With everyone else out the back of the house, it would've been no trouble for Jake to slip out the front door and away. Addison didn't blame the guy, but that didn't lessen the sinking feeling, as if whatever usually held him upright had slumped right out of his body.

It had been an embarrassing and undignified end to what had otherwise been a very memorable evening. Two steps forward, and one step back? At least he hoped that was the case, that they were still further ahead today than they had been this time yesterday.

No matter what he tried to tell himself, it didn't leave him full of warm fuzzies. It kept coming back to Jake and how he couldn't get out of there fast enough. As Milverton's sergeant, his position was a high profile one, always in the public eye, and Addison could understand him wanting to keep his private life private. This morning was anything but that, with not one witness, but three. They might as well have had the entire town there, considering they'd all know by lunchtime anyway.

People could forget those in positions of authority or power lived regular lives behind the scenes. And it's harder to maintain the same level of respect or deference for someone when you're picturing them in their underwear. It was a hit to Jake's professionalism, no doubt about that.

Logically, Addison recognised all this, but he also couldn't shake the thought it might have spooked the sergeant, had him regretting staying over, embarrassed to be seen with Addison.

In a town like Milverton, nothing stayed private for long. Jake had to know this would be the case, right? It wasn't like there was anything shady, shameful, or secretive going on.

Despite recognising the selfishness of it, Addison couldn't help feeling almost *annoyed*. And then he was annoyed at himself for being annoyed.

'Bah!'

The jolt of frustration pulled him out of his mental spiral and he found himself with hands either side of the sink, staring aimlessly out the window.

He picked up the coffee he'd barely touched and took a sip, only to find it stone cold.

'Of course,' he said to nobody but himself, huffing out a breath and pouring the mug's remaining contents down the drain.

Chapter 35

'Someone looks a right misery guts this morning, don't they?'

With the mood Addison was in, he wanted to ask if telling someone they looked terrible had ever done anyone any good. But between the welcoming tinkle of the bell over the door, the wonderful aroma of coffee, and the sight of Lynne's open and expressive face, Addison couldn't bring himself to do it.

He had to concede even his dejection was hard-pressed to endure the uplifting experience that was Lynne's Cafe.

He wasn't about to jeopardise that by spilling all his thoughts, which at present mostly related to the text message he'd received earlier. Jake had kept it brief, thanking Addison for the great night and apologising for rushing off. Addison had immediately drafted a response only to delete the message and try again at least ten times. In the end he settled for saying he'd had fun too, and not to worry about the swift exit, that it was all good.

Addison was less zen about the situation than he'd let on, but he understood Jake's position and hoped it was but a minor blip.

Having made it to Lynne's, what he really needed was coffee, not counselling – though he knew Lynne was great at one, and suspected she'd most likely be great at the other too.

'I haven't had a coffee yet this morning,' Addison said simply, pulling off his bike helmet and running a quick hand through his hair.

'Oh, well, that explains it then,' Lynne said, hands on hips. Her tone suggested that it did not, but also that she recognised Addison was not in the right frame of mind to elaborate. 'Are you having it here or rushing off today?'

'I'd better have it to go, thanks.'

He noticed then that Lynne's apron of the day featured a cupcake with a swirl of pink icing and a cherry on top, and printed beneath were the words 'Life is what you bake it!' If that wasn't the nicest, most sickly sweet way of telling him to stop wallowing, he didn't know what was.

'When you're feeling better, you can tell me what happened,' Lynne said, her face the picture of sympathy.

Addison wasn't so far gone as to fall into the trap of volunteering information that wasn't already known. 'What do you mean "what happened"?'

She looked stern now. 'Am I going to have to have a word with our Sergeant Murphy?' Addison knew he didn't want to know what having *a word* might entail, and certainly wouldn't want to be on the receiving end of it. Also, it appeared his two-man dinner party had made it onto Milverton's social calendar. Because of course it had. It appeared he would also be having *a word*, though his would be with Mabel.

'No, no,' Addison said. 'Jake and I, uh, our date went well.'

'Your face says otherwise, love.'

'It's… it's a long story.' He pulled his lips into a tight line. 'Another time, perhaps.'

Lynne nodded, recognising it was something Addison had to deal with himself. She handed over the coffee, which he had ordered, along with a small brown paper bag twisted off at the top, which he had not.

'What's this? I didn't ask for anything from the cabinet.'

'Just a little treat, on me,' Lynne said. 'I thought you could do with some sweetening up, love.'

***

Addison's past few days had flip-flopped back and forth between using Dominic's death to take his mind off Jake and using his date with Jake to take his mind off Dominic's death. Rinse and repeat.

Coming into the library and getting to work had forced him to hit pause on both and given him something else to focus on, even if rather half-heartedly. Being around other people helped too, anchored him in the present and stopped him wandering off in his own mind.

But after a morning in the library, plugged in to his work, what he needed now was a proper clear-out, some fresh air. He'd been swept up in investigation mode earlier when talking to the electrician, thinking out loud about going to see the DOC ranger. He didn't need an excuse to go for a little lunchtime bike ride.

One last check of his email inbox confirmed nothing immediately needed addressing, and then his work calendar joined the party by being mercifully clear of any scheduled calls or meetings for at least the next hour.

Addison unplugged his headset, snapped his laptop shut, and was packing them away in his bag when he heard his name.

He looked up to see someone with a head of unruly hair and an oversized scarf wrapped around her top half, as if she'd been caught out in a storm and not working in the relative calm of the library.

'Oh, hi, Ariana.'

The librarian beamed. 'You looked so focused, I hate to disturb you.'

'That's all right,' Addison said. 'I can always do with an interruption every now and then.'

The librarian laughed and then tutted, shaking her head. 'Don't tell me that, or you won't be able to get rid of me.'

Addison couldn't help smiling in the face of such cheeriness. 'Working remotely is great for convenience, but sometimes it's nice to chat to someone in the same room as you.'

'Oh, absolutely. The library has such a great range of ebooks and other online resources, but there's nothing quite like coming in and grabbing something off the shelf, is there?' Her eyes glowed, looking around the building as well as all the books on the stacks and the people passing by.

'For sure,' Addison said, nodding in agreement. He felt like this would be the perfect opportunity – a little lull in the conversation – to make his excuses and head out. But Ariana didn't seem in any hurry to move off.

'I, uh, saw Sandra on the news last night. How's she doing?' He didn't really want to get into it, not when he was on his way out to clear his head. But considering Sandra was Ariana's partner, and their only other mutual topic, it was the polite, friendly thing to say.

'Oh, she's properly cut up about it,' Ariana said, leaning against the desk he'd been using, settling in. 'Not that she'd say as much, of course. I do worry sometimes. Sandra's not one for big emotions, but she doesn't quite have the lid on it like she thinks. It comes out in her gruffness. She's all businesslike, keeping busy, getting everything sorted with the family and all that.'

'Yeah, everyone manages these things in their own way.'

'Don't they just? Those two squabbled like it was a competition. You know how it is with siblings.'

Addison did not, but nodded along, as was expected of him.

'Or in their case, cousins who grew up at each other's houses every weekend and school holiday. She was pretty fired up when he scraped the bottom of her car on those rough back roads. And then, when she found out he'd "borrowed" her car again on the weekend.' Ariana had her eyes wide as she shook her head, blowing the air out from her cheeks. 'But next call she gets is from the police, asking her to come in, which is when we saw you.'

'That must have been hard.'

'You bet. She felt so guilty, cursing his name all morning, only for him to wind up dead a few hours later.'

'Was she at home when she got the call?' Addison knew she hadn't been, remembering the mud-splattered hiking boots and hard-wearing work trousers as she arrived at the police station, but it was worth asking to see if the story had changed.

'Oh no, she was at work, out in the field, somewhere up here.' Ariana waved vaguely in the direction of the ranges behind Milverton. 'That's another thing that wound her up at the time.'

'What's that?'

'She was collecting data out in the field, only halfway done when she got the call and had to pack up and head back into town. She knew the data would be a mess and she would have to go out and recapture it all. So that wound her up, but then she heard what the call was about.' The librarian winced, her face all sympathy.

Addison remembered Sandra saying something about working alone, not having the budget for two of them to be out there, but the data she collected would have timestamps and coordinates all over it, which would pin her to a specific location at a specific time.

To verify the theory he'd have to ask some uncomfortable questions and make some uncomfortable implications. And he didn't want to do that unless he thought he had very good reason to do so. He kept that thought in his back pocket though, ready to pull out if required.

'It's tough all round,' Addison said, reflecting the sympathy.

She let out a big sigh. 'Yes.'

Another thought occurred to Addison and he knew he had to ask. 'How'd she get out there if Dominic had her car?'

'Oh, she had a work vehicle. Better for off-road driving, and has all her kit in it.'

Made sense. 'Right, right,' Addison said, and with nothing else to say he grabbed his bag and bike helmet. 'Anyway, I was just heading out for lunch.'

'Yes, yes, sorry! Here I am holding you up.'

'It's no worry,' Addison said, and meant it.

They said their farewells and Addison made it outside

without further incident. Thankfully, Mabel wasn't on the visitor centre desk today. As much as he adored his septuagenarian friend, he wasn't prepared to recap his date, which she would absolutely want to hear all about – both the highs of last night and the lows of this morning.

He wasn't allowing himself to think about that. He had said the same about Dominic's death, but that hadn't survived his interaction with the librarian. He was thinking about it all again now, wasn't he?

So much for clearing his head.

Addison growled in frustration then let out a deep sigh as he stepped out onto the street fronting Milverton Square.

He clicked his helmet in place, swung a leg over his bike, and decided he might as well go and see Lars after all. If he didn't, he knew it would just play on his mind.

This was the next step in the rather straightforward investigative approach he'd adopted: keep asking people questions and collecting information, and sooner or later something was bound to turn up.

Or it wasn't.

And that would be answer in itself, giving him the peace of mind that Dominic's death really wasn't suspicious after all.

No matter which direction it went, Addison hoped some progress on that front would give him the confidence to make enquiries with the other person weighing on his mind: Sergeant Jake Murphy.

Chapter 36

The streets were quiet as Addison set off on his bike, passing Lynne's Cafe on one corner, the fish and chip shop on another, and then the offices of Emily Smith – real estate agent and also his late great-uncle's property manager. A little further along was Go All the Whey, the shop unmissable with all its bright signage. And they still had their branded white van out front in the prime parking spot. Addison rolled his eyes – he'd never understand, but that was their business.

He turned off towards the river and was soon cruising alongside the wide, turbulent waterway. Addison thought he really ought to do this more often. Nothing too strenuous, not pushing to build up a sweat or feel the burn in his muscles. Just a relaxed, leisurely cycle along the riverside pathway.

This section ran along the crest of the embankment, which kept the town to one side and the river to the other. There were a fair few with a similar idea, out for a lunchtime stroll, but everyone still had plenty of space.

Clear skies, a little wind in his face, the sounds of human activity falling away behind the roar of the river and the chorus of bird and insect life. Barely a mote of pollen in the air, and just enough warmth from the sun to take the chill off.

Addison followed the pathway upriver as it continued beyond the town limits before turning away from the river towards the ranges. It was an area with which he was not nearly as familiar, being on the opposite side of town from Harper House.

The path meandered along a section of small, sparse shrubs and recently planted trees. They had mulch around the bases of their thin trunks and sturdy stakes alongside, presumably keeping them upright until they'd established themselves. This had to be the so-called green belt that Mayor Ferguson had pushed for – the 'visual, acoustic, and aesthetic barrier' between the town and the big new road that was planned to go over the ranges.

It was early days yet, but Addison could imagine how the surroundings might look in a few short years, and the habitats created in this rehabilitated nature corridor between the river and the ranges.

No sooner did he have the thought than he was unceremoniously ejected back out onto the old road. He pulled to a stop, noticing a small sign that had been staked into the ground at the end of the pathway. It informed users that the second and final stage finishing the connection was 'coming soon,' and that walkers and cyclists should complete the remainder of the distance to the gorge on the road shoulder 'with care.'

The road was sealed, one lane in each direction with a painted centre line. No kerbs, not even painted lines on the outsides. The sealed surface gave way to gravel on the shoulders and then drainage ditches beyond that. There wasn't a whole lot of room, but then it didn't appear to be highly trafficked now it was a dead-end road. Beyond that point there was only the car park for the gorge trails and the DOC office. Addison put his foot back on the pedal, crossed to the other side and cycled as close to the edge of the sealed surface as he could, and hoped nobody came flying too fast up behind him.

***

Addison coasted across the mostly empty gravel car park, with only a handful of vehicles between him and the bike rack at the far side.

Beyond that the forested slopes of the Manawatū Gorge rose up dramatically. It was quite the sight, but Addison had had more than his fill the previous weekend. Though it felt so much longer ago, he wasn't in a hurry to get back up there.

Back down at the edge of the car park, large signs had DOC's name in both English and Māori – 'Department of Conservation' and 'Te Papa Atawhai' – printed across the top in the organisation's distinctive green and yellow colour scheme.

The signs featured maps of the area, snippets of history, walking track time estimates, details about the huts, access restrictions, safety information, and contact phone numbers. None of it was what Addison had come to find, but then he spotted a small sign off to the side. Behind overgrown harakeke was a laminated sign partially obscured by the tall, wide, blade-like leaves of the flax. The rusted staples in each corner of the home-made sign created runs of orange-brown across the page and had let rainwater in to saturate and distort the paper that was meant to be protected by the laminate. Despite all that, Addison could make out the word 'Office' and an arrow that pointed up a small, overgrown path, clearly not intended for regular public use.

Set a little back and above the car park was a simple structure with dark red corrugated iron walls and roof with a chimney vent poking out the top. From the small timber deck out the front, Addison had a clear view of the car park below, then the river and town in the distance.

He was here, and with nothing else for it he turned and knocked on the door.

The call that came from within was immediate. 'Come in, come in.'

Addison tried the door and found it already unlocked, though it opened with some resistance. He spotted the culprits, a pair of waders, which he nudged out of the way, but then the door came to a soft stop anyway and would open no wider. Addison shuffled sideways through the half-open entrance and discovered behind the door a peg overloaded with coats, jackets, and other wet-weather apparel, all smelling like wet dog.

Threshold successfully navigated, Addison turned to find the entire building appeared to be made up of the one room. And that one room was covered in papers – pinned to walls, scattered across tables, and piled up on the floor. In the corner sat a small, free-standing fireplace which, considering the overabundance of flammable material within the space, Addison was relieved to find was currently not in use.

A man sat at a desk with his back to the door, tapping away haphazardly at a keyboard before hitting one last key with finality and spinning around on the swivel chair to face

Addison.

'You're lucky you caught me,' he said, a relaxed smile on his face. 'I was just about to head out.' A slight accent came through in the man's words, with the 'was' sounding a bit like 'vas' and the 'just' edging closer to 'yust'.

Addison suspected he'd found his man, not imagining there were too many DOC rangers in or around Milverton with Swedish or similar-sounding accents. He looked washed but scruffy, like a man who did everything to maintain sufficient standards of hygiene but then wasn't interested in checking himself in the mirror before heading out the door. The scratches and scars up his tanned arms were evidence of his days spent in the bush. He sported a camouflage-patterned bucket hat, despite currently being indoors, with short, dishevelled blonde hair sticking out underneath.

'I don't bite,' the Swede said, smiling through his scruffy beard. 'Unless you like that, of course?'

'Ah, um—'

'I joke, I joke,' he said, though, again with a softer J sound, which reminded Addison of his eggs at breakfast. He quickly waved away the comment. 'I have a girlfriend. But then again...' He scratched his beard, eyes narrowing and smile widening. 'I joke, again, promise!'

The man laughed, beckoning Addison further in.

'I've seen you before, haven't I?' The man squinted, tilted his head, then shrugged. 'It'll come to me.'

Addison didn't want to pry into where the man might've seen him before, in case it hadn't had him in the best light at the time. So they made their introductions, and Addison was pleased to learn that he had indeed found his man.

'So, Addison,' Lars said, his voice turning gravelly

almost witchy. 'What brings you to my little cabin on the edge of the woods? And what offering have you brought?'

Addison really didn't know if he had the capacity to deal with this guy today. So much energy, he seemed delighted to have been distracted from his task at the computer. 'Well…'

'I joke, I joke.'

'Actually,' Addison said, reaching into his bag and pulling out the small brown paper parcel from Lynne which he hadn't yet had a chance to even look inside.

'I said I was joking, but also, I'm not going to say no, am I? What have you brought us?'

Addison didn't have a clue, but when it came to baked treats, he trusted Lynne absolutely. 'You'll have to open it and see.'

The ranger accepted the parcel and with great fanfare, like a magician pulling a rabbit out of a hat, he produced: 'A custard square! Oh, this is from Lynne's, isn't it? My favourite, honestly. Blew my little mind when I discovered this New Zealand delicacy.'

'I don't know if I'd go that far,' Addison said, somewhat baffled, but also finding the man's enthusiasm a little infectious. He liked a custard square as much as the next Kiwi, but it wasn't on his bakery shortlist.

'It is just like millefeuille, isn't it? But not so fancy, which I appreciate,' Lars said. 'Puff pastry on top and bottom, custardy creaminess in the middle. What a dream. Here, let me cut it.' Lars swivelled back around in search of a knife.

'No, no. You have it.'

'Yes, yes. *We* will have it. Then you tell me why you're here.'

'Sure thing,' Addison said, shrugging, as if he thought he

had any control over the situation.

After the first bite of his half of the square, Addison had to concede Lynne knew what she was doing, though had that ever been in doubt? Lars had already demolished his half, licking his fingertips before wiping them back and forth on his shorts.

'All right, what can I do for you?'

Chapter 37

'I was hoping to get some information about someone,' Addison said, not sure how Lars might react to the topic, thinking it might be best to warm him up first. 'We used to know each other, and I'm just trying to piece together what happened last weekend.'

'Ah!' Lars said with a click of the fingers. 'I suppose you're talking about our – what's the word? – *litterbug*. A bit too cutesy for my liking – the word, I mean, not the man. New Zealanders are very passionate about not littering, being 'tidy Kiwis' and all that. As you should be. It's very good, I approve.' He murmured his approval, nodding along. Then the gesture shifted to a shake of the head, and his murmur to a tsk. 'I take it your *someone* was Dominic Campbell?'

New Zealanders were often accused of taking liberties with the pronunciation of vowels, even swapping a few around. This Swede's vowels were different again. Between that, the melodic cadence of the man's voice, and the rapidly jumping topics, Addison had found himself quite mesmerised, with his comprehension trailing a few words behind. But hearing the name of the subject of his investigation snapped him out of it.

'Yeah, yes, that's him,' Addison said. 'I knew him from back in Wellington, and I'm trying to find out what's been going on up here.'

'Yes…' Lars said, though with another shake of the head. 'How long do you have?'

Addison shrugged, as if he was in no rush. 'Is there that much to say?'

'I'll tell you, and you let me know if that is much, yes?'

Despite his wariness of how forthcoming this ranger appeared to be, Addison was happy to go along with it, at least for now. 'That'd be great.'

'OK, buckle up, buttercup,' Lars said, crushing up the brown paper bag and tossing it into a cane basket loaded with paper and cardboard beside the fireplace.

The DOC ranger recounted how he'd fielded a steady stream of complaints from other trail users about Dominic's aggressive behaviour, how he acted as if he owned the place, and had been witnessed dropping packets and plastic bottles the moment he was done with them. Lars's face was like thunder as he described Dominic's many transgressions. 'The worst though was his use of closed tracks, all clearly signposted, no excuses. We only block off very short segments, and only for a few months each year. Minimises disturbance during nesting season. We have so many wonderful bird species up here in the ranges, but they do need a helping hand sometimes.'

Addison nodded along, taking the tiniest bites of his custard square to make it last as long as possible, and hoping that would encourage Lars to keep up his monologue.

'I live and breathe conservation, you understand?

Everyone deserves to feel safe in their homes – humans, birds, everyone. We all live here. Important to respect other living beings, especially those with less power than us, which for us humans is all of them. Big responsibility. We all deserve to live.' Lars let out a big sigh, shaking his head. 'Though some specific humans may be a little less deserving sometimes.'

Addison paused mid-chew, didn't say a word, only raising one eyebrow.

'Yes, I am talking about Dominic. But whether he deserves it or not doesn't matter anymore, does it? Compare him to the other off-road triathlete who trains up here – what's his name again?'

Addison swallowed and said, 'Kyle Thompson?' If so, this guy really was coming up a lot lately.

'That's the one. He's up here training all the time, days at a time sometimes. Same sport, two very different men. This Kyle doesn't bully other walkers or runners, respects the seasonal track closures, always takes his rubbish with him. Dominic, no good.'

Lars didn't seem as if he was going to elaborate further, so Addison prompted, hoping to nudge his retelling. 'So, what did you do?'

'About Dominic?'

'Yeah.'

'He'd had a few warnings from me and the other rangers. He was on the cusp of fines' – Lars tsked and shook his head – 'not that they'd do any good, I don't think.'

'Not enough of a deterrent?'

'No, not for his type. First warnings, then fines, then prosecution. But we rarely get to that point. They normally get the message soon enough.'

Addison waited a beat, then asked, 'And what if they don't? Do rangers, uh, take matters into their own hands?'

'What, violence?' Lars seemed horrified at the suggestion.

'Yeah,' Addison said, feigning indifference as best he could. 'You know, rough them up a bit? Or at least threaten to?' This was kind of what the electrician had implied the ranger had done – that he'd *had words* with Dominic, *if you know what I mean*. At least that was Addison's read on the comment.

'No, never,' Lars said, his horror at the suggestion clear 'We're not *thugs*. Guys and girls who like to solve things with their fists, they don't get into conservation, do they?'

'I didn't expect so, no,' Addison said. More than anything, it was the outrage which felt so genuine, that had him believing the ranger's protest.

Lars recovered quickly, his amused expression back in full force. 'No, I was thinking of going rogue in a different direction, taking a more *creative* approach.'

He paused, as if inviting Addison to speculate. ' couldn't begin to guess,' he said. 'Go on, tell me.'

'I threatened to hit him where it hurts, right in the sponsorships,' Lars said, looking suddenly very pleased with himself.

'Oh yeah,' Addison said. 'How were you going to do that?'

'Leak a story to the press. Dominic Campbell would be the golden boy no longer. Bullying, bad behaviour, trashing the environment – nobody would want to touch him. Poof no more money, all gone.'

Addison inclined his head, impressed. 'Yep, that ought to have done it.'

'No need anymore, of course.'

'That was something else I wanted to ask about, actually,' Addison said. 'What exactly happened last Saturday? Were you here?' Or were you up in Douglas Glade, lying in wait, ready to solve your litterbug problem for good? Not that Addison voiced that last thought aloud.

'That's right, I was right here. I spotted your friend Dominic actually. I was out on the deck here having a coffee, getting some fresh air. I spend too much time cooped up in this office for my liking, didn't become a ranger to be doing all this paperwork.' Lars shook his head, sighing again. 'Anyway, on Saturday mornings when the weather is good, it gets busy up here with more occasional walkers. So when I saw Dominic heading in, I knew I'd be getting complaints later – there were always one or two, at least.'

'I'll bet,' Addison said, nodding along. 'Did you notice anyone else heading in that morning?'

'Oh, plenty. I do like my coffee breaks, long and often.' He nodded at Addison as if to say *you know how it is*. 'I saw that ragtag bunch who call themselves the Riverside Runners, and the sergeant – with you, wasn't he? Yes! That's where I've seen your face. I got the call and rushed up to the glade – you were there, of course. A bit spaced out though, which is fair enough, I say.'

The ranger spoke the truth, even if he was rather generous with his assessment of Addison's state of mind.

'Anyway, yes – you and the sergeant, hm?' Lars smiled and gave him a wink. 'Why don't you just ask him?'

'What?' Never mind the amused look from Lars, Addison didn't know where to start with what he should've been asking Jake about. 'What do you mean?'

'I've already given the sergeant a list of everyone from

277

that morning. All the comings and goings, at least those I saw, recognised, and remembered. I don't normally keep a list.'

Jake didn't say anything about this last night. And why would he? He really was treating Dominic's death with more seriousness than Addison had given him credit for. And he seemed to be at least a couple of steps ahead.

'Who else—'

'Ah, boring,' Lars said, waving a dismissive hand. 'And useless. So many faces I didn't recognise – and that included you, at the time. The only reason I noticed you was because you were with Sergeant Murphy.' His eyebrows danced for a moment before he shook his head. 'Anyway, after seeing Dominic, I was back in here. Planning to head out a little later, but then I got the call.' Lars pursed his lips and flared his eyes. 'A death in Douglas Glade.'

Addison felt an inappropriate surge of whimsy at the comment. 'Has quite the ring to it, don't you think? "Death in Douglas Glade."'

Lars barked out a laugh. 'I suppose you're right. Very film noir.'

'Coming to cinemas near you,' Addison said, joining in the laughter before cutting himself off and shaking his head. 'Sorry, I shouldn't joke. Um, you got the call?'

'Don't worry about that. It's good to laugh after bad news, shocking news.' Lars smiled to show he could empathise. 'And yes, I got the call. I wasn't surprised, to tell the truth. It was bound to happen.'

Addison waited to see if he might go on, but he didn't seem like he would. 'Because he'd upset so many people? Made too many enemies?'

'What does that have to do with it?' Lars said, his face

the picture of confusion. 'Being a terrible person isn't fatal. No, it was the amount of rubbish he was pumping himself with.'

It was Addison's turn to be confused. 'Pumping himself with what?'

'Nothing from the fresh produce aisle, that's for sure. I'd be surprised if he ever set foot in the grocery store, or even recognised a piece of fruit.'

'Are you suggesting...' Addison scrambled to order his thoughts after the new and unexpected speculation. 'Are you suggesting he died of malnutrition, or something?'

Lars blew a raspberry. 'Perhaps. But I don't know if you could call it that. You know those packets of protein and bottles of electrolyte drinks that he's always dropping wherever he pleases?'

'Yeah?'

'Looks like he lives off the stuff. Sure, there must be something worthwhile in it, for it to be so popular, but you still need to eat a vegetable every now and then. He gets it all from that supplement store in town, Go All the Whey – you know the one, they've always got their van parked out the front? Yeah, they must be sponsoring him or something.'

Addison didn't know about Dominic's eating habits and nutritional intake, but what he did know was that the same names were starting to crop up in unexpected places, and all in relation to Dominic.

'The amount of rubbish he was taking,' Lars went on, 'I wouldn't be surprised if he'd taken it to the *next level*.'

'You mean...'

'Getting mixed up with harder stuff, performance-enhancing substances? I would not be shocked. Maintaining that top spot must be stressful. And he seemed like the type to get into that, if it gave him the edge.'

Addison did not disagree. But using those kinds of things, if they weren't outright illegal then they were at least banned from competition for the very reason that they gave users an unfair advantage.

Lars continued. 'Malnutrition? Overuse of supplements making him overconfident, pushing him beyond the limits of his body? Other, more dangerous substances doing much the same, but worse? Many options. All self-inflicted, sadly.'

'Thanks,' Addison said in a bit of a daze, mulling over the possibilities. 'Thanks so much for all this, so good to learn a bit more about what was going on with Dominic.'

'That's no trouble. And thanks for the custard square – you can come back any time.' Lars smiled before turning serious again. 'You look after yourself.'

***

A bunch more vehicles had arrived while Addison had been in the office, people keen for an afternoon on the trails. It was not for Addison, at least not today. Besides, his lunch hour was almost up anyway, and he had much to consider.

Go All the Whey had come up in conversation, once again. Addison racked his brain for anything Zach or Prisha might have said while he was at their shop, reviewing it from this new angle, but nothing immediately stood out.

What might have been going on with them and Dominic? Were they supplying performance-enhancing or otherwise illegal substances? Boosting Dominic's chances of coming out on top, and with Go All the Whey splashed all over his gear, boosting the profile of the business at the same time? Had something gone wrong with the arrangement, relationships soured, blackmail threatened? Or something else entirely?

Addison's thoughts were only half-formed, if that, but he couldn't ignore that it all kept coming back to the sport supplement store. He knew he had to tell Jake – Sergeant Murphy, he should say – what he'd been up to, and that he suspected Go All the Whey was involved in Dominic's death somehow. He'd hate to be sitting on his emerging theory only for something awful to happen, something he might have prevented if only he'd raised his concerns earlier.

He may have already gone against Jake's past warnings about sticking his nose into what was rightfully police business, but he was not going to be a maverick about it by confronting anyone himself.

Addison was strapping his helmet on and pulling his bike out of the rack when he decided to call Jake, and that he had to do it right away. No putting it off. His feelings about the man's abrupt departure only that morning were far from resolved, but this was too important, and he had to let the sergeant know what was going on.

Addison sat on his bike seat, one foot on the pedal, brought up Jake's number from his recent contacts, took a breath in and out, then hit the green call button. He cycled across the gravel car park, one hand on the handlebar, the other holding the phone to his ear as it rang. He'd almost made it back to the road before the call connected.

'Hey,' Jake said, then before Addison could respond he continued. 'I'm sorry I took off this morning. I—'

'It's fine, it's fine.' It wasn't, not quite, but Addison knew he couldn't deal with it right at that moment.

'I hope you know it had everything to do with me wanting to keep *some* separation between my public and private lives. To keep some moments just between me and those I choose to spend my time with,' Jake said, his voice warm, yet serious. 'I hope you know it had nothing to do with secrecy or shame or embarrassment or regret or anything like that. Nothing to do with the fact I was at your place, with you. Because that was perfect. You know that, right?'

A lump had lodged itself in Addison's throat. He hadn't realised he'd needed the reassurance, or that Jake would do that much and then take it a step further.

It took Addison a couple of attempts to clear his throat, before he managed to get out, 'Yeah.'

'Good,' Jake said, apparently as relieved as Addison to be back on firmer ground. 'Where are you?'

'That's what I was calling about, actually. This morning back at the house, the electrician mentioned Lars had been having dealings with Dominic recently.' Addison could hear the sharp intake of breath from Jake and carried on before he could say anything. 'Hear me out, hear me out. I thought I'd come out to the DOC office here at the gorge, see if I could catch him while he was in.'

Addison could hear the man taking a steadying breath down the line. 'So you could continue your own investigation?'

'I just wanted to see if he had anything to add.'

Was that grinding teeth Addison could hear? 'And?' Jake said.

'He said you'd already been to see him.'

'I have, because that's my job, Addison. Hang on, what's that noise? Why's it so windy on your end?'

'Oh, I'm on the road, biking back into town.'

'Get off the phone,' Jake said with an abruptness

Addison had never heard from him, but whatever he said next was lost in the roar of an engine.

Addison realised it wasn't coming from the phone and had half-turned, catching a glimpse of a white van as it rushed in to fill his vision, clipping his back wheel, wrenching the handlebars from his grip and hurling him forwards, head first off his bike. The world spun and spun until it abruptly stopped and then it went black.

Chapter 38

Addison could see only the sky and hear only the chatter of birds.

'What—' He went to sit up, but the rest of his body took that moment to catch up, sending in reports from all over that *something was wrong*, causing him to suck in a breath. After the initial shock of the pain, he waited for any further reports to come in, and when none did, he made a tentative second attempt to sit up, this time with more success.

Addison found himself on the gravel shoulder of the road, with his bike and bag a little further along, upside down in the drainage ditch. He had bombed out big time, with a bit of a case of the shakes as further evidence.

Slowly he got to his feet to survey himself, relieved to discover all limbs intact. As was his head, his cracked helmet clearly having taken much of the impact. There was a little dizziness, yes, and he could feel a headache coming on, but he hoped it was nothing a couple of painkillers wouldn't take care of.

Looking down he found his jeans had saved his knees and legs from the worst of it, though they themselves were now looking very torn up. Some people paid good money for 'distressed' denim like that, Addison couldn't help thinking.

His hands had not been so well protected and were now covered in cuts and scratches, but it was his left forearm that had come out worst off. The gravel rash had done a number, but it looked much worse than it felt.

There were bound to be more scratches and scrapes he hadn't yet noticed, and the bruises would come, but all up, Addison reckoned he'd got off fairly lightly.

He picked his way over to his bike, gravel slipping out from under his feet. He hauled it out of the ditch and, just as he'd done with himself, surveyed the damage. The handlebars and seat had been twisted out of alignment, and the chain hung loose, all easily corrected. The buckled front wheel was probably beyond repair though. He'd already established his helmet would need replacing, and likely his phone. He'd cast around for it briefly, but couldn't find it and didn't want to spend any longer than necessary on the side of the road just then.

Addison slung his laptop bag over his shoulder and started pushing his bike back towards town. He'd barely made it two steps when he heard the distant roar of an engine. The sound jolted his memory, the flash of white before he'd come off his bike. He hadn't just fallen off, he'd been *hit*.

And that was not something you wouldn't notice, as a driver on an open, lightly trafficked road, surely?

He'd been in a hit and run.

And he'd seen who'd hit him too, sort of. His mind raced. Where had he seen the white van before, and recently too?

And then it clicked – parked outside the sport supplement store, of course. And it had left an impression, because who parked right out the front of their own store, taking up a potential customer's space?

This whole thing had suddenly become much scarier – which he suspected was the point. A glancing blow, not to kill, but to scare him off? He struggled to believe it of Zach and Prisha, but you never truly knew what people might be capable of when they got desperate. What was going on at Go All the Whey?

Lost in his thoughts, he hadn't realised the roar of the engine he heard still hadn't let up until the flashing blue and red lights caught his eye.

A vehicle tore up the road towards him before screeching to halt diagonally across the road, blocking the lanes in both directions, lights still flashing.

Sergeant Jake Murphy launched from the police car and was at Addison's side in seconds. Eyes wide, he frantically scanned Addison from top to toe, his hands hovering as if desperate to hold him tight, but afraid to touch, lest he break him.

'I'm fine,' Addison said.

'You are not fine,' Jake said, his voice and his face seeming to battle between furious and upset. He took hold of the bike and set it aside so he could look Addison over properly.

'Just some scratches—'

'Your arm.'

'Is not nearly as bad as it looks,' Addison said. 'I promise.'

'Let me wrap it – first aid kit's in the car – then I'll get you to the medical centre.'

'I'm fine. I don't need—'

'You do need.'

'Fine, first aid, but that's it.'

'First aid—'

'Yes,' Addison said, 'good.'

'—and then the medical centre.'

'No.'

'If I have to,' Jake said, his voice unyielding, 'I will arrest you, Mr Harper.'

Addison was shocked at the threat, though he had to concede he knew it was for his own good. Maybe he should call the sergeant's bluff? He had to admit getting 'arrested' by Jake was something he'd daydreamed about, and more than once.

No, he'd better not...

'Fine,' Addison said. 'It's in the car, you said?' He started to walk off, to prove he was quite capable of looking after himself. But the move was ruined by the gravel on the shoulder slipping out from under his foot again. He recovered without falling over, but no sooner had he righted himself than he felt one arm across his back and another behind his knees, lifting him clear off the ground.

'What— Put me down! I am not— This is not—'

'Stop squirming.'

Addison growled, outraged, and made even more so by the small smirk on Jake's face. He stopped squirming though, as instructed, and settled on simply glaring at the man. 'I hope you put your back out.'

Jake's smile widened a touch. 'You don't mean that,' he said, which infuriated Addison further, because he was right.

Addison kept up his protest for the remainder of the short journey, because he knew that's what he should do, but... he also kind of loved it? Getting scooped up and carried by this man? He might have been quite content for Jake to carry him all the way back to town if the car wasn't right there and if he thought he could keep up the protests for any longer before it was blatantly obvious that he didn't mean a word of it.

Jake decanted Addison into the passenger seat and went to retrieve the first aid kit.

'Shouldn't you move the car? We're in the middle of the road.'

'There isn't much traffic, and anyone who comes up here can get around if they need to,' Jake said, already back at his side. 'Is this yours? I found it on the ground.'

Jake handed over a familiar device, though it now featured a great crack across the screen, much like his helmet. 'Ah, yes. Thanks,' Addison said, accepting the phone. He gave it a tentative tap, not holding out too much hope, but was surprised to find it lit up, and still appeared to be functional.

Jake dropped to one knee beside the open passenger door and Addison's first inclination was to say, 'Yes, I do,' with hands clapped to his mouth in mock shock. But he immediately and unexpectedly realised this was something he didn't want to joke about. Addison was busy failing to process those thoughts as Jake unzipped the first aid kit on the ground and pulled out a few things. He watched the movements of Jake's hands, captivated as he adjusted the position of Addison's arm, wincing as he rinsed the grit from the graze before patting it dry.

Jake tore open a dressing, set it on the graze, and then stopped.

Did he say something? Addison was about to ask when he found his right hand being guided across his front so the fingers rested on the dressing. Jake held his hand there a moment longer, the message clear – *hold the dressing in place.*

Jake rummaged around in the first aid kit, pulling out a roll of cloth bandage which he wrapped around and around Addison's arm. Addison found himself enjoying the touch, the ministrations, equal parts firm and gentle. But with the bandage fixed in place, Jake moved away and out of his space, all too soon.

Addison came back to himself. 'Thank you for coming,' he said, offering a tentative smile. 'And sorry for cutting you off on the phone.'

Jake gave him a look, clearly not amused. He zipped up and stowed the first aid kit in the back, along with Addison's bike.

'So,' Jake said, as he turned the car around and headed back towards town, 'what happened?'

Addison explained, though there wasn't much to tell – phone call, biking, bang. Not that Jake said anything, but Addison could see the anger and terror in his face, the way he held himself, all over again. The last thing Addison wanted to do was add to that, but he suspected it'd be worse if he kept quiet.

'I don't think it was an accident,' Addison said, then went on to describe his suspicions and the possibilities around Dominic, his death, Zach and Prisha of Go All the Whey, sponsorships, blackmail, and performance-enhancing substances.

Jake's expression darkened. 'The autopsy didn't turn up anything like that, nothing in the bloods.'

Of course they'd already looked into that. The police were professionals, they knew how to do this kind of thing.

'But we can soon check in with Mr Paine and Ms Kumar-

Attwood. I'll get McGiffert and Edwards onto it the moment we've got you to the medical centre.'

'That's really not—'

'You blacked out, Addison. It is necessary.'

Addison knew he didn't have a leg to stand on, and would allow himself to be checked over, even if only to reassure Jake. But if he was going to endure that, he might try and squeeze something else out of it. 'I'll go if you tell me what Sean and Manaia find.'

Jake looked about to reject the suggestion outright, but must've recognised passing on his constables' findings was a small price to pay. He shook his head. 'I'll tell you if you promise to follow the doctor's orders.'

In this little game of tit for tat, Jake was getting more tit than Addison was getting tat, but he accepted the terms as he recognised they really were for his own good.

Chapter 39

'You don't have to wait around.' The medical centre's waiting area was just as sterile and fluorescent as the police station's, but with even more stress in the air, and a near-constant rumble of coughing echoing around the space. The seats were more comfortable though, and they weren't bolted to the floor, which was nice.

'I do,' Jake said, sitting at his side. 'How else will I be sure you don't slip out before being checked over?'

Addison wanted to argue, but Jake had a point. He wasn't great at taking direction, but he had promised. 'You'll have to trust me,' he eventually said. 'I'm a *big boy.*'

'I won't be distracted with comments like that.' Jake's mouth twitched in amusement, but then his frown slowly returned. 'Addison,' he said, turning to be sure he had his full attention.

'Yes?' Addison said slowly, properly worried now.

'I know you think I'm being over-the-top about all this, but it's not for no reason.' Jake took a breath, rubbing his hands on his thighs.

'What is it?'

'When I knew you were on your bike, then you cut out

like that…' Jake said, trailing off and looking away.

The silence lengthened and Addison was weighing up whether or not to say something when Jake cleared his throat, looked back up at Addison and continued.

'When I was at school, my best friend was in an accident. Knocked off his bike by a distracted driver.'

'Oh, no. Were they—'

'He was fine.' Jake started lifting a hand as if to hold off the question, before putting it back down. 'Concussion, broken arm, cuts and scrapes all over, but he was fine – he recovered, physically at least. But he never recovered his confidence. He was still our mate, of course, but he was a different person. And I never want that to happen again to anyone in my life, not if I can help it.'

Jake's eyes were shining and his smile tight. Addison had never seen him looking so vulnerable. He just wanted to wrap him up tight and squeeze until the man couldn't remember ever being sad, but he suspected that was not what Jake would've wanted.

'I'm so sorry,' Addison said instead, placing a hand over Jake's as it rested on his thigh and gave it a gentle squeeze, just to let him know he was there. 'I won't be so flippant, promise. I will take it seriously.'

'Good.' Jake cleared his throat and repeated himself twice more, as if trying to convince himself it was true.

Addison's hand – the one on Jake's – started vibrating. They pulled their hands away and Jake fished his phone out of his pocket. Addison couldn't help noticing the screen showed an incoming call, with the caller identified as 'Edwards'. He could see Jake deciding whether or not to take the call, and if he did, whether or not he could leave Addison alone.

Addison gave him a look as if to say, *Come on, why haven't you answered the phone yet?*

Jake thumbed the screen to accept the call, putting it to his ear as he walked away. 'Manaia, what is it?'

He didn't go far, just to the corner of the waiting area. Far enough from Addison and the others to have a semi-private conversation, but close enough to keep an eye on things. He leant against the wall, glancing up at Addison more than once.

Between the coughing around the waiting room and the distance, Addison didn't catch much, but he did pick up snippets from Jake's half of the conversation. He overheard 'no damage', 'parked', 'denying everything', 'steroids', 'are they admitting', and finally 'no, I can't.'

Jake hung up and returned to the seat at Addison's side without a word, his mind clearly racing.

'If you need to go, you should,' Addison said. 'I'll be fine here.'

'No, I'm—'

'I'm surrounded by people here, Jake. There's no chance I'll drift off or anything without someone noticing. And if anything is wrong, I'm in the best place for them to fix it. I won't leave until I've been seen by a doctor, promise.'

Jake searched Addison's face and saw that he meant it. 'OK,' he said. 'You'll call me if you need anything?'

'I will.'

On the one hand he was proud of himself for not interfering in a police investigation – in this particular, very specific instance, at least – but on the other hand he was *dying* to get involved, to find out what was happening.

Alone in the waiting room, he was free to speculate.

Zach and Prisha were in the mix, somehow. Go All the

Whey seemed legitimate, but was it just a front? Were one or both of its owners running another, less legal business from out the back? If Dominic had been taking performance-enhancing drugs – which wasn't backed up by the autopsy, but for argument's sake – and he was being supplied by Go All the Whey's shady side business, then they were both in the wrong. They could blackmail each other, if it came to it. Was it a cold war kind of thing – mutually assured destruction?

So, what changed? Something just didn't add up.

The evidence suggested Dominic hadn't been on steroids or anything like that at the time of his death. Maybe he had been though, just not recently, long enough ago that it had flushed from his system? That might be possible, but Addison just couldn't imagine Dominic risking it. The potential fines from the sport's governing body, banning from competitions, or at least suspension. Presumably illegal too? Addison didn't know the specifics of any possible consequences, but the reputational damage alone would be shocking. Not something a professional athlete would ever recover from.

Why risk it when he was already on top? Or was he willing to do just that to *stay* on top?

Addison could feel the answer frustratingly just out of reach. And he didn't think his inability to grasp it had anything to do with knocking his head. He was missing *something*.

A less disciplined Addison might have wavered at that point and struck out to hunt down the final piece of the puzzle, but he held fast, as promised.

'Harper.' The call came from someone emerging from a hallway off the waiting area. 'Addison Harper.'

Addison was led to a small room where the doctor poked and prodded and shone a light into his eyes before whipping through a bunch of questions and rattling off a long list of potential symptoms he might be suffering, most of which did not apply, which was reassuring.

The doctor's verdict: 'I don't think you have a concussion, mild at worst. Still, it's important to take precautions.' A pamphlet was thrust into Addison's hand titled *So you've hit your head – what now?*

Together they worked their way down the checklist on the back. 'Now, in case you develop any serious symptoms later today, it's important you're not alone,' the doctor said. 'Do you have someone?'

Way to come out swinging, doc. Addison didn't say it, having already judged the medical centre was not the time nor place for such things. 'I'll make sure I'm not by myself today,' Addison said.

The doctor checked off the rest of the list. 'No naps. No alcohol. No sleeping pills. You're OK to take regular painkillers if you have a headache. No driving. No physical activity.'

It all sounded very manageable, and he said as much.

Addison was encouraged to hold onto the pamphlet in case he forgot anything, or needed to refer back to it, then was sent on his way.

And so Addison found himself stepping out of the medical centre and out onto the street, not entirely sure where to go or what to do next.

He could go to the library. He probably *should* go to the library. This lunch break had been extended well beyond what he'd intended. Though he wasn't going to be able to focus on anything, get any actual work done. Probably best if he called in to say he'd be off the rest of the day. Getting thrown off your bike and sustaining a possible minor head injury met the threshold for taking the afternoon off, surely. He felt bad for his colleagues who'd have to pick up the slack, but he'd built up plenty of favours and could afford to cash in a few.

He could go back to Harper House. The electrician said they'd have the fibre installation all done by the end of the day. But then walking back and kicking around the house meant too much time without anyone else close by, which was against doctor's orders. As much as he'd like to count Keith, he doubted the cat could call the doctor or an ambulance, which was a key requirement for the supervision role.

He could go and see what was happening at the sport supplement store. The police might need his insights? Addison considered that for all of half a second – it would be a mistake, no question. Jake could argue Addison really had squished the last of his brain cells, and he wouldn't be wrong.

After a few false starts, Addison finally struck on something he could do that didn't go against the doctor's orders or Jake's wishes.

Julie Halswell's establishment offered many things. Addison could already vouch for their shirts, underpants, and haircuts, and it stood to reason their other stock would be good too. On previous visits he'd noted the range of hiking, camping, and fishing gear on offer, but most importantly for Addison, they also had bikes. He had to hope that meant they stocked all the bits and pieces that went along with them, specifically replacement wheels and helmets.

If he was to prove to himself that he wouldn't be brought down by this, he couldn't think of a better way than getting right back up.

Chapter 40

On previous visits to Halswell & Company, Addison had only ventured to the left side of the store, which had been given over primarily to their menswear selection, with the barber's chair tucked in the back corner. The chair was empty today, and Addison remembered Seb saying something about only being scheduled for earlier in the week. Julie was in though, helping another customer over by the changing rooms. Addison raised a hand in acknowledgement before going about his task.

Facing the pair of mannequins dressed in some of the latest menswear offerings were another pair of life-sized plastic men. One sported a pair of waterproof waders with straps over the shoulders, a khaki vest with pockets all down its front, and a pair of wraparound sunglasses with multicoloured lenses sitting on the featureless face. The other wore head-to-toe camouflage fleece, with a beanie perched on top.

They fronted the right half of the store which Addison had noted was there, but hadn't had cause to give much thought or attention before. The shelves, racks, and hooks had been dedicated to equipment and supplies for those who thrived in the outdoors – that is, not Addison. Everything for water-based pursuits was closest to the front door – wetsuits, fishing rods, life jackets, to name a few – with land-based pursuits further back – tents, hiking boots, raincoats, camp stoves, knives, dehydrated meals, and all the rest.

Mounted to the wall between the two sections was the space's most distinctive, eye-catching feature: a stuffed deer's head with a very impressive set of antlers. Addison was not a fan of taxidermy, finding the whole thing a bit grotesque, and the hunting trophies so often looked dusty and manky, untended out of reach up high on the wall. But his specimen remained proud, as if maintaining his status as king of the forest, watching over all below, even in death.

Saying that, the beast's prestige was at least a little diminished by the fact a yellow kayak and a couple of paddles had been hoisted upright above a display rack with their ends resting against the deer's neck. A bit undignified, but that was an inevitable consequence of running a store packed with so much stock.

Speaking of, a little further along was what he had actually come in looking for, as advertised by a couple of display bikes. Unfortunately, now that he was faced with all the options, he wasn't entirely sure which one he needed. Who knew bicycle wheels came in so many different varieties? Addison wasn't even sure what size his current wheels were, and he didn't want to grab the wrong one and risk winding up with a penny-farthing situation. He'd have to wait until he could retrieve his own bike from the back of Jake's police car. Still, this was a good start.

As far as buying a new helmet went, he already had with him everything he needed to select the right size.

They had the sporty, aerodynamic bicycle helmets you might expect, and the rounded, BMX-style helmets too. They also had some serious full-face helmets, but Addison found himself drawn to their range of novelty options. He told himself it was silly to be self-conscious about such things – adults could have fun things too – but when he picked up the neon green helmet with a spine of short rubber spikes, like a dinosaur or a dragon, he couldn't help glancing over his shoulder.

Addison froze, staring, confused by the presence of the man he spotted in the store. Grabbing things down off shelves, his movements quick and efficient, he was unmistakable even in profile.

What was Kyle Thompson doing here?

He hadn't heard from the electrician, so presumed everything had been going well back at the house. Surely he would've called when he'd finished the job, to let Addison know how it had all gone?

Did he need something to finish the job? Halswell's covered a fair few bases with their stock, but hardly seemed the place to grab anything for laying and connecting fibre-optic cable.

The guy really had big arms, Addison couldn't help noting once again as Kyle reached for something on a higher shelf. Bulkier than you might expect for a tradesman who trained for cross triathlons in his spare time. Surely that'd build leaner, functional muscle? Not nearly as prominent, as showy. It was almost as if—

Addison gasped as the missing piece – right in front of him all along – slotted into place.

He ducked out of sight behind a rack of bike tyre tubes and hand pumps.

Surely not? It fitted, though… didn't it?

What if he was right about the dodgy dealings and the blackmail, just not who was at the centre of it all? Who kept coming off second best to Dominic, and might just be desperate enough to take drastic action? To artificially, chemically boost his own abilities? To take down the competition, hoping to score those lucrative sponsorship deals that had previously been denied to him?

And, more directly related to Addison in his current situation, who also drove a *white van* for his work?

All signs pointed to full-time electrician, part-time cross triathlete Kyle Thompson.

So… what was the guy doing? After last weekend, Kyle had carried on, business as usual, nothing suspicious going on there. But now? He'd sensed the net closing in and he'd freaked? Was he cutting his losses, stocking up, and going to ground? Heading into the bush to lie low for a while, or to vanish altogether?

No matter where Kyle intended to go or what he intended to do in future, Addison knew where he was and what he was doing *right now*. And he could think of one person much better equipped than he was to do something about it.

A quick peek around the side of the rack confirmed his suspect had shifted to a different shelf but was still in the building.

Addison pulled out his damaged phone and for the third time that day called Sergeant Jake Murphy.

Phone pressed against his ear, it rang and rang and rang. Addison was frantically shuffling through possible backup plans when Jake finally picked up.

'Hey,' he said. 'How are you? What did the doctor say?'

Addison couldn't afford to waste time dealing with the man's concerns for his well-being, no matter how warm that might have made him feel inside at any other time. It would be faster just to answer the question than to explain why he couldn't answer the question. Still, he kept his voice as low as he could. 'The doctor said I'm fine, just can't be by myself today.' Then, before Jake could ask, he said, 'And yes, I'm following orders. But I'm calling—'

'OK good, that's good,' Jake said. 'I can join concussion watch later, if you like?'

'Sure—'

'But right now I have to go, sorry,' Jake said, his mind clearly back on what he was doing. 'We're pursuing a strong lead, currently trying to determine the whereabouts of our new prime suspect.'

Addison paused, sneaking a look at the man he strongly suspected was Dominic's killer before ducking back down again. 'Kyle Thompson?'

The phone line was silent, which was all the confirmation Addison needed.

'Jake?' Addison said. 'He's here, at Halswell's, which is why I'm calling. I think Kyle killed Dominic.' He chanced a glance to re-confirm the electrician's position, and he didn't know what tipped the man off, but they locked eyes from their respective positions halfway across the store from each other.

Addison caught Kyle's shock for a split second before realisation crashed over his features, followed swiftly by a rage Addison had never before seen on anyone. In an instant it made the man's bulk that much more intimidating. One second he was still, and by the next he'd already closed half the distance between them, silently lunging towards

302

Addison, arms up.

Addison stumbled back, not willing to wait and see what the man did next. He lost his footing and his phone in the process, falling into a rack of waterproof jackets, but managed to pull himself upright and fling armfuls of the jackets into Kyle's path.

It didn't stop him, but it hampered his progress, throwing him off Addison's exact position. But then a portable camp stove flew over Addison's head, followed by a volley of small gas canisters, clanging as they bounded off shelves to either side of him, ringing in his ears.

Still frantically backing away, Addison pulled more and more stock off the shelves, hurling it into the path of his pursuer, but he only seemed to be getting his hands on unhelpfully soft items – beanies, coats, vests, woollen socks.

Then he laid hands on hiking boots. They had some heft to them, with hard, rubberised treads. At least one pelted blindly in his wake made contact, resulting in a howl of pain and rage.

The sound spurred Addison on. But between flinging debris behind himself and trying to keep out of the man's grasp, he'd lost track of where he was going. He bolted straight into a rack of fishing tackle against the wall, with toppled shelves to either side. He had nowhere to go, and looking up at his attacker, he could see Kyle knew it.

With a look of pure poison, he pinned Addison in place, stalking forward, his prey trapped. But then the groaning and screeching of the rack at Addison's back intensified, demanding Addison's attention before a paddle whacked him in the shoulder, sending him sprawling. A bright yellow kayak immediately followed suit, swinging down from above into the space he'd been in only a moment earlier but which was now occupied by his wide-eyed assailant. The kayak made violent contact with Kyle, taking him down with it.

Into the sudden stillness and quiet, all Addison heard was his own rapid breathing and thumping heartbeat. And looking up, all he saw was the mounted deer's head, a bit off-centre now, but still fixed to the wall, surveying the chaotic scene.

Chapter 41

Addison had taken up position on a bench just down from Halswell's, but still within the taped-off area. A few looky-loos had started gathering at the police cordon, but were behaving themselves, at least for now. Addison's breathing and heart rate had slowly returned to normal, and he wasn't even jumping at movements out of the corner of his eye anymore.

Constables Sean McGiffert and Manaia Edwards had stopped briefly to check in on him.

'You really had the boss worried there for a minute,' Sean said, pulling him into a quick hug before holding him at arm's length to look him over.

Manaia shook her head. 'Addison Harper, you sure know to pick 'em.'

Then they were back to work, strategically positioning themselves as the paramedics checked over Kyle Thompson - ironically for a suspected concussion – ready to jump in if he tried anything. Not that it seemed likely. From Addison's vantage point, the accused looked utterly defeated.

At Jake's insistence, they'd already looked over Addison the second round of medical attention in as many hours.

He may not have been in Milverton for all that long, but he was on first-name terms with these paramedics – Diana and Scott – considering the number of times they'd tended to him now. They didn't even bother telling him to take it easy, just shook their heads, muttering things like 'unbelievable' and 'walking disaster.'

Despite all the makeshift projectiles and falling outdoor equipment, Addison had made it through the ordeal without hitting his head again. The paddle to the shoulder was the worst of it. And just as with the low-level headache and various other scratches and scrapes, it could be managed with regular painkillers.

Jake refused to leave his side throughout the paramedic's assessment. Addison knew he could've insisted – patient privacy and all that – but after all the day's dramas, he'd been very happy to have Jake right there.

Backing it up by twenty minutes or so, Julie Halswell had been the first on the scene, clearing a path through the carnage moments after Kyle's rampage had come to an abrupt end. And before she'd even had a chance to ask what on earth had happened or if he was OK, Jake was right there too.

Addison gave the man a small, relieved smile, and Jake drew him in, enveloping him with his arms, as if shielding him from any further harm. Addison could've spent all day there, held tight, pressed against Jake's chest, but he knew he had some reassuring to do first, and then some serious explaining to do later too, no doubt.

He promised Jake he was fine – honest, all in one piece, no stoicism necessary – agreed not to venture off, and reminded Jake he had the rest of Milverton to look after.

Addison could see Jake knew it was true, and with one

final encouraging nudge, he switched into sergeant mode. The man was a whirlwind of efficiency, questioning everyone who'd been in the store at the time, instructing his constables, and otherwise taking charge of the crime scene, but still never taking his eye off Addison for more than a moment.

Addison had taken up position on the bench due to it having good clearance in all directions, giving him plenty of notice if anyone approached, but it also gave him space, allowing him to catch his breath and calm his nerves away from the claustrophobia of the overturned store and the chaos of the crime scene. He told himself remaining in clear sight of Jake was to allay the man's overprotective instincts, but equally, Addison took reassurance from knowing Jake was close to hand.

Addison had chosen a spot that afforded him a high degree of visibility, so in what should have been an entirely expected consequence, he was also highly visible.

A familiar face soon appeared at the police cordon and immediately spotted Addison, ducking under the tape to march over.

'Hi, Mabel.' Of course she was here. Why was he surprised that she'd already caught wind of the drama?

She ran her eyes over him, and seemingly satisfied, tutted and shook her head. 'Another one for the books, isn't it?'

Addison scoffed, unable to help himself smiling. 'Are you miffed you missed all the excitement?'

She scoffed then too, batting his hand in admonishment. 'Don't be absurd. I'm just glad that, despite your best efforts, you remain in one piece. Even if you are a little worse for wear. So, are you going to bring me up to speed?'

Addison quickly recapped everything that had happened since their car shopping expedition while Mabel sat with him and the police continued doing their thing. She nodded and shook her head and gasped at all the right places, but otherwise didn't say a word until he'd caught her right up.

'My dear, knocks to the head are serious business. Do you need me to come supervise? Make sure you don't drift off and don't wake up again?'

'No, no. I've got Jake here keeping an eye on me,' Addison said, nodding over to the sergeant where he was speaking with Julie Halswell and the recently arrived Mrs Harriet Ferguson, Her Worship the Mayor of Milverton. He had indeed positioned himself in order to keep an eye on Addison, and presumably now Mabel too. 'I suspect Jake isn't going to let me out of his sight for the next little while.'

'And so he shouldn't.'

'I think this might be a bit beyond his duty of care as sergeant.'

'Least he could do after letting you go off and get run down by a man in a van.'

'There's been a bit of that recently, hasn't there?'

'Don't remind me,' Mabel said, laughing, but in a way that made it clear she knew she shouldn't. 'The roads around here are hazardous to your health, Addison, my goodness.'

She wasn't wrong. He was about to ask how the search for her new car was going when he spotted another friend who apparently had little regard for the police tape Sean had so diligently strung up. Lynne stepped over the top, holding a tray of takeaway coffees aloft in one hand and a few small brown paper bags in the other.

'You know, when I had someone come into the cafe telling me what was going on, I did not believe them.' Lynne settled herself and her supplies onto the bench on Addison's other side.

'Yet here we are,' Mabel said, 'once again.'

'Addison Harper, right in the thick of it,' Lynne said, pausing to share a look with Mabel. 'Once again.'

'I am *right here*, as you say,' Addison couldn't help pointing out.

'So you are. Like a lightning rod for drama, you are,' Lynne said, plucking out a coffee and one of the paper bags. 'Now, not sure if you'd had a chance to grab any lunch, so this mince and cheese pie is for you. And an oat flat white, in case you needed a little pick-me-up.'

'You're a star, Lynne.' He hadn't realised how hungry he was until he opened the bag and caught a whiff of that beautifully baked pastry wrapped around savoury goodness. 'I've only had half that custard square since breakfast.'

'What happened to the other half?'

'I, uh… had to use it for a bribe.'

Lynne burst out with a surprised chuckle. 'Of course.'

'Thanks again for that, by the way. My tab seems to grow by the minute, I promise I'll be in again to settle it soon.'

'Oh, don't be silly, love. But I will be glad for the visit – I feel like we've hardly seen you all week.'

'It has been a bit hectic, for sure.'

'I don't doubt that for one second,' Lynne said. 'I'm just pleased to see my new best customer is still alive and kicking.'

'Long may that last,' Addison said, raising his takeaway

coffee cup in a mock toast.

'Hear, hear. Now, I'd better get back,' Lynne said, levering herself back up. 'Just wanted you to have those and see how you were doing. I'll drop these other ones off on my way.'

It wasn't long after Lynne left that Sean and Manaia took Kyle away, followed soon by the paramedics – each member of emergency services bearing a takeaway coffee and baked treat.

And then Jake was heading towards Addison's bench.

'Hi, Mabel.'

'Hello, Sergeant.'

'Thanks for coming over,' Jake said to Mabel. 'I can take him from here.'

'Can you just?' Mabel's face and tone suggested that she'd see about that.

Jake appeared lost for words, unsure how to take the older woman's comment. 'Uh… if he'll have me, of course.'

Addison struggled not to laugh. 'Stand down, Mabel.'

'Very well, then.'

'Thank you for your company, I appreciate it,' Addison said, with a genuine smile before turning to Jake. 'And yes, I accept.'

'OK then, you look after yourself,' Mabel said, patting Addison's arm, then turned to face Jake. 'And you look after him too.'

'I will, Mrs Zhou.'

Mabel rolled her eyes and tutted before excusing herself.

'So,' Jake said. 'What do you want to do?'

'What? Don't you have to wrap this thing up?'

'McGiffert and Edwards have everything in hand. And they can call if they need me.' Jake sat down at Addison's ide. 'I'm already right where I need to be.'

If the bench hadn't been underneath him, Addison might have melted into a puddle on the footpath right then and there. 'Ah, um… I just want a bit of quiet and a lie down, if I'm honest.'

Jake nodded. 'I'll take you home, make sure you don't nod off. We can get some takeaways delivered a little later?'

'That sounds perfect.'

Chapter 42

In the comfort and security of Harper House, on the couch with Jake to one side and Keith to the other, Addison finally felt up to asking what had really happened between Dominic Campbell and Kyle Thompson. He had the broad strokes of what went down, and why, but a few things still didn't quite match up.

Jake, for his part, recognised Addison's need to know, and required only occasional prompting to add details whenever he tried to skate past any critical points.

Constables McGiffert and Edwards had stopped by Go All the Whey while Jake was with Addison at the medical centre. They'd questioned Zach Paine, the only one present at the time, regarding his involvement in Dominic's death and in the supplying of banned performance-enhancing drugs, both of which he denied.

'But then they mentioned you'd been targeted in a hit-and-run and he changed his tune.'

'What? So it was him who hit me?'

'No, no. They checked the van parked out the front of the store, not a scratch or dent on it,' Jake said. 'Edwards think Mr Paine realised this wasn't over, that Dominic's death wasn't the end of it, and that more people were getting hurt.'

'So he became more cooperative?'

Jake nodded. 'At least until Ms Kumar-Attwood turned up.' His partner, both personally and professionally, Prisha Kumar-Attwood, had arrived shortly after that and tried to change the story, but by then it was too late. And she soon realised they'd be better served by being cooperative.

Dominic had been blackmailing them all – Zach and Prisha, and Kyle too. It wasn't Dominic using the performance-enhancing substances banned in competition, but Kyle – *this* was the piece Addison had been missing, and with it everything else had fallen into place.

'Kyle was cheating,' Addison said. 'And Zach and Prisha had been supplying him with what he needed to do it.'

'And Dominic knew it. He had all the evidence he needed, and threatened to share it if Kyle ever placed higher than him in competition.'

Addison thought back to his conversations with the man. 'Which ensured Kyle never got any real traction with sponsors, and had to pay his own way, funded by his electrical business. But with jobs falling through, was his business coming under pressure? Not able to cover the bills and in danger of falling over? Or even just less able to fund his athletic aspirations?'

'Making the need for sponsorship all the more pressing.'

'Not only was Dominic effectively blocking new sponsorship for the guy, but he'd also nabbed Kyle's only previous sponsor: Go All the Whey.'

'Eventually, Zach and Prisha confessed to supplying Kyle, but insisted they hadn't done so for years.'

'But Kyle was still using?'

313

Jake nodded. 'They think Kyle found himself another supplier. They don't know who, and never asked, didn't want anything more to do with it.'

'So,' Addison said, 'why didn't Kyle stop using when he was caught out by Dominic? It endangered any possibility of a future career as a full-time athlete.'

Jake shrugged. 'We'll be asking those questions, but I suspect Dominic had evidence to hold over him already, so as far as Kyle was concerned, he might as well carry on.'

'I guess.'

'And it's addictive stuff, with all sorts of side effects.'

'He was ripped though,' Addison said, realising now he should've known growing those bulging arms and shoulders and all the rest might have required a little unnatural assistance.

'Maintaining the look might have had something to do with it too.'

Addison knew the potential consequences on someone's physical and mental wellbeing, but wasn't totally sure of the legalities. Luckily he had someone whose job meant he might know such things. 'I know things like that are banned from competition,' Addison said, 'but they're not illegal, or are they?'

'They're legal on prescription—'

'Ah.'

'—which Thompson did not have.'

'Right... So, why would Zach and Prisha get involved in the first place?'

Jake recounted what he'd heard from his constables, that Zach and Prisha only did it in the early years to prop up their business until it was more self-sustaining. And Kyle, out there doing pretty well in competitions with the Go All the Whey logo on his shirt, helped to boost their business profile.

'And somehow Dominic found out, supposedly had evidence and threatened to use it.'

Jake nodded. 'Unless Go All the Whey switched their sponsorship over from Kyle to himself.'

'And that was the arrangement,' Addison said. 'Until…'

'Until Kyle decided enough was enough.'

'He would have so much to gain with Dominic out of the picture. Staging his death as an accident was an extreme step, but he still didn't quite manage it.'

'Too many people were involved for a start, like Lars spotting him heading into the bush that morning. And then he didn't get the chance to finish the job properly.'

'You mean…'

Jake nodded. 'We're still going through the details, but the working theory is Mr Thompson had killed him and was in the process of dragging the body away when we turned up at Douglas Glade.'

Addison's eyes were like saucers. 'And what? Was he waiting in the trees, hoping we'd finish our picnic and leave so he could come back and finish the job?'

'We think so,' Jake said. 'But then you found the body first.'

Addison felt sick. He'd been in more danger than he'd even realised.

'It was all very rushed and untidy. Too many loose ends, which Kyle came to realise today when he felt you were getting too close for comfort.'

'Good thing for me he failed at that too,' Addison said, pulling on a forced smile.

Jake rested a hand on Addison's knee, as if to reassure

himself that he was still there. 'We don't know yet whether he meant to just scare you off, or whether it was an attempt on your life but he had second thoughts at the last moment. I don't know if we'll ever know for sure. Regardless of his intentions, there is a dent in his van now that wasn't there when I saw it this morning after breakfast at your place.'

The mention of their meeting earlier in the day took Addison back, and he realised what he'd done. At the time, he'd been thinking out loud, about how he thought he'd go and see Lars over his lunch break. He'd effectively tipped Kyle off about how close he was to uncovering the truth, then told him where he'd be, and when. The perfect opportunity to dispense with Addison away from prying eyes, particularly those of Sergeant Jake Murphy, who had been very close to hand, even if he'd been in a state of undress at the time.

The friendly, curious, chatty approach Addison took to unearthing information had come back to bite him. It went both ways – of course it did. He really should've been more guarded with his words, but then if he had been, he might never have triggered this whole thing, and Kyle might never have been caught.

'It's not clear yet what he was doing between the hit-and-run and stocking up at Halswell's.'

'Maybe just trying to figure out what he was going to do next?' Addison couldn't even imagine what must have been going through his mind at that point, not that he had much sympathy for the guy.

'I'd say so,' Jake said. 'And it looked like he'd settled on doing a runner, maybe trying to lose himself in the bush? What he planned to do after that, I don't think even he knew.'

Addison let out a breath, like he was finally willing to consider relaxing after a tense day, or week. He laughed. 'At least he finished the job this morning.' Addison had noticed the freshly turned ground marking the line of the buried cable as they arrived back at Harper House, along with the paperwork left on the kitchen bench. To think he'd left Kyle Thompson – full-time electrician, part-time cross triathlete, and now accused murderer – to roam around the house and the property while he was going about his day, completely oblivious.

'Still keeping up appearances by that point, part of his business-as-usual approach, I'd say. If he'd left an incomplete job, people might have started to wonder and connect the dots.'

'But that plan fell apart anyway.'

'Who knows what he was thinking.'

Wow, OK. Addison was sure more thoughts and questions would come to him later, but he had more than enough to process already. Really, it all boiled down to the fact that Dominic had been killed, and Kyle had been the one to do it.

Addison remained deep in thought, barely registering the knock on the front door, Jake getting up to answer it, or Keith repositioning himself to get maximum contact with the outside of Addison's thigh. Absently he patted the cat, only mentally re-engaging once Jake reappeared.

'That smells *amazing*,' Addison said, eyes flicking between the bags Jake had brought back in. 'How much did you order, though? There's only the two of us—'

Keith sat up, no longer tucked into Addison's side, his full attention directed at the bag in Jake's left hand.

'Three of us,' Addison corrected himself.

'Curry puffs, prawn tempura, Thai green curry and rice,' Jake said as he pulled each container out of the bag, then the final one containing stir-fried noodles. 'And pad see ew.'

Jake was about to start opening them up when Addison jumped in, pointing to the mystery bag Jake had left by the door. 'Before we get into the food, were you going to tell me what that is?'

'Just a few things.'

Addison didn't respond, at least not verbally, just gave him an expectant look.

Jake got the message, and brought the final bag over. 'They're for you.'

'For me?'

'Yes,' Jake said, not elaborating any further, only nudging the bag.

Addison had no idea what to expect as he reached in and brought out a brand-new bike helmet – neon orange, with silver reflective strips all over it. 'Wow, very uh... *visible*,' Addison said, struggling to contain his smile.

'There's something else in there too.'

Addison dutifully reached back in and pulled out a matching vest in the same high-visibility orange and silver.

'For you to wear over your clothes.'

'Yes, I know,' Addison said, his amusement now battling with his surging emotions. 'It's very sweet, thank you.' He knew Jake could've taken a drastically different approach with this, but it was clear he knew better. He trusted Addison, didn't want to change him, but couldn't help just trying to make him that little bit safer.

'I've put in an order with Julie for a replacement wheel too.' Jake's fists were balled on his knees, clenching and unclenching. 'Just promise me you won't use your phone while you're on your bike?'

'I don't think that would've helped in this situation...'

'No, but...'

'Yes,' Addison said. 'I promise.'

Jake nodded once, apparently satisfied with the response. 'One more,' he said, holding up a hand to forestall Addison as he reached for the bag. 'Before I give it to you, just know there's no pressure, completely up to you.'

'OK...' Addison drew out the word, more curious than ever.

'I just thought it would be good to have, in case you were maybe interested. Now that you're spending more time up here in Milverton, and not so much in Wellington. No pressure though.'

'Yes, sure,' Addison said, before his hand found what felt like a book in the bottom of the bag. He pulled it out and read the cover. 'The official New Zealand road code.' He looked at Jake, not sure what to make of this *gesture*.

'In case you wanted to get your driver's licence,' Jake said quickly. 'It includes practice questions in the back for the learner licence theory test.'

Addison nodded slowly. 'Thank you. Yep, very sensible.'

'I can help teach you too,' Jake said. 'Only if you want, that is.'

'You are even braver than I thought,' Addison said, setting it aside, not knowing yet how he felt about it but intending to give it serious consideration.

'I'm sure you'd be an excellent driver.'

Addison wasn't so sure, but he appreciated the vote of confidence. 'Thank you, Jake,' he said, and he meant it, leaning in to show his appreciation with a quick kiss.

It only lasted for a moment before Addison pulled back

and smiled at the slightly startled look in Jake's eyes.

'Let's eat first, before I get carried away.'

Jake smiled, letting out a chuckle. 'I'll allow it.'

They piled up their plates under the watchful eye of Keith, and Addison was happily sampling each of the dishes when he realised something.

Investigating his suspicions around Dominic's unexplained death had filled in much of his time and mental capacity, so he'd barely had a moment to reflect on anything else, consciously anyway. With all that behind them now, Addison realised that when it came to the decision he'd been putting off making, there really was nothing left to decide. He already knew precisely what he wanted.

It was something he'd come to all by himself, without any nudging from Mabel or subtle querying from Jake. He'd made the decision, because he knew it was the right one for him both personally and professionally. Though he'd be lying if he said the man sitting beside him didn't factor into the decision, at least a little. And the support he'd received through all the drama – from Jake, his constables, Mabel, Lynne, and so many others – showed he really was in the right place.

'I'm going to accept the mayor's job offer,' Addison said without any preamble, unable to hide the shy smile already taking over his face.

Jake swallowed his mouthful of noodles. 'Oh, yeah?'

'Yeah.'

'To work with her team,' Jake said, pausing a moment before adding, 'in Milverton?'

Addison nodded. 'The brief for the role is broad – to market Milverton – and I'm excited to get started.'

'That is exciting,' Jake said. He glanced down at his

plate, absently nudging a curry puff aside before looking back up at Addison. 'So, I suppose this means you'll be sticking around?'

'I suppose it does.'

Jake cleared his throat. 'Have you told the mayor?'

'Not yet, but I'll do that tomorrow,' Addison said. 'You're the first to know.'

Jake nodded as if this all wasn't the big deal they both absolutely recognised that it was.

'That reminds me,' Addison said, breaking the moment to jump up and grab something from the other room. 'You know how you organised our last outing?'

'Yes,' Jake said, slowly, suspiciously. 'I know the bush walk wasn't your first choice as far as dates go—'

'Hey, I enjoyed it. Up to a point, at least,' Addison said, returning with two pieces of card. 'Well, I have something that's a little more my style, courtesy of the mayor.'

'Oh, yeah?'

'And you've bestowed so many gifts on me tonight, it's only fair I offer these in return.'

'All right, enough suspense, what are they?'

'Two tickets for a new show by the Milverton Community Theatre. It's coming up soon,' Addison said, handing over the tickets. 'Sounds like it might be a laugh, but we don't have to go if you're not interested.'

'No, no. I haven't been to a show in ages,' Jake said with a smile. 'And I'd love to go, as long as you'll be joining me?'

'Of course.' Addison smiled right back, and planted another impromptu kiss on Jake's lips. 'Besides, compared to traipsing through the great outdoors, a night at the theatre will be no trouble at all.'

Addison will return...

Fright on Stage Right
The Milverton Mysteries #4

It's opening night at the theatre and Addison Harper
has front-row seats with Sergeant Jake Murphy.
This might just be his perfect date.

The playbill promises spooky Halloween fun, ghoulish drag
queens, frightening musical numbers, and the scariest thing
of all: audience participation. Of course, the unlucky victim
dragged from the safety of his seat is a mortified Addison.
In a play full of twists and turns, he has no idea what's
coming next but nobody could have anticipated witnessing
a sudden, absolutely unscripted, and very real death.

A dreadful accident? Or was it foul play? As the curtain falls
before a horror-struck audience, Addison Harper finds
himself once again in the spotlight at centre stage.

Fright on Stage Right is the latest in a wonderful cosy
mystery series set in an enchanting small town nestled
amongst stunning New Zealand scenery. Investigate *The
Milverton Mysteries* for a chaotic cast of local busybodies,
delicious baked treats, a demanding and disdainful ginger

cat, a very slow-burn romance with a rather appealing policeman, and of course… murder!

Scheduled for release mid-late 2025.
Pre-order today, or buy now if it's already out:
www.gbralph.com/fright-on-stage-right

Thank you for reading

I hope you enjoyed the story. If you did, please tell your friends – personal recommendations are the best! Also please consider leaving a review wherever you bought this book, and on Goodreads. This is important in making my work more visible to other readers – each review gives the books a little boost, and means others are more likely to stumble across them.

For my latest updates, free short stories, and to be the first to hear when Addison and the good people of Milverton will be back, you can join the mailing list on my website: www.gbralph.com. You can also find my other stories there, and links to my social media if you'd like to drop me a message – I'd love to hear from you!

Acknowledgements

I still can't quite believe the reception to Addison, Jake, Mabel, Keith, and all the other residents of Milverton. It's been truly wonderful. I'm so pleased I get to keep writing these characters and everything they get up to, even as Milverton's murder rate continues to escalate. I joked with friends recently that it might be time to rebrand the series as *The Increasingly Inexplicable Adventures of Addison Harper*. I think this more accurately describes the state of affairs in his life. What do you reckon?

Anyway, on to the thanks! I've had so much support over the past year while writing *Death in Douglas Glade* and promoting *Murder on Milverton Square* and *Poison at Penshaw Hall*. I am so grateful to everyone!

To Tantor Audio for taking on the audiobook adaptation and Philip Battley for his wonderful narration. I'm so pleased we've been able to make Milverton available in a format that is so convenient and accessible for so many readers.

To the readers and librarians of the Palmerston North City Library for showing such enthusiasm for these local stories and this local author. The library truly feels like a second home.

To Louisa, Corey, and the team at Bruce McKenzie Booksellers for taking on my books. It's such a joy to see them on the shelves.

To Craig Sisterson and the Ngaio Marsh Awards for bringing local mystery writers and readers together with their series of 'Mystery in the Library' events. I had such a blast on my first-ever in-person author panel.

To my very talented bunch of local author friends who are always up for coffees and brunches, walks and talks: A.J. Lancaster, Mel Harding-Shaw, Marie Cardno, Anne Kemp, Bing Turkby, and Riley Chance.

To the Word Racers who are there at all hours offering words of encouragement and/or a kick in the pants, whichever may be required at the time: Andrew Chapman, Angela C. Nurse, G.M. White, Jackie Kirkham, J.W. Atkinson, Julian Barr, L.J. Shepherd, Paul Austin Ardoin, Rachel Chapman, Robyn Sarty, S.C. Gowland, and Tom Foot.

To the Speculative Collective for being such a lively and engaged community of authors, sharing all the ups and downs of both the creative and the business sides of writing, editing, publishing, and promoting books.

To those who read early versions of this book and gave brilliant feedback, helping to make it really shine: Angela C. Nurse, Paul Austin Ardoin, Julian Barr, Cameron Jones, Derryk Butcher, A.J. Lancaster, Mel Harding-Shaw, and Chris Zable.

To my partner, my family, and my friends – your support means the world.

And finally, thanks to you, my amazing readers. Your enthusiasm for Addison and his various misadventures is what keeps me coming back for more!

Made in the USA
Las Vegas, NV
05 January 2025